The English Professor

GINA IAFRATE

....

Beate,
May your heart be
touched with this
novel. It did mine
writing it.
Blessing & love
Gino Iafrate

Copyright © 2014 by Gina Iafrate
First Edition – 2014

ISBN
978-1-4602-3013-8 (Hardcover)
978-1-4602-3014-5 (Paperback)
978-1-4602-3015-2 (eBook)

Produced by:

FriesenPress
Suite 300 – 990 Fort Street
Victoria, BC, Canada V8V 3K2

www.friesenpress.com

Distributed to the trade by The Ingram Book Company

My gratitude to the wonderful people in this journey of my life.

First and foremost I need to thank my husband Mario for his never ending patience and love. Many nights were spent watching me type away at my manuscript, becoming obsessed with the final details. You supported my passion and fulfillment of a lifelong dream.

Ruth Troughton – for your encouragement; your positive feedback regarding the development of my story; and, anxiously awaiting my next chapter. You gave me the momentum to continue writing.

My dear friend, Linda M. Walters. Thank you for taking your precious holiday time to answer my inquiries. Armando Di Francesco her husband for his part in supplying some of my photos.

Jody Cunnison, thank you for responding to my questions. Monique Atherton, thank you too for all your answers.

I am grateful to my humble friend Dr. Joanne Lennox, for her knowledge and advice in medicine. As well, a big thanks to Dr. Bruce Lennox, for your explanations, which allowed me to put down the facts with confidence.

Father Chris Czezepanik, for your patience and dedication on guiding our tour to Sicily and by responding to my inquiries. I was able to use the proper terms and procedures as to our Catholic faith. Also, your prompt service with the supply of sceneries of Italy, especially Sicily.

My family, my grandchildren helping with the computer glitches.

Howard Diwinsky, for taking the time to read and comment, but most of all, your kindness. Martin Ritter, for your interest and admiration.

Lorraine Noznisky, thank you for your kind words, your enthusiasm, and your praise.

In all gratitude I cannot ever forget the person who revived the love and passion of composition and writing in me: that wonderful person I know, Mae Denby, dedicated to her students, speaking only with kind words, a positive attitude, and a great listener. Yes, Mae, you encouraged me to toss aside my doubts and plow forward when you said I had a voice.

The angel on my path – Jan Pushkar. Thank you.

Geoff Soch, my manager from FriesenPress. He came on board with sincerity, in true assistance. His great efforts, and dedication helped.

My heartfelt thanks,
Gina Iafrate.

The English Professor

Chapter One

······································

Andrew felt completely drained of energy as he walked out of the old and stuffy university building. Another day of futile teaching had ended for him. Now he faced struggling through the hated subway to reach his flat in Bethnow. He glanced at his watch; it was five o'clock.

The sun must have been behind the gray clouds all day. Shivering in discomfort, he felt the humidity penetrating his bones. His quilted blue trench coat didn't shelter his body from the cold. With his gloved hands, he pulled it closer to his body hoping for some comfort. He could hardly wait to get home where he'd crash for a couple of hours before attacking more paperwork; editing was his second job.

He arrived at his doorstep to find his mailbox overflowing, but before retrieving his mail he had to deal with the rusted keyhole to open the old door. If he didn't hurry, old Mrs. Brooks from the next apartment would start with her annoying questions. Sure enough, her squeaky door opened.

"Hello, Professor, did you have another grand day? It's been so quiet around here; I haven't seen a soul all day. Will you come in for a cup of tea?"

The last thing Andrew wanted was tea with Mrs. Brooks. Although he did feel sorry for her, right now he just wanted to be alone.

"Thanks, Mrs. Brooks, I'll have to take a rain check. Right now I have to deal with this darn keyhole." He continued jiggling the key and turned his back on his neighbor. Finally, with a hard twist he managed to make the key work.

Andrew was living in the old southeast section of London where the narrow row houses were cramped together. His apartment needed a facelift indoors and outdoors. But with Andrew being a procrastinator, nothing got fixed. As far as Andrew was concerned, it didn't matter, and repairs definitely weren't his priority. This was basically him, uncaring for any better existence. He was an intellect at heart; his literature, his books, and teaching were his passions.

Andrew got the door open, emptied the mailbox and walked in. The smell of mold immediately hit his nostrils. He threw the mail on the littered coffee table and reached for a can of air freshener; he didn't care if the chemicals affected his lungs.

Andrew was moody these days. He was easily irritated and bouts of sadness darkened his soul. Since Gertrude left, his place was getting unbearable. He hoped, just maybe, that she might return, but it hadn't happened.

Lately Andrew was turning to alcohol for comfort. This is how he was choosing to ignore the disorder in his life. He filled his glass with scotch and soda. Then settling down on his leather chair, he opened his mail. He knew the alcohol would soon take effect and relax his nerves for a while.

London Row Houses

Shaking his head, he thought, *Nothing exciting ever lands in my mailbox; bills and more bills, junk mail for the wastebasket,* and as for his editorial clients, some of them were so boring he just wanted to throw their work in the wastebasket too. But it took money to live in London. Andrew was miserable and he didn't know when he would hit bottom. Little did he know, from this evening on, his life would take a new turn and change forever.

He noticed a brightly illustrated envelope among the rubbish. Promptly, he retrieved it and tore it open. Inside there were six spectacular postcards of Sicily. Andrew carefully scrutinized each one of them. The pictures were scenic and interesting. *Who sent them?* At the bottom of a card he recognized a signature: Fabiana Taverna.

Yes, she had been one of his students from a previous term. He remembered her well; she was very studious and wanted to improve her English. The Italian girl, pleasant and courteous, had attended his class faithfully. She was an Italian reporter with a strong desire to improve her speaking skills in English.

Andrew often praised her for her dedication and hard work to become fluent. She passed with well-deserved excellent marks.

Now Fabiana, with her family, was extending him an invitation! How kind of them. A month long stay on the island of Sicily. Fabiana's message was respectfully direct to Andrew:

Dear Professor Robertson,

My family with myself, extend you an invitation, to be our guest, for the month of August at our residence in Palermo. We would be honored to have you. This invite is in appreciation of your diligent dedication in helping me when in London.

We look forward to your reply.

Sincerely,

Fabiana and family

Andrew felt flattered. No one had ever repaid him or appreciated him with such a thoughtful gesture. This offer seemed to come at the right time. Yes, he was going to relate this to his students in class tomorrow. Some of them had been friendly with Fabiana. He would be proud to bring the cards to show them. This was the best offer he had ever received in his entire life. With that, he turned over the cards to observe the sites. He reread the note over and over, to make sure this wasn't any mistake. *By golly*, he thought, *this calls for another drink to celebrate.*

Andrew rose from his sofa, in an elated mood and fixed himself another… would he go? *Of course, I will start counting the days.*

The winter had been dreary and long in London. Now, being the end of March, the continuous rainy and foggy days were depressing. It would be great to explore southern Italy for one whole month. The daily classes were getting to him regardless of his love for teaching. Sometimes his dedication seemed unrewarding. He admired his students from other countries;

they were hungry for knowledge. They dedicated themselves to absorb everything with much interest. They motivated him to give more of himself. Some of the local students were taking much for granted. He could feel their lack of participation and their disinterest showed in their eyes. As a result, Andrew had been feeling unrewarded in every which way.

He picked up the lovely cards again. They were enticing. He admired the panoramic view of Taormina, the Greek Theater, the Blue Grotto, the ruins of Agrigento, Isola Bella and Sicily itself seemed to be a beautiful island, separated by the mainland from Mare Ionia in the Mediterranean Sea. Just by observing these cards, Andrew's heart was racing with excitement. He went to bed, for the first time in a long time, looking forward to tomorrow.

He would go to a travel agency and inquire about a flight and immediately reply with his acceptance. He was free at this time in his life. Gertrude, his former girlfriend, wasn't any longer a part of his life. She had recently dumped him and left a big void in his heart. He was approaching fifty and had never traveled much outside of England. This trip would be good for him.

He was alone without any family. He lost both his parents a few years ago, they both died within a year of each other. They had lived in London and he used to visit with them often. Andrew grieved their loss for a long time. He had an older brother Ian, who immigrated to Washington, DC. Ian was married to a redheaded, freckle-faced Irish woman and they had four children. After their parents passed, they hardly ever came to visit. Their excuse was that they couldn't afford taking trips abroad. They phoned occasionally. His brother never failed to lament on how demanding his life was, therefore, Andrew didn't want to impose on them. Their relationship was slowly becoming distant.

Ironically, Ian never failed to make some smart remark in their conversation, "Andrew, you're the lucky one." Andrew hardly considered himself the lucky one. Sometimes he thought his brother was jealous of him for some strange reason. Andrew had inherited the flat from his parents because he was in London to look after them. He wondered what his brother was insinuating. Could it be that lousy flat he occupied, or because he didn't have any family responsibilities? One day he would ask him, but until then, he felt Ian was the lucky one with a wife and sons and daughters to love him. As for himself, he felt no one cared if he lived or died.

This gesture from Fabiana and her family meant a lot to him. *Who knows?* he thought, *maybe Sicily will be my salvation and bring me some luck. I'm a free man and I'm open for anything.* He had to admit, he had been in such poor spirit lately. Gertrude had hurt him badly. She had been uncaring and cruel with her announcement.

It happened one evening when he got home from work. He was totally oblivious to her desire to leave. Andrew had arrived home earlier than usual and found Gertrude dressed to the nines. She was wearing a stunning red dress, revealing her well-shaped body; a side split exposed her bare long legs, accentuated by the pewter high heels. Her makeup was impeccably applied and her hair was pulled back in a chignon propped on her head like a rooster's crest. When she walked to the bar to pick up the tray with the martini glasses, she moved her rear end and hips like a teasing whore. She handed him the funnel shaped glass with a red cherry floating in it.

"Andrew," she said, and as she lifted her glass a fancy bracelet glittered on her wrist. Strangely, she posed like an upper class aristocrat.

Andrew was confused: *Has she gone all out to dress for me? Is this a special evening that I have forgotten?* He had to admit; she looked appealing and provoking. Teasing.

She gave him a quick kiss and then spoke, "Andrew, we are celebrating."

Andrew felt uneasy, her tone of voice sounded imperious.

"Darling, sit down, let's have this drink to us. I have an announcement to make."

Andrew took a sip and was going along, curious, puzzled, and waiting.

Finally, "Andrew, we are celebrating my freedom."

"Oh, freedom, from what dear?"

Sarcastically she responded, "From you, my darling. You and I are through. I'm leaving, I cannot bear to live in this dump any more and after ten years our relationship has run its course."

She continued bluntly with no regard for his feelings, "I have met a younger fellow who is fun to be with. He's willing to adhere to my wishes and fulfillments; therefore, I need to be moving on in my life."

Andrew, completely stunned continued to sip his drink. In that moment he saw Gertrude like a bulldozer crushing him. He felt rejected; like a piece of rubbish for the garbage. But he couldn't stop her. He was a placid man, set in his ways and contented in his usual routine. He asked himself, *What is wrong with me?*

It didn't occur to him that his lack of ambition plus the lack of desire to better his living status was the main culprit. He was six foot two, his gray hairline had started to recede and his eyes were sunken in from fatigue. Plus, his pot belly wasn't exactly complimentary.

Sitting there now, reflecting on Gertrude's episode, he decided it was time to renew himself, especially if he was going to go on this trip. Andrew was likeable, but his monotonous lifestyle proved to be boring and that was the reason he couldn't keep a partner. With all these assessments, Professor Andrew Robertson made a vow to himself. He needed to get his personal life in balance and he then made a decision. All his future actions would be to improve his well-being. He walked to the full-length mirror to review his appearance. "Am I still marketable?" He had gotten into the habit of talking to himself.

The following morning he replied to Fabiana and accepted her family's invitation without any hesitation. Next, improvements both mentally and physically. After work, instead of rushing home to his flat and drinks, he detoured to a fitness center and requested to see a personal trainer.

A tall, blonde, muscular young woman came out to greet him. She introduced herself with a strong handshake, "Donna Smith, welcome to the Bali Fitness Centre."

"Andrew Robertson," he replied, extending his hand.

"Nice to meet you. What can I do for you, Andrew?"

Harrods Department Store, London

"I'm here for a complete assessment of my fitness level and overall health."

"Very well, Andrew," she gestured, "please step into my office."

Andrew was a little taken aback; she portrayed an aura of assurance. She reminded him of Gertrude's personality. He didn't find her attractive, but he had noticed she moved swiftly and looked fit.

Donna asked him to take a seat in front of her desk. The room was a fair size, bright and sanitary. He noticed pictures of people pinned to the walls. They indicated the before and after results.

"Andrew, you need to fill out this form and sign at the bottom. It's necessary for the assessment." She had handed him a questionnaire and he quickly marked all the answers positively and handed it back to her.

She glanced at his answers and stood up, "Andrew, let's move over to the next room." Once there, he noticed all kinds of foreign apparatus that were unfamiliar to him.

"Andrew, step onto this machine." His hands and feet were placed on a computer device electroscope. She sat in front of a screen reading his results with an obscure look on her face, "Andrew, when was the last time you had a physical check-up?"

"I must say, it's been a long time. I can't recall the last time. I prefer to stay away from doctors."

"Okay, I know you're a teacher, what are you doing physically every day for your body?"

"I walk to the subway every day."

"How long of a walk is that?"

"Fifteen minutes each way."

"Andrew! You need to listen to me carefully, besides being a personal trainer, I'm a medical doctor and a certified alternative medicine practitioner. The fact is you're forty-nine years old. Your body has the capacity and strength of a seventy-five-year-old man. You have high blood pressure and I suspect diabetes. Plus, you're overweight with a sluggish gut creeping up on you."

With that statement, she printed a sheet of paper and handed it to him while she continued: "We can start the program soon if you like. I suggest you verify my findings with your medical doctor and we will proceed as soon as you are ready."

Andrew stood up, he never expected this verdict, and the happiness that had been stimulated by Fabiana's card vanished. Donna put an arm on his shoulder and with a serious look on her face warned him, "You need to go on high blood pressure pills immediately. With the sugar combination, you're a candidate for a stroke any time soon."

Andrew was scared. He never thought his health had deteriorated so badly.

To his surprise Donna's voice now sounded gentle and caring, "I don't want to scare you, I want to save you. You're still young and have a lot to live for. Come back as soon as you can. I'll be waiting for you. I promise you, with my knowledge and your cooperation, you will be a new man."

All of a sudden he felt down again, his life had taken a sinister twist. Both his parents had died from cardiac arrest. This was the result of his genes. It hadn't occurred to him before. Andrew wasted no time in calling his doctor. After a visit with him and extensive tests, sure enough they confirmed Donna's prognosis and more. He was placed on a heavy dose of blood thinners and pills to stabilize his blood sugar level. Also, the doctor agreed, a fitness program would be beneficial to his entire body both physically and mentally.

One thing was bothering Andrew, he asked, "Doctor, my libido has gone down the tubes, do you think it is all related?"

"Professor Andrew, I take it you are an intelligent man. In your state eventually everything shuts down. You have some work ahead of you to rectify the situation. If you ignore it … I can't help you."

He told the doctor about the plans for his trip, "Doctor, will I be okay to take this trip for a month?"

"Andrew, get busy, the trip might motivate you. You are going in August, right? You have five months to get yourself rejuvenated and in good health. It will do you good." And with a half-smile, he said, "Between us men, those Italian women are pretty tempting; make sure you take a box of condoms, your libido should be up by then. One more thing, drop the hard alcohol. Replace it with red wine. You could have two five-ounce glasses a day. Good luck. I would like to see you back in a month. Call me should there be any complications with your medication."

Andrew had a big job on his hands. He had neglected himself. Maybe Gertrude was right to leave. He had become a derelict, good for nothing. He knew his truth now. The anger in his soul needed to turn into forgiveness. He had himself to blame. It was his fault.

He made the decision to go and see Donna the following day after school to work with her. Fabiana's invitation had been a godsend. He didn't have any time to waste. He needed to do what he had to do.

To his surprise, after a couple of weeks of lifestyle changes and workout sessions with Donna, he started to feel better. Now, he looked forward to what lay ahead, but he needed to do one more thing. It was necessary for him to brush up on his Italian. He wanted to communicate well; therefore, he would have to take a refresher course.

He had seen the course posted at the university. It was offered on Saturday mornings and one of his colleagues, Professor Arthur, was teaching. He signed himself up without any hesitation. Andrew found the classes pleasurable, the words rolled around his tongue like music, the verbs he emphasized with gusto. They were formed in the reverse order of the English language. He thought how English was much easier in comparison, yet how he loved those sounds when he practiced with his classmates. He felt so stimulated and couldn't wait to get to Italy and show off his language skills to Fabiana.

Andrew was busy these days. He didn't have any time to sit, brood, and drink away his sorrows. He was busy in his new life, his morale was lifting and he was happier. He often took time to engage in conversations with the people at the university. Once again, he had become aware of his surroundings and smiled more. One morning he stepped on the scales and noticed his weight had gone down considerably. Looking in the mirror, he also noticed his gut wasn't protruding as much anymore. He had lost a considerable amount of fat and his clothes had gotten baggy.

Andrew decided it was time for new clothes so off he went to Albam Nottingham menswear to find some classics; he liked to dress conservatively. Then, he visited Norton and Sons to buy fine shirts and Merino wool vests. Next, new shoes. Yes, he always did well at Harrods shoe salon on Brampton Street. Andrew had now gotten into the habit of wandering around the shopping district whenever he had a little time to spare. He wanted to buy everything new for his trip and he was getting more excited by the day. He needed to upgrade his camera in order to capture all the scenes. After all, one could not afford to take trips of this caliber too often.

Donna had been pushing Andrew pretty hard. She had been increasing his endurance in stages and he cooperated well. His hard sweat brought great results. But Andrew was still worried about the results from his doctor. However, the news was good. At his last visit, the doctor changed his medication, put his hand on Andrew's shoulder and said, "You have been an excellent patient, Andrew. Your serious dedication has brought good results. Enjoy your trip!"

Fiuggi Fountains outside of Rome

Chapter Two

....

Finally, the day arrived. On August 1, his flight landed in Rome where Andrew made his first stopover. Here he planned to stay for a couple of days and then continue by train to Calabria and then on to Sicily. Andrew was used to the crowds in London. He had researched Rome in August. At this time of year it was comfortable and not so busy, as most of the locals had left the city for the coastal shores.

Andrew could easily explore the city. Since he was so fascinated by Roman history and loved archaeology, the Coliseum was his first choice of venue. He joined a group of tourists and learned what took place there in the time of Julius Caesar and the Roman Empire. He stood there astounded. Every now and then he would exchange comments with the other tourists, "One could gain so much knowledge by digging deep into these ruins, I'm sure there is still so much buried in here."

All he could do was admire and take pictures; maybe he would show them to his class. His next stop was the Vatican. The architecture was amazing and once he was inside, he didn't know where to look first. The perfectly sculpted marble statues, the art, gilded with gold and silver leaf, the skilled work of Michelangelo. Everyone had told him, "You must visit the Sistine Chapel." Now, here he was touring Rome. There was so much to see and not enough time. He wanted to see it all! Next, the fountains. His passion led him to an excursion to the Trevi Fountains, then to the Tivoli Gardens, a work of art combined with waterfalls, lush gardens both soothing and refreshing and Piazza di Spagna. Andrew, now used to being alone, still had moments when he desired to have someone with him to share these sights. He noticed couples holding hands and others travelling together in groups. A sudden sorrow came over him and he asked himself, *Why am I condemned to be alone?*

Andrew knew better than to indulge in self-pity and quickly shook himself out of it. With a renewed encouragement he noticed the tourists were approachable. He started to engage in conversations whenever he heard English spoken. They were visitors like him.

The aroma of coffee was overwhelming. He couldn't help indulging in an espresso and some mouth-watering pastries. Surprisingly the strong espresso didn't give him the jitters.

"A burst of caffeine is so good for me!" he expressed to a gentleman standing next to him at the coffee bar. The stranger nodded his head in agreement.

In Italy, Andrew replaced his alcoholic drinks with espressos and *gelato* in all the irresistible and sinful flavors. He told himself, *I'm going to treat myself with all the goodies. All the walking I'm doing will take care of my sugar with the assistance of medication.* With that resolution, he was determined to live this month to the fullest and take in whatever life presented.

After a couple of days, he found himself seated on the train to continue down the Italian coastline. He was travelling first class. The cabin was luxurious and comfortable for the long ride to Calabria. He had specifically chosen a cabin with a large window so he wouldn't miss anything as the train zipped through the countryside. Although he wished the speed to be slower, he was still capturing and enjoying the scenery of southern Italy. The rocky terrain along the coast of the Mediterranean Sea was picturesque. The scattered towns were nestled on hilltops and some were sprawled around the valleys. The sea was so blue, the lush foliage was interesting and the olive trees were abundant.

Port of Messina

In no time, he reached Calabria and had to take the ferry into Messina. Once there, Fabiana and her family were going to pick him up and continue on to Palermo. He knew the Sicilians were proud of their island. Therefore, he suspected they would show him their island with all its offerings.

"I'm so fortunate. I have local people picking me up," he exclaimed to a woman sitting beside him on the ferry.

"Oh! I'll say you are! I have to take a cab to Nexus. This is my third trip to Taormina, I just love it here. I flew into Rome from Boston and connected to Lamezia."

He knew it would be comforting to have locals to travel with, plus he was looking forward seeing Fabiana again. He remembered her vividly, a beautiful young woman in her early twenties. A lovely petite girl, bright and intelligent with long black hair, olive skin, and a confident and energetic demeanor.

Andrew was the first to get off the ferry. He didn't have to search for long. He immediately spotted Fabiana with two gentlemen. Beautiful as ever, she ran towards him with her companions behind her.

"Professor!" she cried out as she gave him a hug. Then she turned to her father standing behind her. "Remember my dad," she said, leaning over with an affectionate gesture.

"Of course, of course." Andrew smiled excitedly, ready to greet him.

"This is Joseph my younger brother," she gestured pulling him forward.

"Professor, welcome to Sicily." Joseph approached him delightedly.

"Thank you; so kind of you to come for me."

Even the men embraced him; the Professor found it a little much, however, he complied. He knew that was part of the rich Italian culture and figured he would get used to that. Both gentlemen lent him a hand with his baggage and escorted him to their limo.

Fabiana was very chatty; she was trying to make Andrew feel welcome. Mr. Anthony Taverna her father and the younger fellow Joseph were joyfully participating. They seemed to be pleasant people. Mr. Taverna was a stout man and looked severe, but as he spoke Andrew could detect a kindness in his voice. When Joseph spoke to Andrew, he referred to him as "Professor Robertson."

Several times Andrew said, "Please, Joseph, you have my permission, call me Andrew."

"No, no, Professor, that will be considered disrespectful on my part."

With that answer Andrew let it go.

It was before noon when they started out. Fabiana suggested sightseeing in the area for a short time. They were driving through the city of Messina and into the city of Taormina. Andrew couldn't stop taking pictures to capture the universal beauty along the way. Sicily sits like a jewel among the seas, with a blend of Greek, Arab, Italian, and of course, Roman architecture. The history, the cathedrals, there was going to be so much to see and admire.

Fabiana's family noticed how Andrew was mesmerized as they were driving along the coast with the panoramic view below them. It was getting late in the afternoon and they reassured Andrew that they would make sure he got to see more of their beautiful island. Fabiana hated to break his spell.

"Professor Andrew, my mother and family are anxiously waiting for us. We can come back and sightsee later on during your stay."

"Whatever you decide, my dear, *non preoccupatevi*, don't worry," Andrew said proudly, showing off his newly polished Italian.

It was quite the drive to arrive in Palermo. Andrew continued in awe as he admired the city sprawled around the Tyrrhenian Sea. Soon they made a turn onto a country road that headed toward the outskirts of the city. The car stopped in front of a gated stone mansion where two doormen stood to welcome them. The two automatic iron gates opened and they drove into a circular driveway. A majestic Roman structure, with several marbled pillars held the stretched out three-floored mansion. A gathering of people mingled in front of the entrance.

As he stepped out of the limo, the sound of a waterfall soothed him. Andrew turned. Yes, there they were: two fountains on each side of the mansion. The gentle cascading levels brought a certain peace to his soul. Andrew turned to Fabiana, and exclaimed, "Is this for real or am I hallucinating? Is this a house or a hotel? Am I staying here?"

"Professor, I want you to feel at home. This is our home and you will be our guest."

He had left a flat in Bethnow. This place boggled his mind. He couldn't wait to see the inside, but before he could get in, more people were coming out to welcome him.

He only knew Fabiana as his student. Her parents had visited her in England a few times. He didn't know them well, but he had been casually introduced to them. Yet he could tell they were an affluent, close family. Sending a daughter to study in England wasn't inexpensive. He was going to enjoy what was presented to him and not ask too many questions. He should only be grateful for one month of life in this heaven, but deep down his gut feeling was not at rest.

He was telling his subconscious mind, *Stop this silly churning.* Then Fabiana startled him from his thoughts. She gently put her arm around him and guided him towards her mother, Mrs. Lora Taverna.

"This is my mother. Do you remember her?" she asked.

"Oh, yes!" he said, as he proceeded to greet her.

"Professor! Here you are, how nice," she said, and then gently kissed him on both cheeks.

He recalled her as a lovely lady, civil, and pleasant. She was attractive and petite like her daughter. They shared a strong resemblance. One by one, Andrew greeted many more people. He was slowly being introduced to them all. They were all relatives: uncles, aunts, cousins, and the maid Ersilia. He noticed her black and white uniform. Out of respect, they had all come to meet and welcome him to Sicily.

Andrew was a bit confused as to who belonged to whom, but eventually it would be sorted out once he got to know them better. An elegant lady was the last person to meet, she stood aside, a little quieter than the rest. Fabiana took her by the arm and gently led her toward Andrew for the introduction, "This is my Aunt Francesca."

Andrew shook her hand. He had noticed, it seemed that she didn't really want to be there, but he kept his opinion to himself. With a curious smile, Francesca introduced herself.

Once his baggage was taken to his room, Fabiana showed him his quarters and encouraged him to take a little rest or freshen up before dinner.

Andrew was so excited with everything, he quickly commented, "Fabiana. Are you kidding me! I sat enough on the train, the ferry, and the car. With all this beauty around me, I don't want to waste any time sleeping. I will freshen up all right and be ready to socialize."

"As you wish, Professor. We will serve refreshments and dinner when you are ready, take your time."

"Fabiana, you are such an angel. Thank you."

Fabiana went back to her family and informed her mother and Ersilia that the Professor wasn't going to waste any time. She felt the need to check on her aunt. Francesca still seemed sad and removed.

"Auntie, what is the matter? Let me see a smile on your face. We want the Professor to feel welcomed by us all."

"Easy for you to say, Fabiana, and I love you for it. I miss my boys, I so wish they were here."

"I know, I know, Auntie, but put on a good front, please do it for me."

In no time Andrew, all spruced up, came to join them. A big smile on his face complemented his good humor.

Francesca, from Fabiana's order, approached him and motioned, "Andrew, join the family in the atrium for a drink. You must taste our *amaro*, it's an artichoke drink to stimulate one's appetite. Afterwards we'll proceed into the dining room."

Andrew was only happy to be part of whatever they suggested and followed willingly. After the *aperitivo* they moved to the enormous dining room. Everyone seemed to know exactly where to sit. Andrew was seated beside Mr. Taverna and Fabiana sat on his other side.

Their glasses were filled with wine and Mrs. Taverna invited everyone to recite a prayer to bless the food. They all made the sign of the cross. Andrew just looked on. Then everyone lifted their wine glass in cheers welcoming Andrew to Sicily.

A succulent Sicilian meal was served with all the trimmings and nothing spared. The array of antipasto, from prosciutto, to the cheeses, pickled eggplant and mushrooms, was a feast followed by the main course, more wine, and then desserts.

The wine was flowing freely and voices were getting louder and more animated. A mixture of Italian, English, and their Sicilian dialect was spoken. Andrew tried to grasp it all, but he really needed to pay close attention. The dialect was totally foreign to him. Fabiana sat beside him to be his aide. During the conversation, he found out the family had various businesses in New York, Las Vegas, and Los Angeles, some of their holdings were in real estate and hotels. Sicily was their home base where the family gathered and they were grateful to have him as part of their family. In a way he was overcome by doubt. Something wasn't quite right.

Later he excused himself and retired to his quarters. After admiring his amenities, he felt he was in a five-star hotel. His mind started to wander and he asked himself: *Where does all their wealth really come from?* He knew that property in Italy was inherited and passed on to the next generation. That explained the home, but he had some reservations. He wanted to know more. *Who are these people? How are they earning their living?* And then a dislikable thought came to his mind, as stereotypically, this southern part is known for the mob. *No, shame on you, Andrew.* He immediately dismissed any sinister unpleasantness from his mind. He knew Mr. Taverna and Joseph were hard working people. They owned acres and acres of tangerine and orange orchards, and had big extensions of vineyards.

The following morning Fabiana asked him, "Professor, would you care to go to work one day? We will go down to the valley and pick oranges. It will be an experience for you."

"I would love to do that, Fabiana, considering the hospitality, I should do some work," he answered.

"Oh no, it's for fun only. We have plenty of help."

Fabiana was his guardian angel; she had assumed the role of a guide and with delight ventured to show Palermo to Andrew. They visited the grandiose cathedral, the piazzas, the splendid fountains and the outdoor markets. The prices were so reasonable compared to London. The ladies and the men seemed so well groomed in their southern apparel. He felt it a necessity to improve his own appearance; he wanted to blend in.

Andrew's humor had improved since his arrival and now he was in total bliss with his daily discoveries. Every day someone would accompany him on his outings. Mr. Taverna made sure he was having a good time and that he was safely escorted.

On his first Sunday morning, just after they had finished breakfast, Mrs. Taverna announced, "This morning we will go to church; it is a day of rest. We will attend mass at the Cathedral of Saint Rosalia at Mount Pellegrino."

She asked him, "Andrew, would you care to join us?"

Andrew was not a devoted Catholic, but he promptly replied, "It will be my pleasure." He was not in the habit of attending mass; actually he couldn't remember when he last attended a service. He found it boring and it certainly wasn't his ritual Sunday obligation. But he wanted to oblige.

The chauffeur was waiting for them; on the way they stopped to pick up Aunt Francesca, Mr. Taverna's sister. Her husband was away, out of the country at the moment. The limo pulled up and she joined them dressed elegantly in an ankle length, yellow floral chiffon dress with a blue colored veil covering her head and shoulders. Her appearance was that of sainthood. Andrew couldn't help staring at her.

The chauffeur negotiated the narrow road that climbed the mountain, and the higher they went, the more spectacular Palermo appeared beneath them; the white sandy beach glittered with the midmorning sun.

Once they reached the top, Andrew couldn't believe the size of the cathedral. An enormous rock had been amalgamated into the structure combining mortar and natural stones to create the incredible church. The architecture boggled his mind with the idea that man and nature had created it all. It was here that the Statue of Saint Rosalia was placed: the patron saint of Palermo.

She stood erected on a marble altar lit by flickering blue spot-lights. Massive arrangements of white roses, with deep green leaves, were layered at her feet. The scene was heavenly and religious. Andrew felt he had been transmitted into another world: the singing was mesmerizing as was the praying and chanting.

While he was taking this all in with admiration, his eyes glanced at a figure knelt down in front of the statue. Her head was tilted, she was looking up at the statue and holding her hands together in prayer. It was Francesca! There she was in front of the altar of Saint Rosalia. He suddenly felt a strong desire to be in her thoughts. She didn't seem happy to him, she appeared mysterious. He noticed a certain sadness in her eyes. Andrew had also detected it with the tone of her voice.

Cathedral of Monte Pellegrino, Palermo

Poor soul, he wondered. *What could be troubling her?* He considered talking to her in the hope that he might cheer her up. What Andrew didn't know was that married Sicilian women didn't engage in long conversations with other men unless they were related. It was also not their custom to keep company or have male friends, especially a married lady with an absent husband.

Fabiana had informed Andrew she was going to have lunch and dinner with them, since it was Sunday. This was their custom. Andrew was puzzled and intrigued by Francesca, he wanted to know more about her. She appeared to be a lady in her forties, he thought, although she looked younger for her age. Her long black hair adorned her face; one could detect the lines of stress on her fine skin. She was petite and attractive and she certainly had panache.

Andrew admired the closeness with family ties. He couldn't help but make comparisons with his own family. He seriously thought of his brother; his family didn't give a hoot about him or his well-being.

As the days passed, he became more and more intrigued with this mysterious lady. He had to admit to himself that she was mighty appealing, even in her aura of misery. When Francesca was with them, he felt that in some strange way her presence filled the void in him. The days were passing by fast; Andrew was getting used to living in luxury and wealth. He was also getting accustomed to Mrs. Taverna's meals; they were such a treat for him. Andrew knew his taste buds would be in for a shock once he returned to London.

Chapter Three

....

On Thursday of the same week, he found out that a celebration was going to take place at Francesca's house on Friday evening. They were all invited, including Andrew. Francesca had stopped by and extended an invitation to him personally, "Professor," she said, "please make sure you join us tomorrow night, dinner at my place, okay?"

Andrew protested a bit saying, "Maybe I should remain behind, I don't want to impose on your family."

"Nonsense, I want you to meet my husband and my two young sons. You must come."

Deep down he wanted to go, "I will be delighted to meet your family, Francesca." He loved to say her name; he emphasized the "sca" making it cascade at the end.

Andrew couldn't help notice how upbeat and happier Francesca sounded. In high spirits she related to him all about her boys and her husband, "My two boys are attending school in Boston. Now being August, they're returning for a vacation."

Andrew listened attentively. Fabiana had given him a brief preview about Francesca's family, but he felt privileged that Francesca was relating this to him personally. He accepted the invitation willingly. Actually, he was curious now. He looked forward to meeting these people – especially Francesca's husband.

Friday evening arrived and Fabiana suggested, "Professor, why don't you and I walk over? It will do us good. Joseph and my parents will drive over and meet us there."

He had noticed from going to church that Francesca's home was within walking distance. "Good idea, Fabiana. I'll be ready."

Fabiana had served as his chaperone since he had arrived in Sicily. He was getting to know her better and was fond of her. Actually, he admired the father-daughter relationship she had with Mr. Taverna. Sometimes he felt bouts of regret for having never married and had a family. The numerous relationships he had had in the past had been fruitless. He considered Fabiana like a daughter, and she in return, had a lot of respect for him.

With Fabiana at his side, Andrew arrived at Francesca's home feeling reassured. Once inside, he noticed it wasn't as elaborate as the Taverna's place, but it looked just as prosperous. Francesca, radiant and smiling, had greeted them in the foyer. Her long royal blue silk dress added to her femininity. She was indeed a very attractive lady, Andrew observed with keen eyes.

Francesca promptly led Andrew to meet her sons, "This is my son Diego."

"Nice to meet you, Professor." Diego promptly extended his greeting with a handshake.

"Likewise, Diego, the pleasure is mine."

Another young man stood behind, he seemed pleasant, yet timid.

"My son Daniele," said Francesca.

"Daniele, how nice to meet you, too!" he encouraged with a big smile welcoming his handshake.

"Welcome to Sicily, Professor. It's good to have you with us." He blushed, turning his facial expression even more likeable.

After meeting the boys, Francesca's husband joined them, "Professor Andrew!" he said extending his hand, "Angelo Frarano, welcome to our home."

"*Molto piacere* – with much pleasure," Andrew felt compelled to impress him with his Italian.

"*Il piacere e' mio* – the pleasure is mine," Mr. Frarano replied with a strong assertive voice.

Andrew's knuckles were hurting from his strong handshake. Angelo looked like a powerful man, but he wasn't going to pass judgment with his first impression. These people were receiving him in their home, this in itself showed kindness; therefore, he was discarding any feeling of negativity. Back in London, no one ever invited him for anything, except Mrs. Brooks with her tea offers, which he knew she was only doing it out of her loneliness and to fulfill her own desire to gossip about the neighbors.

Angelo was a big man in stature. His dark hair was brushed back, making him appear quite severe with his receding hairline. Andrew noticed that Angelo had a scar on his upper right eye, plus an extended beer belly that swiveled around as he walked. The boys gathered around their cousin Fabiana affectionately, he could detect their close relationship. After all, they were close in age and had a lot in common. The boys were fluent in English and he felt a great sense of pleasure among these young people. Andrew wondered what Angelo Frarano was like as a husband to Francesca? The sons seemed genuine and innocent. He would like to get to know them, but the father, he wasn't so sure. It was questionable.

In observing the boys during the course of the evening, he noticed how polite Diego was. Like his mom he had good features. Daniele looked so young, a polished young lad with a nice smile and big brown eyes. In Boston, Diego was studying law at Harvard University, and Daniele on his first year of architecture was also at Harvard.

They exchanged information and compared everything from lifestyle to food and the education systems of the two countries.

Andrew commented, "Regardless of which country or school, you need to study diligently. Once you retain the knowledge, you are empowered."

The boys listened attentively, nodding in agreement.

He could see why Francesca was all smiles as she gazed admiringly at her two young sons. Andrew had to admit, they appeared to be two fine young men indeed.

Letizia their maid had served a fabulous meal. Once they finished dinner, Francesca motioned them to move outdoors onto the terrace. In the warm evening breeze they could indulge in espresso and *tartufo*, with tropical fruit soaked in amaretto and sambuca. Francesca radiantly sat herself beside her husband and lifted her glass cheerfully, "I want to propose a toast to my Angelo, for coming home, to my sons, and our honorable guest Professor Andrew. Cheers!"

Then Francesca's brother Anthony, asked in a disturbing tone, "Angelo, how long are you going to stay in town this time? You need to spend more time with my sister, here in Sicily, don't you think?"

"Anthony, what is the matter with you? You know the hotel industry. I need to be in New York. Don't be ridiculous and try to make me feel guilty."

Francesca knew he would only be in town for two days. He had told her, "I'm here hardly long enough to warm the bed as I need to get back to business. I have to fly back to New York on Monday. The boys can stay to keep you company."

As long as she had her sons she was happy. Francesca stood up and moved over to put her arms on the shoulders of her sons, smiling between them she said to her brother, "Anthony, don't worry about me, I have Diego and Daniele. I'm fine as long as Angelo calls me every night. I will be fine. I will wait for him."

Andrew looked at the family with admiration. However, at the same time he couldn't help but feel intrusive in the family's conversation. He gathered Angelo's work was his priority.

The evening had been great. The Sicilian food, sumptuous again. He drank more than two glasses of wine and felt pretty relaxed. It was time to depart. Since Angelo was going to be leaving, Andrew wanted to say his goodbyes and thank him for his hospitality. But he sure was looking forward to seeing Francesca and the boys again … soon, he hoped.

Andrew then approached Mr. Frarano, reluctantly extending his hand, as he did not want his knuckles crushed again. "Mr. Frarano, it's been a pleasure to have met you. You have a safe flight back to New York and thank you, thank you for having me in your home."

To his surprise, Mr. Frarano responded with a hug, "Professor, if you're a friend of my family, you're a friend of mine too, and most welcome in my home. It has been an honour to have you with us and at our dinner table."

While he spoke, he kept striking his shoulder with his strong hand. Andrew had a fearful thought, *As long as I don't end up with a dislocated shoulder.* But his kind words were reassuring and made him feel good. As he walked home with Fabiana, he asked her, "Your uncle. He isn't as tough as he looks."

"My father and my family are very protective of my aunt and concerned for her well-being. He gets into arguments with my uncle in that respect, but he resents being controlled by my father. "

Indeed, Angelo Frarano didn't care much for Francesca's brother. Who was he to tell him when to come and go? It wasn't any of his business; he didn't have any authority over him just because he was married to his sister.

But it seems Angelo did have a bit of business to do before leaving, which no one knew about. Angelo figured before he was to leave again on Sunday, he better have another meeting with Miliano Cardone, his informant and watchdog. He paid him well to keep an eye on his wife and boys when he was out of town.

The next morning he went to his favorite coffee shop *Il dolcetto* (The Sweets), which was around the corner from the four fountains at the center of Palermo. He knew Miliano would be there for his freshly brewed espresso.

Palermo Bay

Angelo walked in and immediately spotted him sitting on his usual stool by the coffee bar.

"Eh, Angelo," Miliano shouted as he saw him, "how are you doing? I knew I was going to see you here."

"Miliano, I know where to find you on a Sunday morning. Do you think I go to church looking for you? You crumb!" With that he smacked his shoulder in a friendly gesture.

"I'm fine, I leave on the morning flight from La Mezia to Rome, then on to New York."

"Eh boss, nothing to report. All has been going well here."

"Miliano, I have something that I need to get off my chest. My brother-in-law has been getting on my sweet nerves more and more. And lately he's always making smart remarks. You be vigilant and keep your eye on him! *Mi capisci?* You understand me?"

He certainly didn't want him or his family talking about him in his absence. He had no problem keeping Francesca dutiful, as long as they didn't fill her head with crazy thoughts. He knew

Anthony had never been in favor of Francesca marrying him and his feelings had not changed in time.

"Don't worry, boss, I'm dutifully at your service. Leave it to me."

With that they shook hands in agreement and Angelo slipped fifty million lire into his hand. Miliano grinned with pleasure. Angelo gulped down his last drop of espresso and left.

In his mind he felt justified. He was a good provider for his family. No one was ever going to harm or bother Francesca while he was away. He secretly protected her. It was okay for him to stay away from her; after all, he was attending to business. She was terrified of flying so she couldn't go to the United States. It all worked in his favor.

***

Once back in his bedroom Andrew felt restless. He couldn't keep the vision of Francesca out of his mind. But he reminded himself, *I must not fancy her, she's married and I must put those thoughts of her to rest.* Guilt started to churn in the pit of his stomach. He knew it was unfair to Angelo. Agitated, he slumped his body onto a soft leather chair and picked up his book on the side table hoping to relax. It wasn't quite working so he decided to step out onto the terrace for some fresh air. He sat and meditated to calm his mind. Finally, he returned inside and hit the pillow. Gradually, sleep took over.

A couple of days later, while he was reading outdoors under a fig tree he could hear Mrs. Taverna complaining to Fabiana, "Two days have gone by and no sign of Francesca. You better check on her, she hasn't called us over for pizza or coffee. That's not like her."

Fabiana remarked, "Mother! You forget, Aunt Francesca now has her boys; she doesn't need us as much. Leave her be!"

Andrew felt guilty eavesdropping, but he continued to listen; his ears perked up when he heard them mention Francesca's name. Andrew also wondered when the boys were due to leave; deep down he hoped it would be soon.

He missed her and enjoyed her company. He noticed her sadness when her husband and sons weren't around. Then he reminded himself that it was none of his business.

The next day Fabiana asked him, "Professor, tell me, what do you think of my Aunt Francesca? Do you approve of such a long distance marriage?"

Andrew responded, "I feel in my heart that she isn't happy. A middle-aged woman with an absent husband, and her two sons so far away from her must be lonely."

"You are right, Professor, this is why my father is perturbed at their marriage arrangement."

"I understand."

He knew only too well how it felt to be alone and abandoned. He couldn't help but wonder, why wasn't she going with them? What was the mystery holding her here? Surely, she wasn't afraid of flying?

"Fabiana, why doesn't she go abroad with her husband and family?"

"Good question. We think he likes it that way. He has the best of both worlds."

Chapter Four

Andrew would soon be returning to London to his simple Bethnow row house and all this would be a memory: Sicily, the Taverna family and the Frarano family. Francesca was only to be admired as the most wonderful lady he had ever met. She certainly did not encourage him, or give him any sign of anything beyond friendship; she was in a world of her own. He would keep in touch with Fabiana and the Tavernas of course, he was grateful for their hospitality and this wonderful vacation they had granted him.

One morning, the sun was beaming and the weather was hot and scorching. Andrew had swum some laps in the pool and after his workout, he glanced at his watch. Pleased with himself he thought it was time to relax with his mystery book. He sat under the fig tree, which was his favorite spot in the garden and immersed himself in reading. The tree this year was not producing any fruit, as Anthony had explained. It was leafy and rich in branches producing dense shade for relaxation. A fresh breeze was blowing occasionally up from the sea and he found it rather pleasant to be there.

Fabiana startled him, "Professor Andrew, would you like to join us for an espresso and *cannoli Siciliani*, which is a special dessert? Aunt Francesca and my two cousins are here."

Andrew jumped up closing his book immediately, "I'd love to!"

Francesca and the young men were delighted to see him. Greeting Francesca, Andrew felt a jolt in his heart. He knew he couldn't help the desire to be in her company. She had been in his thoughts and his dreams. He yearned to see her. Andrew was vulnerable. Yes, he realized more and more that she was not available. Nevertheless, he could not help his feelings.

He had questioned Fabiana once, "What does Francesca think of me?"

Her reply had been curt, "That you're a fine Englishman."

Simple as that, he thought, *do I even enter her mind?*

Francesca seemed totally absorbed in her sons. After the refreshments, Diego announced, "We came over for two reasons; one is to visit with you, and the other is to invite you, Auntie Lora, and my dear cousin Fabiana and you, Professor, to Cefalù for a week. We're going to take my mom and we're asking you to join us, especially you, Professor Robertson."

Daniele continued referring to Andrew, "This would give you an opportunity to explore Cefalù, enjoy the rugged coast above the sea and the countryside."

Francesca followed, "They have booked rooms at the Hotel Pozzetti. It's situated on a hill overlooking the Mediterranean with the barrier of the mountains behind. The combination of fine mountain air and the sea is a healthy retreat."

Diego, now turning to Fabiana added, "A week there will rejuvenate Mother and beside it's our yearly thing. We must go to Cefalù. Please come with us. It will be another experience for the Professor."

Andrew was at Fabiana's mercy, he welcomed any opportunity to be in Francesca's company and he hoped she would accept. He would be delighted to go along. He was holding his breath in the meantime.

"Yes, of course," said Fabiana, "It will be great for the Professor if he would like to go."

Andrew quickly responded, "Fabiana, I would love the opportunity to explore Cefalù and I am grateful to be included with your cousin's family, as long as I'm not imposing."

Mrs. Taverna interrupted, "We're familiar with the coast and have been there many times; why don't the five of you go? I prefer to stay behind and help Ersilia look after Anthony and Joseph with the meals. Diego, you mean well. I know your uncle likes it better when he finds me at home to greet him and Joseph from their hard day's work."

"Aunt Lora, you are so devoted; does my uncle know how lucky he is?"

"It's my duty dear, no question about it."

Fabiana was quick to reprehend her. She knew her mother was old fashioned.

"Mom, I know dad and Joseph are busy, but you can join us if you want to, can't you?" she insisted.

Mrs. Taverna continued excusing herself, "Diego, and, Daniele, my dearest. I appreciate you wanting me. But I also know that Anthony and Joseph need to oversee the workers and go back and forth to Castellammare. It is better for me to stay home to welcome them. You boys with Fabiana are perfectly capable to take care of your mom and show the Professor a good time."

Andrew couldn't have been happier.

Two days later a limo pulled up in front of their home and they were off. The ride was great fun, the young people's laughter was absorbed by Andrew in good humor. Discreetly he glanced at Francesca. Then, his guilt would set in and he would turn quickly to admire the countryside. Cefalù wasn't far from Palermo. Driving along the coast was spectacular. The boys were right about the soothing climate; it was rejuvenating. The mountains, the deep blue sea, the beauty of nature – it was a touristic haven for any visitor.

They arrived at the five-star hotel and the hospitality and comfort was that of utmost luxury. Andrew had never been happier. Here he was with three delightful young people and a lovely Sicilian lady who stirred a flame in his heart. He was like a young boy having his first crush; the only obstacle was that she belonged to someone else.

When he was alone, he found himself fantasizing about Francesca. He would like to reach deep into her brain to see what she was thinking. From his encounter with Angelo, he had come to the conclusion that she couldn't be happy with her husband. Maybe, just maybe, he would have a chance to talk to her. He knew deep down it wasn't going to be easy. The women here were reserved, domesticated and totally dedicated to their families. Francesca was the perfect image of the statue he had admired at the altar of Saint Rosalia.

Cefalù was a place of inspiration. One could indulge in any activity, it had so much to offer: horse riding, strolling along the countryside, admiring the olive groves, enjoying the impeccable beach, the piazza for coffees and *gelato,* and the outdoor dances and the discos for the young. The Olympic size swimming pool was delightfully inviting. As they were in the south, the evenings were warm and comfortable. One could easily swim late at night, as the warm breeze would be refreshing.

Three days went by fast. The days were spent exploring and the evenings were celebrated with superb meals and aged wines. Andrew was not accustomed to the hot sun. This evening he felt more tired than usual, therefore, he planned to retire early. Meanwhile, Fabiana and her cousins wanted to go and check out the club *Della Luna,* a local place for the young at heart. Francesca excused herself right after dinner. She announced that her husband was going to call and she would go to her room and wait. She embraced her sons and Fabiana, gave Andrew a gentle handshake and off she went.

Andrew was alone again. Self-pity kicked in. He wondered whether the announcement of Francesca's phone call had triggered a migraine, or questioned whether it was the wine. Instead of going to his room to read, he decided to go for a stroll. *The fresh mountain air might help*, he thought.

There was a walking path around the hotel that was illuminated with lights and the full moon. Other guests were milling about, socializing and gregarious laughter could be heard among them while others were just sitting in peacefulness.

Andrew sat down and lost track of time reminiscing about his journey and his experiences in Sicily. He was just thinking to himself how lucky he had been to have Fabiana in his class. Now he had been gifted with this extravagance. He had been walking for almost an hour as he checked his watch. Now he was ready to retire to his room with his book, but by some force of instinct he strolled a little further. At the side of the semicircular path there was a white ornate bench: Francesca was sitting there. He looked once, he looked twice. Was his vision playing tricks on him? No, she was there, for real. She was holding her face in her hands. At first he hesitated. Then slowly, feeling the heaviness in his footsteps he approached her. He noticed she was crying.

Andrew simultaneously, was both shocked and happy. He stopped beside her. He didn't know what to do or say at first, "Francesca, lovey," he took a deep breath, "what is the matter?"

Francesca started to sob louder. Andrew didn't know how to react, so in an act of kindness he gently put his arm around her. Overcome by tears, Francesca was crying and talking at the same time, which made her difficult to understand. She was blabbering with all kinds of words in broken English and Italian.

Andrew gently tried to calm her down. He was wiping away her tears with a fresh handkerchief he had pulled out of his pocket. Afterwards, he sat down beside her trying to understand.

"Francesca," he said, "I want to be your friend, please tell me, what is wrong? Please let me help you." He held her tightly while she sobbed.

Finally she spoke, "I waited and waited for my husband's phone call. When it didn't arrive, I decided to call him. A woman answered the phone, his mistress. When he came on the phone, he was in a mad rage telling me, how dare I call him when I had been warned not to. In a loud voice he said, 'I would have called you when I was ready, woman. You do not understand do you? When are you going to learn to do as you are told?' "

She was a mess from crying. Andrew felt so sorry for her; she didn't deserve to be treated like that. He knew now why the sadness was in her eyes. All of a sudden he could envision Angelo pushing his weight around. He envisioned him with his loud voice, verbally slashing this poor woman. Andrew felt bad for her. Why would a man abuse this kind soul, innocent and merciful? He cared for her so much and it was beyond his belief that anyone would take her for granted like that.

If only Francesca would allow it, he wanted to make it up to her. He had not wanted to give in to the feeling of uneasiness for Angelo, but now he had no respect for him. He was a brute. Maybe there was hope for him after all. He was fond of Francesca, this poor woman needed to be loved, just like he did. He understood what rejection meant, therefore, he related well to her feelings.

"Francesca, my lovey," he said as he was embracing her again, pulling her closer to his body. He held her tenderly for few moments. Then, he turned her face gently to face his. She was so vulnerable at this moment. Andrew's desires were being stirred by her closeness. But he knew he would respect her. Oh how he dearly cared for her.

He was not going to be a selfish man who would take advantage of her. He just wanted to soothe her with his kindness and make up to her the love and protection her husband lacked giving her. He felt a strong desire to bash that brute of a husband of hers for taking her for granted.

"Francesca, how can he hurt you so? What kind of a man is he? Why do you stay married to him?"

"Most of us women in Sicily, once we marry, we remain married, and we abide by our marriage vows, regardless of the circumstances. I know I suffer but I keep it in silence."

"My poor, Francesca," he murmured while caressing her silky black hair. He felt so much compassion towards her. You could read it in her eyes that she was a gentle soul; she certainly didn't deserve any malice. He had not wanted to admit it to himself, but he had felt a certain dislike for Angelo from the first moment he met him.

Francesca seemed to have calmed down a little. Suddenly she abruptly pulled away from him, "Professor Robertson. *Mi scusa* – excuse me," she said. "Sorry, I let myself go. I'm a married woman."

Embarrassed for her weakness, she tried to regain her composure. On the other hand, Francesca also realized that it felt good to be close to another male human being, especially a nice fellow like Andrew. He felt warm and reassuring. She was starving for love; her husband had never showed her real affection.

She knew he had married her for his own convenience. She was his commodity when he arrived home; the perfect wife to give him two sons. Yes, his two sons would carry on his name. An honor for the Frarano family, having produced two sons was considered a legacy.

Francesca's life had been very sad. She had all the material necessities, but the emptiness in her heart and soul was devastating. She felt trapped in a loveless marriage with no escape. The only joy she felt was seeing her two boys. Inconsiderate of her feelings, her husband had managed to take them away from her by insisting they attend university in Boston.

"My sons will come to the U.S. I want Diego to graduate from Harvard. Without a question. I will call my buddy, Professor Delgato to make sure they are accepted. Daniele will go to Harvard also and do as I say."

"Angelo," Francesca had begged, "Agrigento has the best educators and the best university right here in Sicily. I would prefer for them to be here."

"Francesca, don't try to turn my boys into sissies under their mother's skirt. I want them to be real men and they need to fly the coop away from their mother. End of discussion."

He ruled and Francesca had to obey and keep quiet. He was now robbing her of her time with her two precious young men.

They had been tutored in English all through high school so they were fluent when they moved to the United States. The boys never went against their father's wishes.

Oh, how she loved them. As for her husband, no she had no love for him. Her parents had dictated that she marry him. It was a marriage of convenience. She soon realized his unfaithfulness. The affairs started soon after they had been married. She had no control or say about it; she had to accept and live with it. Francesca had been suffering for many years.

Her duty was to be a good wife and mother and take care of the household affairs. She would pamper her two boys, and as for her well-being, she was well provided for. As he saw it, she should be grateful to him for that and continue to be a dutiful wife.

On this night, Francesca's emotions had gotten out of control and she had broken down from her own starvation for love and affection. Andrew offered to walk Francesca back to her room, feeling tender and desiring her now even more. When they got to her door, Andrew, forced by natural instinct embraced her passionately. Francesca overcome by the same instinct responded by the will of nature. Before they both realized it and, driven by an unnatural force, they locked themselves in a long warm kiss. Andrew didn't ever want to let go.

He begged her with his languishing eyes, "Francesca we need each other, we are both starving for love, let's not throw this night away."

Francesca seemed to be caught in a spell. She put her arm around Andrew's waist, leading him inside her room and closed the door behind them, "Oh, Andrew..." she exclaimed lifting her face to him.

Overwhelmed, Andrew responded vehemently. They spent the night in each other's arms, in the bliss of lovemaking, wishing it into an eternity. Little did they know that their time together had been recorded and videotaped. Miliano Cardone had made sure of that.

As for Fabiana and her young cousins, they had come home very late.

Andrew was awoken the following morning as the rays of the sun were cast through the curtains of the window. He needed to discreetly make his way back to his room. He turned one more time to admire his lovely Francesca. He knew he adored her so. The force of his emotions had finally exploded with his passion. He knew she had played magic on him ever since he had laid eyes on her. She looked peaceful and serene as she slept, and he watched her as he sat on the side of the bed.

"Francesca, am I dreaming? Or is this for real?"

He couldn't believe that he was beside Francesca, in her bed, and they could now be lovers if she was willing. He had a lot of planning to do, as there were only a couple of more days left in Cefalù, and then his vacation would come to an end. How was he going to leave without Francesca? *I love this woman; now that I have found her, I will not let her go.* Love-struck, he continued to kiss her gently, afraid to let go, but he needed to slip out of the room before it was too late.

Outside, around the corner in the hallway, a man was taking a long drag on a cigarette. Miliano Cardone, blowing the fumes high, pretended to be an innocent bystander. But he was diligently doing his job as had been assigned by his boss. Andrew paid no regards to the smoker and quietly headed for his room. Mesmerized by his newfound love, Andrew never realized he was being watched and in serious trouble.

Chapter Five

....

Miliano Cardone was only doing his job keeping vigil on his boss's family. The day before, under false pretenses, he had managed to bug Francesca's room when he had walked in as the air conditioning repairman. The device would record any conversation or goings on. Andrew hadn't even noticed a strange man snapping photos of them; a lot of tourists were taking photos. It was normal for anyone wanting to capture the beauty of Cefalù. Cardone was an expert at his job. He was muscular, six-foot four and dressed in light beige pants and a white linen shirt. His weapon of choice: a high-end camera hanging around his neck.

His first reaction was not to waste any time in placing a phone call to New York. He had some juicy news to report and this news would be rewarded with a lot more money. "Mula, mula, Mr. Frarano," Money, money in his slang language, he happily chuckled to himself. Finally the lamb went to the wolf. He checked his watch; there was a six-hour time difference between Italy and New York. It was now five in the morning in Sicily, so that made it close to noon New York time. Why give Boss Frarano the news at lunchtime? He decided to wait for later in the afternoon.

Francesca had no idea that her husband kept such tabs on her. She had felt like a young widow most of her life and she had been a faithful wife up until now.

Francesca often recognized that needy feeling deep in her heart. She felt so deprived and she fought with the unfairness. In the end, she chose to resign herself and be the martyr. The two boys sympathized with her and were well aware of their father's liaisons. Often Diego and Daniele protected their mother. They despised their father for his poor role as a husband. In the meantime, they obeyed his rules. They had no choice.

When Francesca woke up a big smile circled her face. But as she looked around her room, panic suddenly struck her. She soon realized what had taken place in her bed had been real. She could still smell the scent of Andrew's cologne; it was all around her. She recognized it the first time they met, it was her favorite. *Pino Silvestre*, produced from pine trees of the North. To her, the scent was erotic; it worked to stir up her inner emotions.

"Oh my God," bringing her hands to hold her head, "what have I done?"

Her body shivered. How was she going to face the Professor? How was she going to live with herself as an adulteress? Guilt and shame soon engulfed her. She wanted to go back to sleep and never wake up. She thought of the recent incident with her horrible husband. But now she was wrestling with her feelings, blaming herself. The only justification to her was that she must have lost her mind. But now what? She could not erase the night. The desperate sex she had engaged in was revenge for her poor existence from neglect and loneliness. Yes, her husband deserved to be punished with what had happened between her and the Professor. Regardless of her justifications, she fought with her guilt. The men in town would have never dared to approach her. They were well aware she was a married woman, knew their customs and knew the dangers.

She shamefully decided to apologize to Andrew. *I will implore him to erase the event from his mind, to forgive me for my temporary insanity and weakness.* As for herself, she would be in denial. She wouldn't reveal what happened to anyone. Francesca would go to the church of Saint Rosalia and pray for forgiveness. She would confess her sins to Father Alfonso and diligently do her penance.

Once the realization set in she got up and walked around her room in a daze. She couldn't face Andrew and had no wish to see him. She had to admit to herself – this English Professor had fulfilled her needs. Deep down the feeling in her soul was real, that she liked him. She also asked herself where it would take her. She was doomed and committed until death to a man she didn't love. The Professor would soon be returning to England and forget the one-night fling they had both enjoyed. Now she was going to pay the consequences, she didn't feel pure and worthy of her two handsome sons anymore. Francesca was a Christian and "I shall not commit adultery" was cemented in her faith. But now she had.

Andrew had other plans. He was determined to have Francesca in his life. He wanted to make up to her all those years of non-existence. He was approaching fifty and a free man. Francesca was in her early forties, married with two grown sons and a tyrant for a husband. They were both mature and still young enough to fall in love. This love was not going to be easy. With his strong will and determination he felt somehow he would convince her to follow him. Over the next couple of days Andrew lived his waking hours seeking Francesca's company. He relived that night again and again. But now she was avoiding him, which was driving him mad because the remainder of their time together was limited and precious.

Fabiana and her cousins were busying themselves meeting new people, playing tennis, swimming, and going to the disco at night until late hours. They were having the time of their lives. The boys were attentive to their mother Francesca, but they were young and carefree and on their own quest of girls around them and there were plenty.

Francesca sat alone in her room. She continued to wrestle with her emotions, assuming blame, taking it all personally. Little did she realize or suspect much bigger problems were in store for her. Cardone was hard at work. He kept his distance, but his camera and watchful eyes were constantly on the two subjects of interest now. What had taken place the other night had finally sparked some excitement. Now his work would be motivating and rewarding. He knew this was worth big money for him. He needed to be precise and not lose sight of Andrew and Francesca. It had been so boring watching Francesca for such a long period of time without any action. Her monotonous life and daily routine was enough to drive anybody bonkers.

In the past he had told Mr. Frarano that Francesca was such a good wife and mother. He had nothing to report. But he was kept on as her watchdog for her safety. Cardone churned ideas in his head on what to do with his information. On second thought, he decided, he wasn't going to hurry and inform his boss. He decided it would be best to keep his new findings to himself for a while. Then he would best decide how to put it to work, for his own benefit.

Chapter Six

····················

While they were there, *Il Festival Internazionale Del Gelato* in Cefalù, a three-day celebration of ice cream was taking place in the main piazza. People from the surrounding areas along with the tourists invaded the main street of the piazza to indulge on the variety of ice cream flavors. Vendors competed with one another to show off their flavor creations. Supported by the citizens, everyone celebrated.

Fabiana was quick to inform Andrew of the event. She wished him to experience it with her and the boys, "I will find Aunt Francesca. We will take the hotel shuttle to the piazza."

Andrew's heart flipped with joy. Finally, he was going to see Francesca. What on earth had come over her? She wouldn't talk; she was avoiding him now. He was on time and ready at the front lobby, desperately searching and waiting for Francesca to appear. There, she finally appeared, beautiful as a picture.

"My two cousins will meet us there," Fabiana had informed him. "They met a couple of girls from Switzerland and they will come together."

Andrew needed to control his emotions in wanting to embrace his Francesca. He wanted so much to seal her lips with a passionate kiss. He didn't know how to behave. He held back and decided to settle with a handshake. He needed to talk to her. He was anxious, and wondered where he stood in her world. Were they lovers? Were they strangers? How was he to react? He knew she was married, but if she was willing they could be lovers. On his part he wished she could belong to him and him only. Andrew had never fallen head over heels like this before. All the other women in his life hadn't stirred him up like Francesca. Why was it? Could it be because she was so different and seemed so holy? Unavailable?

Andrew was so naive. Little did he know his infatuation with Francesca was big trouble. *You don't fall in love with a mobster's wife and their wives don't engage in love affairs.* She was forbidden fruit. Was this why Andrew desired Francesca so much more?

To Andrew's surprise Francesca seemed cold and indifferent. This made him sad. He couldn't wait to have a chance to talk to her alone. He needed so badly to talk to her. Maybe the evening would divulge in some private time for the two of them. Then he would have to tell her how desperately he had fallen for her. In the meantime, Miliano Cardone was at work keeping a close distance.

Andrew only had eyes for Francesca. He didn't notice Cardone or anyone else as far as he was concerned. Once they got to the piazza, Fabiana stood in the center holding Francesca's arm on her right side and the Professor's on her left. She was a devoted niece; she loved her aunt. She was explaining to Andrew about the customs of Cefalù and its people. Andrew would smile and nod but he wasn't listening.

In his thoughts he had Francesca, so near and so far. He started to panic because he only had one week left in Sicily. How was he going to leave with this infatuation in his head? He needed to convince her to go with him, but he knew that would be difficult. Could she at least allow him to tell her how much he cared? He needed to find out if she cared for him. He wanted to believe that yes, she did fancy him. He would implore her, confessing his love for her. Maybe – just maybe – if not at this present time, later on in the future there was hope for a relationship.

In a moment of panic, Andrew thought to disclose his secret to Fabiana, but then he decided to wait. First he needed to ask Francesca if there was a little room in her heart for him. However, he didn't have any luck that night, Francesca's sons arrived and they kissed their mother respectfully. They were taken with these new girls and had their own plans of getting acquainted with them. The evening seemed jolly for them. Everyone held ice cream cones in their hands. Fabiana and Francesca had coffee chocolate, the boys had a peach flavor, and their companions and Andrew chose the famous *cassata* Sicilian. That was the number one ice cream that any foreigner would choose. Andrew insisted on paying. Being the eldest he wanted to portray a father figure.

Miliano Cardone, was waiting for action and watching them eat ice cream was boring for him. It was eleven o'clock when they returned to their hotel. The young people weren't ready to call it a night, so they informed Francesca they were going to an outdoor disco and off they went.

After kissing them good night, Francesca announced she would retire to her room and call it a day. Andrew's ears perked up, a slight hope in his inner being told him maybe this was his chance to have a few words with her. But while he busied in his goodbyes with Fabiana and the rest of them, Francesca disappeared in the lobby before his eyes.

Once in his room he couldn't make himself go to bed. He yearned to talk to her. He picked up the phone and dialed her room number, "Francesca?"

He waited for a moment; he needed to read something in her voice. Was she happy to hear from him? Or was she annoyed at his forwardness? A moment later he heard her voice, "Andrew?" Just to hear her mention his name, he imagined her lips and it sent shivers down his spine.

"Francesca, please let me come over. I need to see you; I need to talk to you. Forgive me for calling you at his time. I'm desperate because we have so much to discuss and such little time." He held his breath waiting for a response.

She was silent; there wasn't any response.

"Francesca, are you there? Please answer me, tell me that you want to see me too, that I am not mad."

He waited... finally, "Andrew, I'm sorry what happened the other night. I must have been insane. I am asking you to erase it from your mind and pretend it never happened. Please never reveal it to anyone. I don't know if I will ever forgive myself. Goodnight, Andrew."

With that the phone went dead and Andrew's heart was crushed. He felt like a young teen in love for the first time. He wanted to cry. How could she waste this little time they had? How could she refuse him and be in denial? He knew deep down that she wanted him. He felt it as sure as his blood ran through his veins. But what could he do? Who was going to help him? He wanted to dial again, but he was fifty not seventeen. *I need to behave like a man.* He could not understand why she was so dutiful to waste her life away negating herself the pleasure of their love.

Andrew looked around his room; the walls were suffocating. He needed to step out of this room. He decided to go to the bar down in the lobby and have a stiff drink. It would temporarily calm his nerves and maybe help him sleep. The bar was full of tourists, the music was blaring.

He placed his order, "A Scotch on the rocks, please." In an instant he was being wooed by girls with short skirts, high heels, big heavy thighs, and breasts half popping out of their tops. They were trying to get his attention. He wasn't interested. He felt disenchanted by their aggressiveness. He had desires that could only be fulfilled by the woman he wanted: Francesca. He realized why, because she was such a modest human being and she wasn't for sale.

He had taken a couple of sips from his drink when a stranger sat beside him. The man wanted to start up a conversation, but Andrew wasn't in the mood. He was going to finish his drink and try to get some sleep, hopeful that his luck with Francesca would change for the better the following day.

The stranger was Cardone and he was getting irritated. He wanted to record more juicy stuff for his ammunition. Instead, he had to finish the day with a phone conversation that didn't offer much to his advantage. The boss's wife had declined to get involved; it was looking like a one off.

He followed Andrew to his room and when the lights went off, he called it a night. Francesca's room was quiet, other than the sound of her gentle breathing. But Cardone figured that sooner or later his job was going to get more interesting. By observing Andrew he knew he was a troubled man in love.

The next couple of days proceeded without much action. Andrew looked somber. Fabiana had noticed the change in Andrew and asked, "Professor, is something wrong? Are you getting homesick? Have you had enough of Sicily and us?"

Andrew responded, "On the contrary, love. I'm sorry to be going home. You know, I'm fond of you and your family. I will miss you people so much when I return home."

Fabiana expressed her intention of returning to school in London for the next semester. She asked, "Professor, I would like to do my PhD in linguistics. Will you help me to enroll?"

Andrew's mood suddenly changed. He knew that Francesca and Fabiana were close. Once Fabiana would be in London, maybe Francesca would find her way there even for a short visit. "Of course, Fabiana, I will do anything to help you, you just need to ask."

Fabiana was thrilled; she liked London and its people. Soon she would recommence her studies.

***

Cardone was disappointed, but his instincts told him to wait. No. He would not call Angelo yet. That fool will be caught, reeled in like a fish. He smirked in delight muttering to himself, "I must wait until the fish is in my bag."

The clock was ticking and the days were passing quickly. They had returned to Palermo from Cefalù and Andrew's chances of seeing Francesca were now numbered. The boys had taken a flight back to Boston to commence their school year. Francesca was alone again. No husband, no sons. If only he could find his way to her home and talk to her. *What a difficult task*, Andrew thought.

He plotted and looked for an opening. Two days had gone by, yet no Francesca. He was growing restless, because in three days he would leave for London and the distance was going to complicate the matter more. He felt he needed to make his quest not only for his sake, but for hers also. She needed to be rescued from her insignificant existence. A distinguished lady like Francesca needed to be loved and he wanted to love her, if only she would allow him to.

On one of his final afternoons, while Andrew was in one of his favorite places under the palm tree, Fabiana asked him, "Professor, would you like to go down to the beach this afternoon? We could pack a picnic basket and spend the rest of the day by the freshwater lagoon."

Andrew perked up with hope one more time, "Yes, Fabiana, that's a great idea. Who is going?"

"We could ask Aunt Francesca to join us, she's alone now. My mother wants to remain home to oversee the meals with Ersilia. Dad and Joseph have to attend to some business transactions in Agrigento. It will just be the three of us. My brother Joseph might join us later, should they return early from Agrigento."

Andrew took a deep breath, "That sounds great, Fabiana. What time would you like me to be ready?" *How lucky*, he thought. Fabiana was marvelous to come up with such a proposition.

"In an hour?" she replied. "Ersilia will prepare some snacks for us to take and we will be on our way."

"Great, I can't thank you enough, Fabiana. You have been so kind."

"My pleasure, Professor. I want to show you everything and make sure you have a good time here."

He was so grateful that this sweet, kind girl had come into his life. He could hardly wait.

As planned, everything was proceeding well, and on time. Andrew dressed in his best summer attire: light beige pants complemented by a sky blue shirt, a beige straw hat to protect him from the direct rays of the sun, and some comfy shoes, which would take him to any treacherous adventure of whatever terrain he encountered. His duffel bag contained flip-flops, and swimming attire. He stepped out in front of the house to find Fabiana beaming and waiting for him. He noticed she was radiantly dressed.

"Fabiana!" he called out, "You look like a model that stepped right out of a magazine, very nice."

"Oh, thank you, Professor, this is typical beach attire here."

An elegant ankle length dress, in a bright print of orange and yellow flowers, covered her slim figure, complemented by an orange wide-brimmed hat. It covered part of her face, only to reveal her big brown eyes when she chose to lift her head. There she was holding the door open for him.

"Professor, you take the passenger seat at the front. You know I don't want you to miss any of the scenery. We never took this route with you. We will have Auntie sit at the back."

"Fabiana, my dear. Are you sure? I feel disrespectful toward your aunt."

"No, no, she likes the back seat, don't you worry."

Fabiana confidently took the wheel and off they went with the radio blaring. A little too much for Andrew, but he was with the young at heart. He did not dare complain.

Once they arrived at Francesca's house Fabiana took the initiative to blow the horn in harmony like a little girl calling her best friend. Andrew had gathered that the two women were quite close. That made him happy for Francesca. She wasted no time in coming out; radiant as the sunshine in bright beach attire. Monochromatic in yellow. Her yellow hat, trimmed in green accentuated her essence of mystery.

Letizia the maid followed behind to place a picnic basket neatly in the trunk.

Andrew gallantly put his manners to work. He wanted to help Letizia; she was well trained in her duties. He resorted into extending his hand in helping Francesca into the car as he complimented, "You look radiant, Francesca."

"Thank you, Professor," she answered keeping her head low barely showing her face beneath the brim of her hat.

Once they arrived at the coast, they found themselves in the splendor of the sky and the sea. The long beach extended in front of them to infinity. The white sand gleamed in the sun like diamond dust.

Francesca announced that they would go on the far side where they had their private beach hut and once there they could settle down comfortably. The hut consisted of a few commodities appropriate for the beach. There was a well-stocked fridge, a stove, a love seat, a few canvas chairs and a tiny coffee table.

The afternoon was perfect; there wasn't a cloud in the sky. It was blistering hot. Andrew excused himself; he decided to go for a swim. He needed to freshen up. Afterwards he would sunbathe, his skin wasn't so pale now. He felt the need to escape from this heat that he wasn't accustomed to. That would also give the girls some space. Francesca and Fabiana chatted away with much laughter. Francesca seemed to be in good humor. Andrew was waiting for his chance to make a move on her. But how was he going to without any privacy? He didn't realize that his privacy was worse than he thought. Cardone had followed and was well in tow.

Chapter Seven

Cardone had discreet plans; he was keeping his distance and promptly on guard with his camera. He needed his photos and didn't want to miss anything interesting. It was hard for him to conceal his vigil, as the place was secluded and private.

Andrew's body welcomed the freshness of the lagoon's calm waters. The water felt soothing and invigorating. While swimming he had a notion that someone was watching him, but he shook off the feeling to focus his thoughts on Francesca. He needed to come to terms with her. He needed an agreement before leaving. It was a must. He was going to take her away from that husband of hers. He was determined to win her over, but of course he needed her cooperation. The placid water of the lagoon with its peaceful surroundings gave him a certain calmness. The giggle of the girls coming toward him interrupted his thoughts. He was so glad to see them making their way in his direction.

"Come in and join me," he called and waved to them, "the water is great."

Fabiana didn't hesitate; she plunged in immediately. Francesca remained sitting on shore busying herself with a blanket and a basket of goodies for snack and drinks. She was taking the domestic role. Fabiana joyful and laughing kept calling out to her, "Forget about setting out the food, come cool off, Auntie."

She listened to Fabiana and as she was just about ready to step in, a howling scream stopped her in her tracks. She turned around, but couldn't see anyone. The screams were definitely from a man in pain, and were coming from the opposite direction.

Suddenly they all heard the anguished calls for help. Immediately, Andrew and Fabiana swam towards the direction of the screams; Francesca remained ashore perplexed. She watched them swim to the other side of the lagoon. She did not feel comfortable to cross; her preference had always been to keep close to shore.

Andrew and Fabiana were now ashore on the opposite side. Someone was in distress from behind a large gray rock. Fabiana and Andrew ran towards the location and what they saw stopped them in their tracks. A man lay there contorted in pain: screaming. He was as pale as a ghost. Fabiana and Andrew froze: a big black and gray cobra was wrapped around the man, with its jaws lodged in the man's leg.

For a moment they were startled, speechless and terrified, especially Andrew. He had never seen anything like it. The snake, after being disturbed by them, started to unravel and stood up on its tail flipping the forked tongue from his mouth, ready to strike whoever came near. But slowly it retreated into a hole under the rock where it must have come from.

Breathless and speechless Andrew and Fabiana looked at each other. They knew they needed to help the stranger immediately. The man had passed out. He was lifeless. The poison would soon take over his body and there was no time to waste. They had nothing with them.

They looked around and Fabiana stated, "We need to tie his wound to stop the poison from travelling through his body." She knew what to do. Andrew pulled a couple of strong green twigs from the surrounding high grass and tied it tight around the stranger's leg, containing any venom from the bite within a local restricted area. They needed to take him to a hospital fast. They needed an ambulance and it was all a matter of time.

Francesca was on the opposite shore not knowing what had happened. She wasn't a strong swimmer; therefore, as much as she wanted to go, she didn't trust herself to cross the lagoon. She waited anxiously as Fabiana ran as fast as she could to the main road where she flagged down a passing car. They called for help, but it was going to take a while for an ambulance to arrive. The driver of a car stopped and remained on the highway while she ran back to Andrew and the stranger. It seemed an eternity for everyone.

Miliano Cardone lay there motionless. Thanks to Fabiana and Andrew he was taken to the emergency at the hospital in Palermo. Cardone, in his pursuit, had found a great hiding place. When he spotted the rock he thought this was his perfect hiding spot to spy and watch his prey without him being discovered. Luck was against him; or perhaps it was divine intervention. The snake had come out of its hiding place to put a halt to his mission. Ironic, considering he was there to bring harm to the very people who now had come to his rescue.

Francesca, once she heard of the incident, offered to pray for him. The drama had definitely put a damper on the splendid afternoon they had planned, but Francesca tried to cheer them up. After the ambulance left and they swam back to her, she took care of them and made sure they had plenty of food and drinks. They snacked and opened a delicious bottle of rosé wine. This helped to relax their nerves.

For a short time, Andrew hadn't thought about Francesca while he was trying to keep the stranger alive. Now, he had returned to his thoughts and he wasn't giving up on her. He had almost revealed his secret to Fabiana. He needed her help and given Angelo's relationship with her father, he was sure she would understand.

Francesca, having been spared seeing everything, was in a better mood than Andrew and Fabiana. Playfully she turned to Andrew and asked him, "Professor, I have not been in the water yet to swim. Why don't we go in for a dip? I could use a little release from this heat."

Andrew stood up immediately, "Francesca, the pleasure is mine."

Fabiana admired the two of them as they walked to the shoreline. She was happy her aunt was having some fun, she almost wished her to be married to the Professor. She knew deep down that Francesca must be lacking the affection a woman needed. There was no doubt in her mind that she was in a loveless marriage. Francesca seemed to be in a better mood today. After watching the two of them in the lagoon for a while, Fabiana thought to leave them alone. Intentionally, she excused herself and went back to the cabin.

Andrew knew the clock was ticking and he needed to talk to Francesca. He was determined to win her over. He wanted to hold her in his arms again, feel her soft flesh and make love to her... with all his passion. He playfully tried to get close to her. If she could read his eyes, he thought, she would know how much he desired her.

He knew Francesca was not a liberated woman of the modern world. She belonged to another era. He realized this was his one opportunity to convince her. He gently put his arm around her. She did not push him away.

Encouraged, Andrew moved closer and with longing eyes said, "Francesca, come away with me. I love you. I cannot bear to leave you behind. I need you. I know you need me too. Now, that we have found each other let's not waste any time. Please, I implore you. Let me be with you."

Silently they just stood there, staring at each other. The ripples of the waves were soothing their warm bodies. The lagoon was calm and serene. Francesca's body was trembling; she had tears in her eyes. A torrent of emotions engulfed her body.

She finally spoke, "Oh, Andrew. I have been denying myself the pleasure I feel when I see you. Yes, I'm in love with you too. How will I survive my loneliness once you are gone?"

Andrew couldn't believe the words he was hearing. With that revelation, he embraced her and their lips locked in a passionate kiss.

"Francesca, we must find a way to spend the night together. We have such little time left. I want to make love to you, to last forever."

She hesitated, finally she responded, "Andrew, I know it's so wrong. But I'm tired of being sensible and duty bound."

"Francesca, we need each other. Let's not punish ourselves."

"Okay, Andrew. Tonight I will wait for you outside the gate at midnight when the rest of the Tavernas have gone to bed. You find your way out."

Chapter Eight

The day had ended on a good note. Andrew was grateful to Fabiana, for the opportunity she had given him. He had this inner feeling that at the lagoon Fabiana had left them alone for a reason and did it on purpose. He knew Fabiana wanted her aunt to have a life. She seemed pleased when she saw Francesca smiling with him.

The evening seemed to go by so slowly for Andrew. Mrs. Taverna and Ersilia, as usual, had prepared a hearty Sicilian dinner, but Andrew wasn't too hungry tonight. The anxiety played havoc with his appetite.

"Professor," called out Mrs. Taverna, "tell me how you enjoyed today's outing? The lagoon, isn't it marvelous for swimming?"

"Mrs. Taverna, the lagoon, the hut is a heavenly retreat. Your family is so fortunate… thank you for sharing these splendid earthly possessions with me."

In the meantime, Fabiana kept nudging Andrew to relate what had happened with the cobra and the stranger, but his mind was on Francesca. As much as he liked Mrs. Taverna, he wished she would stop her chatter and just let him be in his thoughts. The anticipation to be with his love Francesca was tantalizing.

Mr. Taverna and his son Joseph had arrived mid-dinner. They had spent the day in Agrigento. The journey had rendered them tired. Soon after dinner, they both announced they'd be retiring early. Andrew was relieved. Mrs. Taverna was the only one full of energy tonight. He knew Fabiana would soon excuse herself to go to her room. She liked to read, plus the sun and the excitement of the day with that horrendous sight of the snake and that stranger had been quite an ordeal for her. He didn't want to be rude but cut Mrs. Taverna short on her inquisition and politely made an excuse to retire to his room.

It was now ten thirty. In the privacy of his own room, Andrew wondered how on earth was he going to get out of this fortress undetected. His desire to be with Francesca was escalating. Francesca had promised to be outside the gate to pick him up and he was going to be there at midnight. All he needed to do was to get there. The hired help would leave the premises by eleven. He had the controller for the automatic gate. Restless, he walked around his room with mixed emotions. He nervously waited for the timed outdoor lights to go off. Total darkness would be in his favor.

The moon tonight was at its quarter. "Good," he muttered, "I am in luck it seems."

In the meantime he splashed himself with fresh cologne, the same Pino Silvestre that brought him luck in Cefalù. He glanced at his watch again. It was now eleven thirty. In his euphoric confusion… suddenly he thought, *what about the alarm system?* He remembered the property was securely equipped with an alarm system and cameras.

"Good heavens." He was pacing the floor and talking to himself. "What was I thinking?" He realized he needed help. He should have opened his heart to Fabiana and confided in her. He suspected she would have understood and helped him. Now he felt trapped. *Francesca, oh my Francesca,* how was he going to get a message to her? The situation was getting more complicated by the minute as his anxiety was skyrocketing. He looked out the window to the gate. Desperately seeking for a solution his brain was getting cloudy and he didn't know what to do. With his jittering, again he glanced at the time. It was ten minutes to twelve. He turned the light off in his room and looked outside. In the dark a white Lamborghini with the motor running was parked to the side of the big gates. Oh yes, that was Francesca's sports car. He just stood there motionless for a few minutes and wished himself invisible in order to get to Francesca. How on earth was he going to get himself there? His feet were planted to the floor, afraid to move. Suddenly, a white figure came out of the car, with her clothes flowing in the wind. She was walking to the gates, they opened, she entered, and she was holding something in her hands.

Francesca was making her way to the front door. Andrew turned his lights on hoping she would see him. He waved to her frantically. She was looking up now, he whispered a sigh of relief, *She knows that I'm here.* She was waving back, motioning with her hand for him to come down. *It must be okay*, he thought. *I'm sure she knows this place better than I do.* Slowly, tiptoeing, he went down the stairs.

His heart was racing. Wearing socks and carrying his shoes, he moved like a prowler in the dark. It seemed to take forever before he found his way to the front door. He was thankful that Mr. and Mrs. Taverna's bedroom was in the far wing of the house. They couldn't see him or detect anything, but he thought about Fabiana and Joseph. They were closer. Was there a chance they could hear his footsteps? He tried to reassure himself that young people usually slept soundly…

He finally got to the foyer, the doors opened automatically and Francesca was right there waiting for him like a Madonna in white chiffon with a veil covering her from head to toe.

He wanted to speak. She promptly put a hand on his mouth to silence him and pulled him out of the house by his free hand. Francesca was swiftly pushing buttons on an electronic device she was holding in her hand. As the doors closed shut behind them, Andrew felt Francesca's arm around him.

"*Andiamo* – let's go," she whispered to him. Andrew couldn't wait to put distance between him and this place for a while. Once outside he felt liberated. He could only attribute it to the late night and the liaison running together, like two eloping teenagers. In no time they got into the safety of her car.

Francesca pushed a red button in her car and the gates closed without a squeak. She drove a couple hundred feet and pushed another button. Andrew didn't have a clue what was going on. She seemed to be well in control and very gutsy.

In admiration he turned toward her, "Francesca, I can't believe it, I'm here in your car and with you. I considered myself trapped; I was going insane in there. I was concerned for you, too. You appeared and my despair turned into courage. Here we are together."

"Andrew, I would not leave you waiting," she replied.

"But Francesca, how did you manage to bypass the security, the cameras, the lighting?"

She smiled, "Andrew, sorry I caused you anxiety. I had no time to explain anything to you before."

Chapter Nine

Francesca explained how she had no trouble getting in and out of the residence. "Andrew, my brother is my blood. I was born and raised in that house. It's customary that a son inherits the original residence. After my parents died he became the heir. But he gave me the key, and said, "Sister, my house is your house.""

Andrew listened attentively, he understood well. He liked the Tavernas all the more and said, "Francesca, you're fortunate to have such a devoted brother, including his family."

"Oh, believe me I know. Okay, enough about my brother's family."

She took his hand in hers and said, "Well, Andrew, let's cherish our little time together. You and me."

They parked and walked into *il soggiorno* (the family room). He looked at her, passionately, holding her hand like a young teen madly in love.

"I feel, this night I could almost call it our wedding night, Francesca, can we go back outside? Let me carry you in. Darling, I've never been married. This is what I feel like doing for you. You have given me life."

She was thrilled to hear his words, and laughed while bent over with joy. She said, "Andrew, it's a nice gesture, let's not waste any more time, sit on that big relaxing leather chair. It's Angelo's chair, it's hardly occupied."

"Francesca, I'd rather sit close to you."

He moved close to her. He locked her body in his arms with a strong embrace and sealed her lips before she could respond. They fell together on that big chair.

"Is this close enough?" she teased him.

Quiet dominated the residence. Andrew felt they were the only two on this earth and this is the way he preferred it. Then he asked, "Francesca, are we okay? Where is your help?"

"Andrew, this is our last chance together. I gave them the night off. I do that every now and then. I really don't need Letizia here at night. That was my husband's idea. At first Letizia hesitated, after my insistence she was grateful to go to her own home. Maurizio, poor Maurizio, he could use a night for himself."

"My love, you mean to say we are totally alone?"

"Andrew, don't underestimate me. Yes, we're alone."

Letizia had prepared a tray with chamomile tea and biscuits; they were nicely placed on a dish. She did this every evening for Francesca. But Francesca walked to the bar, opened the huge crystal doors, turned to Andrew and asked, "What will it be?"

"My love, you decide."

"The heck with chamomile tea, the night is ours and we want to live it to the fullest."

She noticed a bottle of exquisite champagne that Angelo had brought home, "This bottle was meant to be for a special occasion; it's a bottle from 1967. It's our special night and here goes this bottle."

Andrew was detecting a different personality from Francesca. He could feel her resentment and anger directed towards her husband, plus he felt her courage at the same time. He figured her husband must have driven her off the deep end. He wanted her to feel sincere love for him, not some rebound love affair. They opened the champagne and drank happily together.

Francesca seemed well in control of herself, reasoning "Andrew," she said while hugging him, "do you think I am a bad woman?"

"Lovey, no, not at all; why would I think that? I adore you, Francesca."

"All I wanted in my life was a man to appreciate and love me for me, I have never had that. My husband won me over with his charm when I was young. I have paid the price all these years. Believe me."

"Francesca, let's enjoy our time together."

"Yes, Andrew, let's."

She took his hand and led him to the marble staircase up to her bedroom. She put her hands on the two gold-plated locks and pushed open the double doors. Behind the Florentine doors they made their way to an impressive *Baroque* style king size bed with all the trimmings of fine bedding.

Andrew exclaimed, "Francesca, this is a room? It is fit for royalty." He had never admired such richness before.

"Andrew, this is my matrimonial bed, here is where I want you to make love to me. When you are gone I want to re-envision you and imagine you're here with me."

"Oh, my love, you are so precious."

"Andrew, my lonely heart has been crushed over and over in solitude by these walls."

Andrew irresistibly took her in his arms; he kissed her passionately and took her breath away.

"Andrew, my eyes have shed many tears in this room. I will pretend tonight is my first night of marriage with you, my love. Let's shut the rest of the world out."

Andrew's desire was getting out of control; he could hardly wait to make love to her.

"One moment please, Andrew." She teasingly slipped away.

She excused herself and disappeared into the dressing room. A few minutes later she emerged in a white virginal translucent nightgown, which played havoc with Andrew's senses. He was perplexed on how his libido had returned since he had been in Sicily and around Francesca.

They locked their bodies, embracing, and with no reservations, they wildly gave in to the starving love burning in both of them. They held each other breathlessly becoming one.

Andrew whispered in her ear, "I can feel your heartbeat, I'm so afraid to let go. You must come away with me, my love."

Francesca knew this was a one-time night of love and pleasure for her. She rightfully deserved to indulge, especially with this gentle soul who had come into her life. Francesca could feel his sincerity and he made her feel so special, plus, she was also flattered that this kind and wonderful man would care for her.

She broke away from him for a moment and said, "Andrew, you need to get back to your place by four in the morning, so let's not talk about that now."

"Why so early?"

"My brother gets up at five and leaves the house by six-thirty for work. My sister-in-law insists on having coffee with him. Ersilia their maid arrives at seven. You need to get back in your room before that. It's now two o'clock, we only have two more precious hours together, my love."

Andrew answered, "Francesca, my darling, I want to make love to you again and again until my body is drained. I only have two more days left, can you go away with me?"

Andrew didn't seem to understand the situation. He thought it was just as simple as that. An ordinary unhappy marriage could be easily brought to an end, a partner could walk away and separation or divorce would follow.

Neither he nor Francesca knew or realized what they were up against. Andrew never suspected that the stranger he helped earlier that day was the big enemy ready to harm him and Francesca. Lucky for the both of them, Miliano Cardone lay helpless in Palermo's hospital *Casa di Cura*. Cardone had suffered cardiac arrest and was fighting for his life.

Chapter Ten

....

The following morning the newspaper *Il giornale di Sicilia* ran the story on the front page. Fabiana was now reading it out loud to her mother and Ersilia.

"Mom," she said, "it's a good thing we were there. He would have died right then and there if we hadn't intervened. What a horrible sight, but he's alive, though in critical condition."

Sympathetic, Mrs. Taverna responded, "You poor souls, it must have been frightening for you. What about the Professor, can you imagine having to watch something like that?"

Fabiana answered, "I hope this Cardone fellow survives, now we know his name. I haven't ever seen him before. He must be a photographer, he had a camera hanging around his neck."

Andrew had discretely made it back to his room. He was happy, fulfilled with knowing Francesca loved him too. He needed to work on convincing her now. He had only two days left, he needed to act. He thought of Fabiana and wondered… would it be safe to confide in her?

A knock on the bedroom door startled him from a deep sleep, confused he answered, "Yes?"

"Professor, it's Fabiana, it's quite late, are you okay?"

"Oh, Fabiana, sorry, I must have slept in. I'll be down for breakfast right away."

"No trouble, Professor, take your time as long as all is well."

Andrew jumped in the shower to get ready for the day. He had to admit that after the entire night's performance, he could have slept all day.

Mrs. Taverna was always pleasant and ready with her goodies, "Good day, Professor, you must be hungry."

"My apologies, ladies, I slept late and lost part of the morning."

"You're entitled," said Fabiana. "You're on holidays after all."

"What are you and my daughter doing today, Professor?"

"Fabiana always comes up with something good, I will miss her. She is such a good hostess, a sweet girl."

She quickly replied, "Professor, do you feel like driving to Catania today? We will check the orange groves, the lemons, and the tomato fields. We will drink fresh juice. You can watch the operation in progress. The experience is educational and will do you good. You will be able to tell your students all about it."

"Great, it sounds good, who is going with us?" He hoped Francesca would be included.

Fabiana answered, "We will find dad and Joseph working there today, I'm sure they'd love to show you around, they're harvesting the bloody oranges at this time."

"What about you, Fabiana? I don't want you to be stuck with your boring old teacher," he was hinting.

"Professor, you are far from boring; however, if you want I can always ask Auntie to come along."

"That would be nice, love. She is good company, especially for you, Fabiana."

Fabiana promptly called and found out that her aunt was out with Maurizio to check on her car and had gone to church afterwards. "Oh well, Professor, I guess you're stuck with me."

Andrew had one day left. *I need help to move forward with Francesca.* Now he was getting worried, nervous, and restless.

They headed for Catania; they would be there the rest of the day. Andrew was silent and in his thoughts. Fabiana, watching him asked, "Professor, are you okay? What's wrong? You don't seem interested in the scenery."

"Fabiana, honestly, I feel sad because my time is over. I leave tomorrow, I will miss all of you."

"Professor, you can always come back for another holiday. We will miss you too, but don't forget I will be starting the second semester in January."

"That's great and you can count on my help."

"Cheer up, Professor, my family is fond of you and you can come back anytime."

"Thank you. You are so dear, Fabiana. Your parents are so fortunate to have such a daughter."

In the meantime, his thoughts returned to Francesca. *Where is she today? What is she doing? What is she thinking? Am I a part of her thoughts?*

Francesca was at the church. She knew Andrew was going to leave the following day. She had loved being with him, but it was over. She had to go to confession as soon as possible. Father Alfonso would listen to her, in secrecy, he wouldn't judge. Afterwards she would recite her penance and hopefully the weight of it all would be gone.

Andrew and Fabiana arrived at the orange groves early in the afternoon. Mr. Taverna and Joseph were hard at work. Upon seeing them, they immediately came over to greet them.

"Professor, I'm glad you took time to come and see our operation. We have thirty-six hectares to harvest. Our trucks export to countries in northern Europe."

Andrew walked around, escorted by Mr. Taverna and Joseph, it was quite an impressive setup they had. They employed many people: Sicilians, Africans and people from Tunisia. They all lived close by in farm buildings made of mortar and stone. Andrew knew now why Mr. Taverna and Joseph had to get up at dawn. If they didn't pick the fruit on time, it would result in a big loss. Mr. Taverna explained that the combination of the perfect climate and the mineral soil was what the citrus needed, which was why they grew the best bloody oranges.

He explained, "This is all due to the brewing Mount Etna, the lava and the volcanic soil provide the perfect conditions for growing this particular orange."

"How interesting," Andrew was truly intrigued with the local process.

Andrew and Fabiana joined in picking the oranges. The farmers gave him a few instructions on how to identify if the orange was ready to be picked and in no time his basket was filled. Andrew had even challenged Fabiana to a race.

"Professor," she called out. "You are doing so well here in Sicily and adapting so easily, you could pass for a native if it wasn't for your pale skin."

"I'm happy here, Fabiana. This island and its people are inspiring."

The thought of Francesca had disappeared for a while as they conversed but then soon returned. A sharp pain zipped through his gut at the thought of leaving without her.

What could he do? He was years away from retirement and until then he needed to teach in London. If only Francesca would join him, he would try his utmost to please her. He needed to find a way to talk to her before the following day.

* * *

Back at the hospital, Miliano Cardone had been removed from intensive care, but his condition was still critical. His speech had been affected. The coronary arteries were badly damaged; therefore, his recovery was poor and long term. In his greed, he hadn't placed the call to Mr. Frarano. He was eager to really dig for something better and bigger to pin down the two culprits or even blackmail Francesca. His intention was to claim more money. Now he was far from able in his bad state. As per tradition, his job would soon be passed to another once Mr. Frarano got word of his misfortune. The pictures he had taken were well-tucked away, safe, along with his recordings. However, for the time being, his family, especially his wife, were just grateful to have him still alive. The Englishman with Frarano's wife was far from his incapable mind. The nurses were monitoring his condition. They needed to remain vigilant. They had told his wife there wasn't much hope.

In the meantime the kitchen at the Taverna's household was busy. Ersilia the housekeeper and Mrs. Lora Taverna were baking and cooking up a storm. They were planning a goodbye dinner for Andrew; and afterwards some relatives were coming over for espresso and dessert.

Fabiana and Andrew returned from the orchards later in the afternoon. He was restlessly pacing around the mansion in circles. He decided to go for a walk, but really, all he was looking for was Francesca. He knew the way to her house now and it was within walking distance. He was going to casually drop in, just like the locals did. On his way Andrew kept reciting what he would say to her. All he could do was hope. He had never been in a situation like this before. He had had many relationships in England; the ladies were always ready and willing. But of course, they weren't married. Before he knew it, he was at Francesca's gate. He rang and Letizia soon answered on the intercom.

"*Pronto, Buongiorno.*"

"It's Professor Andrew, Letizia, I just came by to say goodbye."

"Do come in, Professor. I will get Francesca."

The gates opened and Andrew made his way in.

Letizia greeted him at the door and invited him in, "Francesca is in the library, Professor."

Andrew had taken a certain book with him. He knocked and opened the door. There she was, comfortably curled up in a large leather armchair. Startled, Francesca looked up. She smiled in pleasure; though only momentarily. Then frowning in concern she jumped up and asked, "Andrew… what a surprise. Where is Fabiana?"

"I came alone, I walked over Francesca. I wanted to see you so badly. I was going mad thinking that I will be leaving tomorrow and I need to speak to you. I need to know where we go from here, my love."

"Andrew, please speak quietly. Letizia and Maurizio are around. God forbid they should hear you. You took a big chance coming to see me here alone."

"Francesca, I need you. What am I to do?"

"I will tell you what you will do. You will go back to London and forget you ever knew me. The little Sicilian lady does not exist anymore; it was just a dream, Andrew. *Capisce* – do you understand?"

"Francesca, you can't possibly mean that."

"I don't have a choice and you're making life more difficult for me than it already is." She turned her back to him and then burst out crying.

"I have written a letter to you, because I didn't know if I would have a chance to talk with you privately before I left. It's here in this book; I am leaving it with you as a keepsake. I have written my address, phone number and my office number. I will wait for you. I want us to be together, please get in touch."

"Andrew, you don't understand do you? I simply can't be with you. What we shared is a memory. Goodbye, Andrew."

Andrew felt helpless, "Francesca, let me hold you in my arms one last time please."

He was pleading now.

Francesca embraced him and they locked in a breathless kiss. Francesca forced herself to be in denial, she searched for strength from the depths of her soul and pushed Andrew away from her. "Go, my love, go. Please go. You mustn't remain here any longer."

Francesca was worried that Letizia or Maurizio would get suspicious; it wasn't their custom for a man to visit a married woman alone.

Andrew walked away somber with his head down like a broken man. Francesca stood by the window and watched him walk away. He was out of her life forever. She knew how he felt. She wanted to run after him, console him. When the gates closed behind him, she said to herself, "Goodbye, my love, our life together is divided by a barrier of strong iron gates."

She turned to face the four walls of the library. *Welcome back to your solitude,* said her inner voice. Here she found refuge. She had been reading a lot lately. Fabiana and Andrew influenced her; they loved to talk about literature. Her spark of interest in some new novels had kept her from going insane from boredom, besides it made her feel closer to Andrew. She held the book he had given her close to her heart.

She was going to keep this book as a souvenir from him. She sifted through the pages and found an insert on page thirty-six. It was a note written in his handwriting, in gold ink. He had artfully written his address and phone numbers. This could be the open door to a new world. She turned to the front cover, the cover showed the back of a woman stepping forward on an infinite road leading to the unknown. The title of the book: *Alone on my Path. Oh,* she thought, *I will put it beside my night table and start reading it tonight.*

As she walked up to her bedroom, Letizia called out to her, "Francesca, has the Professor left?"

Francesca very casually responded, trying to erase any suspicion.

"Oh yes, he just dropped by to give me a book. You know he and Fabiana are bookworms. He wanted me to have this book before he left."

"He seemed determined to see you, although I noticed he's a little shy."

"You know those two are scholars, they want to influence me to be like them."

"I must admit he's a good looking man. I am surprised he isn't married and a woman hasn't latched on to him yet. He probably has someone back in London."

Francesca blushed, if only Letizia knew the truth.

"Letizia, you're a married woman, have you been eyeing him?"

With that she burst out laughing, "Oh, Francesca. If I could only recapture my youth then just maybe he wouldn't escape my pursuit."

Francesca laughed and wished Letizia wouldn't ask so many questions, but she could not risk being rude to her. Since the boys were born, she had always been a devoted housekeeper. She was older and Francesca felt she couldn't be disrespectful.

She decided not to go and join the Tavernas for dinner. It would be better to distance herself from Andrew. Seeing him one more time was only going to deepen their pain. By staying home she would suffer less. The awkward behavior towards each other might give them away. Therefore, she was better off avoiding him all together. They could be discovered and she didn't want to find herself in a tempting situation.

The last evening at the Taverna's proceeded with the formalities. With a heavy heart Andrew pretended to be cheerful. The evening was moving on and Francesca didn't show up. His mind kept drifting off and every now and then he was way off topic in answering Mr. Taverna. The relatives who had come to say their goodbyes all brought little Sicilian tokens for him to take home as souvenirs. Mr. Taverna handed him an emblem of Sicily, *la trinacria* representing Tan-pa-normi. "Andrew, you keep this for good luck from Sicily."

"Oh my goodness! You have spoiled me with your kindness, now gifts as well. You are the kindest people I have ever met. What can I say? I am speechless. Thank you so much."

The next morning he said his goodbyes to Lora Taverna and Ersilia. They were getting ready to leave when Fabiana asked him, "Professor, do you want to stop at Auntie's to say goodbye?

I'm surprised she never showed up last night, but I know for a fact she doesn't like goodbyes."

Mr. Taverna, intervened, "Fabiana, we're running late, the traffic is horrendous at this time of the day. We don't want the Professor to miss his flight."

Fabiana reluctantly agreed. She fetched Joseph and the three of them accompanied him to the airport in Catania. He would soon be in London.

"Fabiana," he said at the airport, "I expect to hear from you. I will be much obliged to assist you with applying for your PhD. See you in London."

He considered her like family now and he was sincere.

He said his goodbyes, thanking all of them profusely stating he would never forget their kindness.

In no time British Airways landed in Heathrow Airport and he made his way out to Victoria Station. He stopped for a moment and looked at the crowd moving, hurrying and fretting in every direction. *So*, he thought, *this Is London. Welcome back, Andrew.*

Chapter Eleven

....

The lavish serenity he had left behind in Sicily certainly didn't exist back home with millions of people.

He wondered if he was getting too old for this rat race, or did he just need a change? He was committed to the university; he needed the paycheck. What choice did he have?

He arrived home to his simple flat and he was more disturbed than ever before. The Tavernas had given him a taste of the rich life, and now back here, nothing soothed him. He thought of Francesca. Looking around he realized more and more that he had been insane to beg her to come here and be a part of his life. That brute of a husband provided well for her and their sons. What could he offer her in London? He lived from paycheck to paycheck. *You're doomed, Andrew, teaching is all you know.* All these unpleasant thoughts were going through his mind. He sank into his sofa in solitude, fighting the urge to resort to drinking.

He reminded himself of the doctor's advice: no hard alcohol and only a couple of small glasses of wine per day. Oh well, tomorrow he would visit Donna and hit the gym. With her stern punishment whipping him, she would snap him back on track. Yes he needed to get back to the fitness club; it would help him mentally and physically. He needed to get disciplined again. After all between Ersilia and Mrs. Taverna's meals he had put some weight back on.

While Andrew tried to establish himself back into his routine in London, Miliano Cardone was trying to reclaim his life in Palermo. Cardone, at his wife's insistence, had just been discharged from *La Casa di Cura,* the hospital. His wife and family had taken him home. The massive heart attack had left him with his speech impaired and poor blood circulation to his extremities, especially his legs. No doubt, Miliano was in bad shape. The family had been told he might not ever recover. They wanted to have him home in the hope that with some personal care and rehabilitation his body would respond, and in time maybe he would get better. If that was possible. Francesca and Andrew didn't even realize that this man's misfortune had been to their advantage.

Francesca's days were spent in sadness. The spark she felt in seeing Andrew had surprised her. She had to admit, he had brought some life to the Taverna's home and hers. She was born in Palermo and nothing here excited her any more. It was fun to watch him being so impressed with the island. It was September, her brother was really taken with the harvesting of tomatoes, the different kinds of oranges were being harvested in stages, and the grapes would follow.

The only person available to her these days was Fabiana. *Thank goodness for Fabiana,* she thought. *Without her my life would be empty.* Some of the town ladies were cordial, but she wasn't close to anyone in particular. She was involved with the church, but the women there were much older and everything was so formal. Most of her husband's family lived in New Jersey now; one sister and brother lived in Messina, who she saw on occasion for weddings and funerals.

She was grateful that after her marriage, one thing she had won over her husband was for them to remain close to her family. Her parents were alive then and she wanted to be near them. Her brother's family and sister-in-law with their children, were her life. Her husband had obliged without arguing.

Meanwhile, Fabiana was getting herself organized to return to London. Francesca knew with Fabiana gone she would be even more desolate. Lately, Francesca had been spending a lot of time reading, she often would hold the book Andrew gave her close to her chest. She thought of Andrew over and over again. She used his little note as a bookmark. By reading it over so many times, she had memorized all his information.

The book's theme had touched her soul. It was a self-help book. It gave her encouragement. She had been married for twenty-three years. She thought of Andrew... *if only you could have appeared in my life way back then. Now it's too late.*

Chapter Twelve

....

In New York, Angelo was up to his eyeballs giving orders. He was so busy, involved in the turmoil of his affairs, as he was opening two more hotels, one in New York and one in Las Vegas. The construction was behind schedule, and he was yelling and putting pressure on the engineers. The hotels were supposed to be ready to be opened by the end of November. They had taken reservations for the holiday celebrations. There was a lot of money at stake. He was a bully and tongue lashing everyone involved.

Every now and then he would place a call to Francesca, between mistresses. At the end of the day, he would retire to his penthouse suite where one of his mistresses waited for him. They would assist him in his demands and he reimbursed them well. Most times he preferred masseuses. One of his favorites was Lula Showorz. She had strong hands and a body to drive any man to the moon. He would rub his hand down her exposed large breasts panting, "Lula, have your way with me baby, will you? Bring my body to ecstasy, like usual. My muscles are in knots and need to relax. I have been put through the wringer today with those brainless idiots." She obeyed like a robot.

He checked on his sons regularly and kept them on their toes too. They knew better than to disappoint their father; therefore, they worked at their studies in order to earn top marks.

They knew they would be spending their Christmas holidays in Sicily. They were writing their first term exams and hitting the books. They loved their mother and called her regularly. Francesca waited for their calls and listened to them attentively when they did.

For her, the days passed slowly. It was now the middle of October and the climate was still warm during the daytime, but the nights were getting cooler. Francesca was not feeling so well, her appetite had vanished and she was having stomach pain. She didn't think much of it, and she didn't take it too seriously. She thought it was just a bug she had picked up and it would flush itself out with lot of fluids.

However, it persisted. Once into November, suddenly she was alarmed and a tremendous fear came over her, *Could it be possible that she was pregnant?* Her period hadn't arrived and it was now two months, going on the third. She panicked. *What am I to do?* She brought her hands to her head in total fear, *I know I was insane to do what I did, but now should this be true, my life is over.*

All these horrible thoughts were wrestling in her mind. She took a deep breath and tried to calm herself down. She couldn't sleep; torment had taken over her entire being.

Letizia was relentless in her questioning. Francesca wished she could just disappear from the face of the earth. It was almost the end of November now. Since Andrew had left, it hadn't been easy for her, but now it had taken a turn for the worse and her days had turned into a real hell. *Okay*, she said to herself, *let's look the devil in the eye. I need to see a doctor.* She figured, just in case her doubts were verified, she couldn't see her own family doctor in Palermo. She would become the talk of the town. Where was she to go? Messina? No, her in-laws were there. Catania? No they were well-known there, too. She chose Agrigento; she was going to seek a doctor there. Then on second thought she reflected, *This could be a tumor or something. Why am I jumping to conclusions?* She got an appointment for the first part of December at the women's clinic, Santa Maria.

Francesca was familiar with Agrigento, she went to school there. Maurizio insisted on driving her. He was quiet and not inquisitive. She went in alone while he waited for her outside. The receptionist escorted her to a woman doctor who was very businesslike and showed no sympathy. The doctor requested a urine sample and gave Francesca a quick checkup. After she looked at the results she informed Francesca, "Congratulations, Signora Frarano, you're three months pregnant."

Francesca felt faint. The doctor said, "Mrs. Frarano, you have two boys. Hopefully you will get your girl this time."

Francesca was speechless. She didn't respond. It was almost as though the doctor could read her mind. She changed her facial expression in an amicable way and said, "You'll be fine, you might be a little disappointed now because of your age, but you're perfectly healthy."

"It's a surprise. I didn't expect to be pregnant at this time in my life."

Oh, my God. Francesca screamed in silence. In a daze she got up from the chair, got dressed and walked out in a confused stupor. If the doctor had told her she only had days to live, she would have taken it better. *What now?* She had been faithful to her husband for all these years. What had possessed her to be driven to adultery was now beyond her comprehension.

Maurizio was patiently waiting for her and with great respect got out and opened the door for her. He was always polite. She knew Angelo paid him well. This is how Angelo felt justified he provided for her. Oh God! His thinking was so warped. If only he recognized what she really needed then she wouldn't have been in this mess.

"Mrs. Frarano, may I ask, is everything all right? The doctor, I mean, did she give you good news?"

"Nothing serious, Maurizio, women's stuff, I will live!"

Francesca didn't know which way to turn with her mind. She spent that night pacing in her room. She did the math, her husband hadn't been in town since the first part of August. She was three months along, and she figured she must have conceived that night with Andrew, in her matrimonial bed. Right at the end of August. *Why was I so careless? How stupid of me.* She was a devout Catholic, contraception was totally against her religion. Why would she even require it in the first place? Well, all the reasoning wouldn't change things now.

The next morning she woke up totally engulfed in fear. She wanted to be alone and think. After breakfast she got in her car and sped away. Where was she to go? She drove around like a lost desperate soul. Her destination: a road to nowhere. She drove towards the beach, parked her car and she stepped barefoot on the cool sand. She stood there watching the waves rushing to the shore. She thought of walking against the white caps, immersing herself in that white foam until her body disappeared into the depths of the seas.

Francesca kept walking into the sea until her wet dress clung to her body. A voice inside her kept echoing, *Francesca turn back, turn back Francesca, you are about to crash.* She stopped. A big wave knocked her down. She was disoriented and it was hard to regain her footing. She wasn't a strong swimmer. She burst into tears and furiously ran back to shore as if a monster from the sea was running after her. She kept stumbling and running. She was going insane. Finally, she reached her car, got in and slammed the door shut. She wanted to hide. She needed to find refuge. She cried hysterically until her eyes had no more tears to shed. Totally wiped out, she threw her head back and closed her eyes.

A knock on her window startled her, she had drifted off and at first she didn't know where she was. For a moment she thought she was waking up from a bad dream. But looking at the blue uniform and the silver badge on his chest, she recognized him as the local beach patrol.

He motioned to roll down her window. Her arm felt heavy as she tried to comply.

Confused and fatigued, she rolled down the car window.

The man asked her, "Is anything wrong, madam?"

Half groggy she forced a response, "Oh, officer, I'm fine. I must have fallen asleep, all is well, thank you."

"Are you sure? Can I be of any help?"

"Oh, no, sir, I am perfectly fine, thank you. I must have dosed off after my swim." She forced herself hard to respond and trying hard to regain her composure.

She didn't know how long she had drifted off. Her dress was damp and her hair hung around her face. She looked in the rear-view mirror; it didn't look like her. She looked more like someone who had just escaped from jail, or a mental institution.

Pull yourself together, she scolded herself. She couldn't return home and face Letizia's inquisitions. Francesca knew she would probably explode and lose her temper and she couldn't risk that. She sat there staring at the empty space in front of her for the longest time. After desperately searching for an answer she decided to take a drive up the mountain.

Yes, why had she not thought about it before, the church of Saint Rosalia; wasn't it there where she always found peace?

She turned on the engine and headed for the church. The narrow road seemed even narrower this time. The higher the car climbed in elevation the lighter her head felt. Once she arrived up there, she noticed the large heavy wooden doors were wide open including the rectory. Francesca made her way in and knelt in prayer at the altar facing the statue of Saint Rosalia where she had prayed many times before in despair. In deep prayer, she begged for forgiveness. In this holy place of worship she felt calmer, the world around her didn't seem so dark. Although she felt so much protection, she knew she couldn't remain. She had to face her truth. In prayer, she invoked a resolution, but there seemed to be none. Her knees had been glued to the marble floor; her bones were aching. Her aching body got up to walk out, when by the corner of her eyes, she noticed a sign by the confessional.

Confessions were heard from two to four. Francesca looked at her watch; it was now two o'clock. She hesitated; did she really want to confess? Yes, without reservation she headed towards the dark walnut confessional. She did not care who was on duty that day. Father Alfonso was usually here, but she hadn't seen him. With this horrible mortal sin sitting deep in her soul, she was ashamed and reluctant. Regardless of her guilt, it had been committed. Slowly Francesca forced herself to find her place and knelt inside the confessional.

Immediately a little slide door brought a gentle voice to her ears, "In the name of the Father, the Son and the Holy Spirit, amen. May the Lord be in your heart and on your lips, so you can truthfully confess your sins."

Francesca recognized the voice as that of Father Alfonso, and knew in her heart that her confession would be safe with him or any other priest because they had taken their vow of secrecy. Her words weren't coming out so the priest questioned, "Yes, my child of God…"

"Bless me, Father, for I have sinned. My last confession was… I did receive absolution and I did my penance. I now ask for forgiveness because I have sinned."

"In what way my child have you offended God's commandments?"

"I have committed a mortal sin, Father, adultery, and I want to repent my soul. I'm at God's mercy."

Even in the confessional Francesca felt tears streaming down her face. The priest felt her anguish and asked, "Talk about it, my child, if it makes you feel better."

"Father," she informed him, "I'm pregnant with another man's child. It is my fault."

"My child, God with his merciful love forgives all our sins, I bless you. Recite the act of contrition and for penance recite

Holy Mary and Our Father ten times. Our merciful God will be with you always."

He made the sign of the cross, blessed and dismissed her.

Francesca did her penance kneeling until her knees felt raw on the step of the cold marble altar. Reluctantly she got up. If she could only hide in this grotto and disappear to nothingness, this was her desire right now. But strange as it seemed, she felt protected and safe here. In slow motion she forced her body to walk out of the church, got back into her car and drove down the mountain. As the car maneuvered the winding roads she began to feel queasy. Her eyes glanced at the rugged cliffs. She stopped the car on a small enclave and got out to get some fresh air.

The waves were slamming against the rocks. It was intimidating. The sun had vanished behind the clouds and a strong wind was furiously blowing. A storm was brewing from the coast. Up here, the elements seemed to be in a crescendo. Again that awful desire came over her. All she had to do was get back in the car, push the gas pedal and before she knew it, she would disappear in that white foam. It would all be over. No more suffering, no more pain.

She was about to proceed with her resolution, when a sharp movement in her body distracted her thoughts. Automatically she lowered her hand to caress her tummy. Was this a message or a reminder from the life growing inside of her? Or a voice from her subconscious, *I'm here too it's not only about you.* "God help me, guide me," she implored looking up at the cloudy sky. A force seemed to lead her back to the car and she drove home.

Her timing was perfect; Letizia had left for the day. *Thank God,* she thought and hurried upstairs to lock herself in the privacy of her bedroom. She went straight for the shower. She let the water run over her body for the longest time, she closed her eyes and thought, *if only this water would wash away my sins then my soul would not feel so obscured.*

She had not eaten all day, weak and dizzy she looked in the kitchen to see what Letizia had prepared for her, but her appetite these days was not in her favor. After forcing herself to nibble on some food from the fridge she went straight to bed.

Francesca with no doubt was slipping into depression. The days that followed were dark. She remained in bed until late afternoon. The waking hours were painful; she preferred to drown herself in her sleep. The days and nights followed fruitlessly in obscurity. Letizia was there, offering her help, and sincerely caring for Francesca. Her refusal was adamant; her preference was to be in total quietness and alone.

Letizia was getting worried; she asked Francesca's permission to call her husband or to alert the Tavernas.

"Francesca, I am concerned, can Maurizio take you to the doctor here in Palermo. What is going on? We need to know."

"Letizia, I am just run down, I will be fine I just need some time to myself. Please, the last thing I need is for you to call my husband and please do not worry my family."

Letizia with her good intentions was relentless. Francesca thought she better come to her senses before her housekeeper or Maurizio summoned her husband and the boys and end up alarming them on her account. She did not want to see her husband; the boys didn't need to be upset.

Francesca pulled herself together, and started to function the best she could hiding any malady. Besides, Christmas was approaching; her husband and boys would soon be home for the holidays. For so many years she couldn't wait for them to come home. Now, on the contrary, she wished they wouldn't be coming at all. How was she going to face them?

She needed help. The only person she could confide in was Fabiana. Fabiana would be shocked and disappointed in her aunt, but she had no choice. They were close and somehow she would understand the madness that had driven her to adultery with the Professor.

They were into December, Angelo and Daniele and Diego were to arrive on the twenty-third. Francesca knew she was running out of time. Normally, at this time of the year she would be busy in the kitchen making the special Christmas pastries. The boys had always brought her so much joy. At this time of year even her husband was kind. Oh how she looked forward to those family gatherings, but this year she wished Christmas would never come. She feared their arrival and their stay. They would need her love and devotion once they arrived. She wasn't in any mood for festivities. Her private world would be invaded and her thoughts of despair might give her away. How was she to manage these two weeks?

She called Fabiana the next morning.

"Fabiana, I need to see you. I have to talk to you, can you come over?"

"Of course, Auntie, is everything okay?"

"Yes, I'm fine. I need you here at my place."

"I'll be there by eleven; maybe we can go out for lunch?"

"Fabiana, let's decide when you get here."

Fabiana sensed the strange urgency in her aunt's voice. She hurried with her chores in order to get to her place on time. Francesca preferred the safety of her home; her emotions were running high. Besides, she was afraid to talk in public just in case someone overheard their conversation. She would send Letizia out of the house just in case she would be eavesdropping.

Fabiana arrived, cheerful as usual, with a basket of grape tomatoes.

"Mom wanted you to have these tomatoes for your salsa."

"Thank you, sweetie, I will give them to Letizia when she's back from the market."

"Auntie you look pale… are you all right?"

"The best I can be at this time, Fabiana. I really don't know myself anymore."

"What do you mean? Nothing serious I hope."

"Fabiana, let's go in the library where we can be alone."

Concerned, Fabiana followed her down the hall. As Francesca entered the library she grabbed Andrew's book and pressed it to her chest as if that would protect her and calm the terror rising in her heart. She closed the door behind them and said, "Fabiana, sit down, I am going to shock you."

Fabiana held her breath and wondered, *What could be so bad?* She noticed Francesca's eyes were red and swollen. For a moment she thought someone had died.

"I'm so sorry to unload on you. I know I'm burdening you with this big problem, my problem... I'm pregnant."

"You are! What a surprise and you are unhappy... why?"

"Fabiana, it's not my husband's child."

Fabiana wasn't sure she heard right. Her aunt, the saint wasn't sleeping around was she? "What do you mean it's not... I don't understand. Who is the father?"

"I hate to tell you. It's your Professor."

Fabiana burst out laughing, "I don't believe it. Professor Robertson!"

"You better believe it. I'm almost four months along."

"Are you sure?"

"As sure as I am standing here, Fabiana, "

"How do you know? Have you consulted a doctor?"

"Fabiana, I am forty-three. I'm a mother to two young men. My husband has been away. A few days ago I almost committed suicide and that would have put an end to my misery."

"Oh! Auntie, my God! What are you saying? Why didn't you call sooner? You scare me."

She hugged her aunt with deep affection, holding her for a long time, while Francesca sobbed incessantly.

"I am sorry, Fabiana, sorry, I know I must have been insane to do what I did."

Fabiana listened intently; her aunt's suffering was serious. And she knew she had nowhere else to turn, and that everyone would scorn her. Plus, if her uncle found out... she didn't want to think about it. The honor, for them it was all about the family honor. Fabiana asked, "Have you told the Professor?"

"Oh, no, why would I?"

"Why would you? It's so important, this is a serious matter."

"Fabiana, you don't understand."

"I think he should know. He's a good man, Auntie, too bad you're married and divorce is out of the question. He would make you happy."

"Fabiana, I was furious with my husband and I was so vulnerable. Andrew felt for me, he begged me to go to London. He can't comprehend my situation. What can I do?"

"Oh, Auntie, I know, I know. This is why I don't want to get involved with anyone here."

"Fabiana! How am I going to conceal my pregnancy? In a month or so I will not be able to hide my growing belly."

"We will think of a solution, but I think the Professor should know."

"Please, Fabiana, it's our secret, I'm so sorry to do this to you."

Fabiana asked, "Auntie, I think we need to tell Mamma and Papa. You need help. You can't go through this alone. Together we will decide what to do."

"Fabiana, please no. I'm so ashamed. I'd rather die. My brother does not deserve this drama. He has always been so good to me and look how I have repaid him."

"Nonsense, you know Dad has never liked Uncle Angelo, because he knows he hasn't been a devoted husband to you. He feels for you since you are alone and neglected."

"Thanks, Fabiana, for being so understanding and for your good logic, but let's keep it to ourselves for now, especially until after Angelo leaves."

Fabiana gave her aunt a big hug and promised, as she wished, to keep her secret.

Her boys arrived and she tried hard to appear cheerful for them while concurrently preparing for the festivities. Angelo, followed, loaded with gift-wrapped boxes for everyone, especially for Francesca. He made his entrance bubbling and he hugged and kissed her. Any one present would be convinced that she was so lucky to have such a sacrificing hard-working husband.

"Wait until you open your present this time," he said.

"Angelo, you know I don't need anything."

"Hush, hush, it's not up to you to say what I want you to have."

He put an arm around her and tried to be amorous, needless to say Francesca found him repulsive with his touch. He felt her rejection, and asked, "Eh! What is the matter with you? You don't seem happy. Are you sick or something?"

"No, I'm fine, just a little tired and I have a terrible migraine."

"You do know I'm leaving right after Christmas?"

"Yes, I do," she answered.

"I want you to be happy while I'm home. Have you taken anything to feel better?"

"No, you know how much I feel about drugs."

"I come home expecting to find my wife in top shape and you look drained. What is going on? Is Letizia not doing enough for you? Is it Maurizio? Maybe I have to shake them up a little."

"They are working fine, it's not their fault just because I have a headache. Angelo, do me a favor, don't worry about me. I will be fresh as a daisy after a good night's sleep."

Francesca was relieved to hear that he was leaving right after Christmas. It meant not having to put up with him for New Year's Eve. *He probably has a date with one of his mistresses in New York or Boston or Las Vegas. One can only guess.* After so many years of deceit, she didn't care anymore. The sooner he was out of sight the better. She knew she was safe with her sons for the time being. She would easily hide her developing body with her wardrobe.

The lively movements that had started to butterfly inside of her served as a constant reminder. It brought her back in time. Her past pregnancies had brought her celebration and happiness. Especially for her parents, and yes, her husband had been happy too. After all, in their culture, having children was so important for a young married couple.

Back then, anxiously he had asked, "Francesca, what's the news from the doctor?" Graciously, he had held her hands and she had detected affection in his eyes. Francesca innocently thought the honeymoon would last forever. She smiled as she remembered how they joked and laughed together when they had discovered she was pregnant with their first child.

She remembered how he had jumped up with so much pride. Lifting her up in his arms he hugged her and then twirled her around the room, kissing her in a glorious fashion. His words resonated in her mind now, "Francesca, I will love you always, my doll. I promise I will provide well for you and our children."

She was sincerely proud to be Mrs. Frarano when they were first married, but slowly he became colder and distant as her pregnancy advanced. The trips he was taking abroad were getting more and more frequent. Her complaints of missing him, were met with condemnation instead of sympathy.

"Francesca, I'm working like a dog to provide for you with your luxuries. I am kicking butts out there. Do you think I'm having fun? What do you think? Tell me."

At a certain point she got tired of arguing with him, but to her surprise after the baby was born his behavior changed, at least for a while. He was proud to have a son and he was kinder towards her and came home more often. Francesca felt the baby had helped replenish her marriage. She was happier in those days, dedicating her time to Diego. Her parents were still alive at that time and they adored their new grandchild. Her faith in her husband was soon restored; she was a forgiving soul. She blamed herself, maybe he was right, and maybe she had been a nagging wife.

She remembered the time he surprised her. On her birthday he came home. It was the sixth of January, also epiphany, and the day when presents are given. She was sitting in the nursery rocking Diego to sleep. Suddenly, she heard the rumble of a car pulling in the driveway. The horn blowing in urgency. She looked out the window to see Angelo sitting in a brand new Lamborghini. She opened the window and said to him, "Why didn't you tell me you were coming home? What a surprise!"

"It's your birthday isn't it? Come down here," he ordered.

She knew better than to ignore him. She gently placed Diego in his crib and made her way downstairs to welcome him home. He hugged and lifted her off the ground, gave her a breathless kiss and said, "Happy Birthday, *bambola*." Doll was his nickname for her, when he was in a pleasurable mood.

"How do you like this little machine, doll? It's all yours brand new. I had it delivered this afternoon from Milano. I warned that idiot at the dealership in Via Borghese. You fuck around with this order not being on time I will kick your front teeth in. It's my wife's birthday gift. It better be on time. So, here it is, baby."

Francesca admired the car and he was like a little boy putting so much emphasis on possessions.

She replied, "It's magnificent, I love it. I can't wait to show it to my brother!"

"Get in, take a look at the interior, your color, eh? Let's go for a ride and show your family."

"Angelo, the baby, I can't leave the baby. Let's go later."

She was thankful that he complied and went straight up to see his son.

That was a long time ago. She got pregnant again and slowly, slowly he slipped deeper and deeper into his own world of greed. He was addicted to material things; he became worse than an alcoholic. Francesca slipped into her own misery. She knew there was no reasoning with him. He was a stubborn mule and she knew better than to stand in his way. He became a very successful businessman at the cost of his family. As far as he was concerned money conquered all, everything could be accomplished with money and it gave him power.

Francesca detected other women in his life, she knew and felt it. The boys knew it too as they got older. They spent time with their father and traveled abroad with him. Francesca and the boys were his privileged family. He, very rightfully so, expected honor and respect from them.

Now here she was pregnant again at this later stage, and with another man's baby growing in her womb. If Angelo would have the slightest idea, he would go berserk. Today she wanted the earth beneath her to open and swallow her or somehow, to vanish in the abyss of the universe. Terror engulfed her with every movement. Once he was gone she would have to decide which direction to go. Since she was a devout Catholic, abortion was out of the question. For the ten millionth time she wished to die. With the help of Fabiana, as soon as the holidays were over they would put a plan in place.

Chapter Thirteen

....

Angelo didn't have much time to spend in Palermo this trip, but he hadn't heard from Miliano Cardone. He thought he better check up and see what was cooking before he departed. He drove to his preferred coffee shop, the espresso bar at the piazza and to his surprise, Miliano wasn't to be spotted anywhere.

He checked with the bar attendant, "Gennari! Have you seen Miliano lately?"

"Miliano! Haven't you heard? He's a very sick man. Miliano had a massive heart attack from some incident. From what I hear he is in bad shape, he is speechless and confined in bed and on slight occasions he can get in a wheelchair."

"Oh! What a *strunz*, no one told me anything."

Angelo didn't care what had had happened to him. He was disturbed for not having been told. Miliano knew the deal. If he was incapacitated, the next person in line was to take his place.

"Good for nothing *stupido* fool." Now he needed to replace him. This was another job he had to fill before he left. With these thoughts, he decided to drive to the fool's house and look after business. He wasn't concerned with Miliano's troubles; he was only concerned for his own affairs.

Angelo knocked on his front door. When Miliano's wife let him in, she was hospitable and believed this fellow had concern for her husband. Other than his family, not too many people had showed up to visit him. She was happy to meet him at last.

Angelo took one look at Miliano and saw how pathetic he looked slumped over on his wheelchair, saliva drooling out the side of his mouth. He was disgusting to look at. Angelo didn't want to waste much time here. As far as he was concerned he was history. He forced himself to be polite and left shortly after he arrived. He had to think. Who was the best replacement? After searching his brain he thought of Miliano's brother-in-law, Fausto Tarantano.

The next day Angelo had a meeting with Fausto and gave him the same instructions he had given Miliano. Fausto was glad to take his brother-in-law's job.

Angelo and Fausto shook hands, "We have a deal, Fausto, eh, and no failing."

"Boss," Fausto Tarantano promised faithfully, "you can count on me, my word is my honor."

Two days after Christmas Angelo said his goodbyes. He preached to his boys, "Look after your mother, these few days eh, guys. I don't want hear complaints from that uncle of yours that you're coming home in the wee hours of the morning, and no drinking. Don't worry your mother."

He knew Francesca called her brother when she worried about her sons. Angelo was good at giving orders, and with that he left for New York. Yes, his favorite Lula was going to have the hot tub ready for him. The foam bubbles, with the marvelous scents, would stimulate his body. He depended on Lula and her touch.

Francesca felt so relieved when her husband finally left. The boys would be leaving right after New Year's Eve to return to Boston and then she would return to her private world of worry. Andrew had brought a little excitement and pleasure to her, but she was now paying for it. God only knew where she was going from here. She occasionally thought of Andrew; without the guilt.

Her boys were loving and kind, but it made her feel worse. She was overcome with remorse; she felt she had betrayed them too. At the same time they knew their mother wasn't well, but nothing was said.

The New Year came and they were gone. Francesca was gaining weight. *How am I going to hide my body... and what am I to do now?*

Fabiana had called her the day after the boys left, "Auntie, I think I should come and sleep there for a few nights, I don't want you to be alone."

Fabiana hadn't said anything to her parents, but they had noticed how bad Francesca looked and were concerned. Over the holidays her father had said, "My poor sister, with that selfish husband of hers. He has always abused her good nature and taken her for granted for so many years."

"Dad, believe me, I know," Fabiana added.

"If my father was alive, he would put a bullet right through his head."

There was silence at the dinner table; everyone felt his anger. He continued, "The guys at the coffee shop were making jokes about how many women he has around at the Vegas casinos. They call him the big Don Juan."

Joseph, usually quiet, pitched in with his own comments: "Yes, Papa' I heard him bragging about some Swedish woman..."

Lora said, "It's embarrassing and disgraceful as far as I am concerned."

"You see, Mom, Dad, this is why I am afraid to get serious with anyone here," stated Fabiana.

"Never you mind, Fabiana! There are some nice young fellows out there. Your Uncle Angelo is one of a kind. Take your father for a good example," her mother argued.

Her father asked, "How do you think that poor girl feels? She has to know."

Fabiana, with her secret buried in her soul, didn't dare say one thing more. She wouldn't reveal anything without her auntie's permission.

Now, Fabiana was even more disturbed after the discussion that had taken place with her family. If they only knew. The next morning she called her first thing, "Auntie, get ready, I'll pick you up and we'll go out for lunch."

Francesca hesitated; she didn't feel like dressing or grooming herself these days. But on Fabiana's insistence, she stopped protesting and finally agreed to be picked up. Francesca had lost her luster. She just didn't appear radiant anymore, both physically and emotionally. She walked out sloppily dressed, without wearing any make-up. This wasn't the Francesca Fabiana knew.

They drove to the east side of Palermo where it was quieter. Fabiana knew this quaint little bistro that served exquisite grilled calamari; Francesca's favorite. Fabiana, being very astute for her age, knew her aunt needed to talk.

"Auntie, listen to me, you can't go through this alone. It's impossible. We must tell my parents and eventually the Professor. Regardless of what you think, my parents will not scorn you."

Francesca listened attentively; she had no energy and really needed someone to take over.

"Fabiana, I can't. Maybe in time things will change."

"How are things going to change? You have a baby inside of you. You need to make plans. I'm leaving for London in a week's time. I want you to come with me."

For a moment Francesca cheered up at the thought of seeing Andrew again. It brought hope. But how could she? "Fabiana, I'm happy for you. You're a brave girl to continue your studies. I will miss you so. As for me, I just don't know which way to turn. I know I can't go with you."

"Auntie, why not? It's perfect timing. You can help me get settled and it will do you a world of good to get away from here."

"My husband, Fabiana, he is coming back next month and I have a doctor's appointment in Agrigento again."

"Okay, but how are you going to hide your pregnancy with your husband? Can the baby pass as his? Have you told him? What about my cousins?"

Francesca listened in denial. Fabiana was right. She needed to come to her senses.

Fabiana continued, "Auntie, you're going to have a baby, a human being, you need to tell your family."

"Fabiana, lower your voice please," said Francesca. She continued, "No, how can I? I got pregnant right at the end of August. He had left by then, he was definitely not at home, besides when he's home for only a night or two, he's tired, he blames the travel so he doesn't make love to me. Fabiana, I hate to tell you this, believe me, he is used to professionals, I am his boring wife for his old age."

"This is complicated. So, what are you going to tell him that you got pregnant like the Virgin Mary? And he is going to believe it." Fabiana knew she was being sarcastic, but how else was she going to convince her.

"Aunt Francesca, this is what we will do. I will rent a two-bedroom apartment in London. You will come with me, or come later if you insist, after you see the doctor. We need the Professor's help. He must know."

Francesca responded, "I think I can hide my pregnancy until March. The baby is due at the end of May, I hope I die by then."

"You are talking crazy now, you know you're not going to die. Prepare yourself to embrace your newborn baby. We will start by telling my parents, then the Professor. You know, I'm happy the Professor gave you a little taste of pleasure, you deserve it. I must confess, I knew he had fallen in love with you."

"Fabiana, how did you know?"

"The way he looked at you and I could sense that he wanted to be around you. He was so much happier whenever you appeared."

"I have become an adulteress, that's what I am."

"Oh, Auntie, stop with your church statements and your beliefs, after all, you're human. Every human being is entitled to have the pleasures of life. You've been denying yours, accepting to play the martyr."

"Yes, Andrew showed me what real love is. I'm glad I experienced it, but I am paying for it now."

"Don't think that way. It's because you are so stuck on your marriage vows. Why don't you liberate yourself and go where your heart tells you? You're a beautiful woman, Auntie Francesca, why wouldn't my professor fall for you? If you want to throw that away it's up to you."

Francesca remained stunned. Her niece belonged to a "matter of fact world". She belonged to the new generation while she was stuck in an old school of consciousness, ingrained by the customs and small world beliefs of their island.

Chapter Fourteen

Fausto Tarantano had followed them from a distance. Since Angelo had hired him, he hadn't seen anything out of the ordinary. He sincerely thought that Angelo Frarano must have a screw loose in his brain. *What was there to catch with this poor woman?* But as far as he was concerned, he had agreed to take this job strictly for money to survive. This *braggalone* (bragger) Angelo Frarano; if he wanted to burn his money, it was entirely up to him. This was certainly an easy job.

Fabiana drove home disappointed at not being any further ahead from when they started off in the morning. Francesca's complicated dilemma was still completely unresolved and now Fabiana was going to be leaving.

A few days later Fabiana said her goodbyes and left for London.

***

Andrew was so happy to see her and have her attending classes at his university. He thought of Francesca, maybe he could find the courage to tell Fabiana how much he loved her aunt. He hoped just maybe she might decide to come and visit her niece. He longed to see her. He had become obsessed with her.

The distance had made his heart want her more. Maybe Fabiana could help him if he told her his truth. He couldn't do it now; he needed to give her some time. After all, she had just arrived in London and had to get settled into her new place. Plus, her classes had started and she didn't have much time to spare. He felt obligated to help her in any way as he promised. Fabiana was a very capable young lady, and with her parents' money, she wouldn't have any problem. As for his own life, there wasn't anything to be proud of.

At my age, I guess I'm just an average professor making a living. I cannot compare myself to the wealth of the Tavernas or even Francesca. At the same time, Andrew hadn't given up on Francesca. He promised himself to go look at a new real estate development in the northeastern side of London. He was going to upgrade his living situation, just in case Francesca considered coming to London. Yes, he would do anything for her.

Fabiana had settled herself in a hotel in the center of London. She opted to stay there until she found an apartment near the university. She was busy with her school; in the meantime she kept thinking of Francesca and hoped she would come to her senses. Her lips were sealed until her aunt granted her the right to move forward. Francesca had been like a second mother to her.

Back in Sicily, Francesca was struggling with her existence. Every morning she woke up in sadness. Everyone was asking questions, Letizia was inquiring ten times a day, "How do you feel, Francesca? What can I do for you? What is wrong?"

She felt like saying, *Yes, Letizia, you could just leave me alone and mind your business.* But instead she answered politely, even thanking her. She knew her staff meant well, her sister-in-law called daily and invited her over regularly. Plus, her brother was checking in on her on his way home from work every night.

She wondered if they knew. Her body was changing daily; she was a mess. She looked forward to seeing that lady doctor again. She thought of Andrew, if he was to see her now he wouldn't think that she was such a prize. She was wrestling with all these ugly thoughts going through her mind. Then realistically she asked herself, *Really, how long can I go on living with this lie?*

She thought of confessing to her sister-in-law. She would be shocked. Like her, she was old fashioned. It was easy to talk to Fabiana, since she was younger and more liberal. Anthony. How could she break it to him? And they would probably hate Andrew. Who knew how they would react. Her sons, she didn't want to cause them shame. What a mess she had created.

The one person she didn't think of was her husband. She didn't care to think of him at all. After all, he hadn't been there for her. She didn't care about the extravagant gifts. Was that the way a man was to love his wife with objects and possessions? He was a sick man as far as she was concerned. She was his wife, the mother of his children. The women he was keeping company with were probably impressed with all those meaningless objects. She was thirsty and hungry for what had been missing in her marriage.

No wonder she had turned to Andrew. He loved her and she could tell he was sincere. She felt like screaming at her husband instead of hiding her pregnancy. She wanted to tell him from the top of her lungs, "I'm pregnant. I am carrying another man's baby and this is the result of my love for him and not you!"

And to Andrew she wanted to say, "You appeared in my world suddenly and briefly and now you're gone. I miss you so, my darling."

Fausto Tarantano felt foolish keeping an eye on the home and moves of Francesca like a hiding thief. He was due to place a call to Angelo in New York to bring him up to date on his report.

"Boss," he said.

Frarano liked that, it made him feel big.

"I have nothing much to tell you; your wife is a good woman, she goes to church regularly, all is well. I hate to take your money, but it's up to you if you want me to continue."

"Fausto, you do what you have to do, don't worry about my money. It's well spent, believe me."

"As you wish, boss, goodbye."

Fausto, got off the phone and with all the unemployment, he was thankful for the income.

Francesca woke up in a very languishing state. She forced herself to get dressed and decided she was going to pay a visit to her sister-in-law. Thoughts of suicide were haunting her. She often thought about swallowing a bottle of aspirins and being finished with her nightmare, but suicide was very much against her religion also. She thought of the baby inside of her, what fault did he or she have to be punished like that?

Francesca dialed Lora's number, "Lora, hello, it's me Francesca. What are you doing this morning?"

Happily she responded, "Francesca, nice to hear your voice. I'm so glad you called. I'd love to see you."

"Lora, I want to come over, have an espresso and chat with you."

"Francesca, I will put the coffee pot on. Get here as soon as you can."

"Okay," she answered and hung up the phone. Lora was thrilled that Francesca was finally reaching out, just maybe she would now find out what was going on.

Lora welcomed her with open arms and with an apron tied around her she looked very domestic. She was a down-to-earth person, humble and kind. Francesca knew she was very fortunate to have these family members close to her.

"Lora," she asked, "where is Ersilia? Why are you fretting in the kitchen? You work too much."

"Francesca, I like to keep busy, especially since Fabiana has been gone. There is a big void in this house. Never mind me, let me take a look at you. We've been so worried about you."

"I'm fine… I guess. Lora, this is why I came over to talk to you."

"Francesca, believe me, your brother is beside himself. He was so angry with Angelo over the Christmas holidays. When it comes to family, you know how overprotective he is. After all, you're the only family he has left."

Francesca's temporary courage was starting to vanish, she doubted confiding in her sister-in-law.

"Tell me, Francesca, how are things going with you? Have you been checked by our family doctor?"

"Lora, look at me, take a good look. Do you notice a difference?"

Lora frowned and scrutinized her sister-in-law from top to bottom.

"I don't know, Francesca, I don't see anything different. What am I supposed to see? Wait a minute turn around."

Searching hard she said, "Francesca, you're not pregnant are you?"

Francesca went ice cold. She froze. *Oh my God,* it was becoming real if her sister-in-law could tell. Where was she going to hide now?

Her fear was taking over again. Lora stood there waiting for Francesca to speak and give her an answer.

Lora didn't wait. She hugged her in support and tried to console her. "I know you're not happy because of your age and everything that goes with it. But, honey, if it's God's will, then there is a good reason."

Francesca was trying to catch her breath. *Wait until I tell her it isn't Angelo's,* she thought.

"Francesca, of all people, you should know; you live in the church and are so devoted. Never go against God's will."

"Lora, if you can tell I am pregnant, I need you and your help. Listen to what I am going to tell you and don't faint on me. The baby I'm carrying isn't my husband's." She took a deep breath before continuing, "The Professor and I slept together. This baby is the result of pure love not only from him but from me, too."

Lora didn't know what to say at first. Then she asked, "Does he know?"

"No, Lora, he does not."

"Why not? You need to inform him."

"He begged me to go with him to London, he loves me, Lora." She turned away, walking towards the open window. She needed some fresh air to strengthen her heart and clear her lungs.

She was actually seeking for answers and hoping her sister-in-law would have them for her.

"Where do I go and what will I do with the baby? Fabiana knows all about this too, and she has also offered to help."

"Really? Let me think. We will sort it out, Francesca. You can't go through this alone. I need to tell Anthony, he will understand."

At the mention of Anthony's name another stab went through her stomach, "That poor brother of mine. This is how I have repaid back his kindness, by shaming him."

"Francesca, nonsense, Anthony knew you were love starved."

They talked and talked, Francesca felt somewhat lighter as she shared her truth and problems. Angelo would be home again mid-February. She would be better off in complying with him for few days, until he went off again. It would be obvious that she was pregnant. What would be the outcome? Her doctor wanted to see her again and she must keep that appointment especially if she was to move forward.

Lora said, "Francesca, you can always make it look like you put on weight, with the right clothes, you can camouflage your hips and your tummy. You asked me to really look at you, don't forget I have been pregnant myself; therefore, I know what to look for, but your husband home for a couple of days, he won't look that deep."

"Thanks, Lora, I guess I will have to do some sewing. I must admit, I have not been thinking straight lately."

Confiding in Lora brought a little relief. Francesca would take the next step, with her advice.

In the next few days she made a trip to the fabric store, in the piazza in Palermo. She had earned a fashion degree in Agrigento, although Angelo had never allowed her to work: "No wife of mine has to work for a living. I'm the bread winner in this house, your job is to look after the children and keep a good home for me and the boys."

She had argued, "But, Angelo, I like to create. I want to be a designer and go to Milano, Rome, Paris…"

"Do you need to do that? Don't I provide enough for you? You have a full-time job right here in this house. Francesca, end of story, forget it."

After she had given birth to the boys she found herself becoming very busy, and her interest in fashion slowly drifted away. Occasionally she would make an extravagant outfit for herself when her heart desired. She was clever, now with the right design she could help conceal her growing figure.

Once at the fabric store Francesca's knowledge kicked back in. She was enjoying the soft silky feeling of the fabric in her hands. Francesca thought with a trick of the trade she could create an illusion that would make her look slimmer and taller. She was going to buy several pieces of fabric, for a few outfits. Francesca made her choices and made her purchases like a little girl buying dresses for her favorite doll. She needed to get them done before her husband arrived back home. She had to fool him. After all, she was a part of his collection. Part of his possessions. Yes, she would look her best for him. She had been feeling a little better lately. She was dreaming of seeing Andrew again. A relentless flickering flame was ready to burst in her heart. Maybe after – one step at a time – after Angelo leaves.

Fabiana's words resonated in her ears, "Auntie, you're too stuck on your vows." Yes, she was right. She was trapped in this marriage. Walking out of a marriage was unheard of in her family. Maybe for a city woman, from the mainland yes, of course some did, but they were labeled and scorned. If she left, Francesca would become one of them. Then there was the church: she would be excommunicated. How could she risk her faith? It would affect the immediate family. These thoughts made her feel miserable. Lora checked on her well-being every day. It was a relief knowing she could open up to her and share her misery, which gave her some comfort.

February had soon rolled around. She was at home and heard the rumble of a motor. She looked out the window and saw a white delivery van. A young man bounced out, walking quickly while whistling. Letizia had gone out for fresh produce, so Francesca went to the door and the man handed her the biggest bunch of red roses. She opened the little envelope, they were from her husband. It was Valentine's Day. He thought roses would take care of things. She looked at the beautiful roses, without any emotion. She wanted to pitch them in the garbage. Instead, she picked a vase and filled it with water. She placed it on the console by the entrance foyer, should Angelo arrive.

Years ago she used to be thrilled to receive flowers. Now she was mature and his roses had become meaningless. Returning to her sewing room, she went back to her work of art. It gave her something to do and her energy started to shift her out of her depression. She asked herself, if it was the will of God.

She still prayed every night before retiring; even in her sin she felt a little peace. She couldn't wait until her husband would come and leave again. Then, the day arrived and he was there. Happy as a lark, he merged into the house picked up Francesca and twirled her around like a yo-yo. She was supposed to be happy to see him.

"*Bambola*," he said, "I'm going to be here three days. Sorry baby, eh! You know I need to get back. I wanted to make you happy for Valentine's Day."

"Angelo, I am used to it by now don't you think? Whatever makes you happy," she mused nonchalantly hoping to hide her panic.

Three days weren't going to be so long. She could pretend to be the devoted wife. She doubted he would get suspicious or ask questions. Lora had coached Francesca; she was going to follow her advice.

"Francesca, when he arrives pretend to be delighted to see him, turn on your charm, you'll see. It will work to your advantage. For those three days, you make sure you dress well and be in good humor. You will see, it will turn out all for the best for both of you."

"Lora, it's hard after having stored so many years of resentment."

"Now, now, Francesca. You are good at forgiving, let go of any of that stuff, you are the one who gets hurt in the end. Stop the harboring… you can do it for few days. Pretend *bella mia*. You will see; before you know it, you will feel better."

"Thanks, Lora, you are precious. I shall try."

Lora was her best friend now. She admired her sister-in-law's qualities. Lora was a model wife and mother, but her brother was a devoted husband and father. So it was easy for her. Angelo, on the contrary, was a restless whirlwind who only cared about going to the piazza for his cappuccinos in the morning and espresso bars in the evening to shoot the breeze with his buddies. With them he played the big macho man, whom they thought of as the big star flying in and out of town.

Tonight, to Francesca's surprise, he was behaving like a new husband in love and referring to her with graciousness. She knew the wolf hadn't shed his skin. She was going along in compliance to be safe. When he suggested they go out for dinner, just the two of them, at the grand Hotel Scaglione overlooking the Mediterranean Sea she got very worried. *Pretend, pretend,* she reminded herself. With a cheerful voice, she excused herself to get ready for the evening.

She had decided to make an effort for her husband. She sat in front of her vanity and applied her make-up using the best dark blue eyeliner with shadows of lighter tones to emphasize her eyes. Her clothes had been meticulously completed and she hoped they would conceal her growing figure.

She chose to wear the white and navy striped layered outfit; topping it with an off-white shimmering shawl. With her black hair piled on top of her head she appeared statuesque and self-assured. Courageously she was ready to walk down her own imaginary runway with an admiring crowd.

Angelo was dressed in his tuxedo. When he saw her walking down the stairs to the foyer his eyes sparkled in admiration, "Francesca! You look stunning; you are my treasure. My number one doll, the mother of my boys. This is why I love you so." He walked over to embrace her, but she stopped him with her left arm.

"Angelo, what about all your other dolls, the ones you keep around like mannequins, what do you say about them?" She was on fire, like a volcano, she erupted.

"Francesca, you know they don't mean anything. Don't start being stupid. You will ruin a beautiful evening. After all, I flew home for Valentine's Day, doesn't that mean anything to you?"

"Angelo, I'm through being impressed with you. If you really want to know the truth, I don't really care what you do anymore, who you see, or when you come or when you go. After so many years of putting up with your nonsense… I'm tired of it all."

"What kind of talk is that? Are you rebelling? Where has my sweet Francesca gone?"

"Yes, Angelo, I am rebelling. I have been at your mercy for too long."

"Francesca, don't get smart with me, I expect you to be the devoted girl I married."

"She died, Angelo, you killed her. All the love I had for you… well, you did a good job of destroying it. The little girl grew up, Angelo. You're not going to suffocate and suppress me anymore."

"Eh, I don't like the way you're talking to me. I am your husband remember? Have you forgotten what I do for you? I work so you can live like a queen, eh! Tell me?"

"I don't have to tell you anything. All I can say to you is, the blood in my veins is running murky, Angelo, and you have turned it that way."

"Something isn't right with you. Are you cheating on me? Are you seeing somebody, Francesca? You know, if you are, I will carve his heart out. And as for you, well, I won't mention what will happen. You know me well. No wife of mine will make a fool out of me."

For a moment Francesca reflected, *How foolish I've been, I'm giving myself away to him*. She quickly retracted, "This is ridiculous, I thought we were celebrating Valentine's Day. Instead we're getting heated in a fighting match. Let's go and have our dinner." She walked over, put her arm under his, and led him out the door. All the way she rehearsed how she was going to pacify him. Angelo was quieter the rest of the evening, but civil. Francesca was making animated conversations and smiling at him teasingly, but the strain was obvious.

Angelo was a control freak and it bothered him to lose control. He liked a passive woman, and this wife of his lately was revealing a different side of her. Yes, he had detected a change in her even from their phone conversations. At Christmas she was not well and now she was being mouthy instead of grateful. He wasn't too happy with the way things were going.

A delicious dinner was served; from entrées to dessert, followed by brandy. The air was warm, the sky glittered and the moonlight reflected on the calm sea. The setup was perfect for a romantic evening. Except Francesca was with the wrong man. How she wished Andrew was there instead. She sat there and hoped that the brandy would make him drowsy and put him to sleep as soon as they got back home.

She had fallen out of love with him. To her surprise she didn't even care that he was the father of her two precious boys anymore. She wished her body would respond to him, but it had been so diverted that she could not help herself. When they got home, she forced herself to respond to his advances, but to her relief he was soon overcome from fatigue and drifted away to sleep.

The next day Angelo thought he better check things out with Fausto Tarantano. He knocked at his door. "Boss," they shook hands while he continued, "when did you get back in town?"

"Only last night. How are things going with you, pal?"

"Not bad, not bad. Wish the economy would improve though, no jobs at all. Once the harvest is done, it's brutal."

"Tell me, has anything new developed; do you have anything to report? Is there anything for me to be concerned about?"

"Boss, I told you before. You have a saint of a wife, I feel bad taking your money. I have nothing to report. You're a lucky man."

"I'm glad to hear that. For a moment, I was in doubt. You made my day, Fausto. My brother-in-law, I want you to keep an eye on him, does he badmouth me?"

"No, no, that poor fellow and his son are working day and night. We don't see them hanging around the coffee shops much."

"Tell me, your brother-in-law Miliano, how is he doing?"

"Not good. He's just hanging on. The doctors have written him off. He has been reduced to a vegetable and better off dead."

"Is that right? I know he didn't look well when I saw him, too bad."

Angelo patted his shoulder, as his way of saying goodbye and happily made his way home. Tomorrow he would be gone and Francesca would be left alone again. If Francesca wasn't terrified of flying he would ask her to go with him, but so far she had not been able to conquer her fear and in the past it had served to his advantage. He could come and go without a wife hanging around his neck.

Those women he had in every city, he paid them and they had to keep quiet and go along as he wished. Francesca was a different story. She was the privileged wife, the image of a stable and real family. He was getting older and she was looking younger, it worried him a little. Now she was surprising him by protesting and speaking firmly. Francesca was changing. Maybe he needed to come home more often and spend more time with her. He wasn't ready yet; the business needed him. In a few years, when the boys graduated, then they could take his place and he would semi-retire. After all, wasn't this why Diego was going to law school? And Daniele to be an architect? That is what he expected of them; he had built this empire for them. Who else? And Francesca should understand, he had sacrificed himself to benefit their boys and it was their responsibility to carry on the legacy he created. This is how he justified his life and it was perfectly fine as far as he was concerned.

However, he was still ready to leave the next day. Never before had he requested Francesca to see him off at the airport. Strangely enough, this time when he hugged his wife he held her for the longest time kissing her over and over again. He took her face in his hands, and said in a passionate voice, "Francesca, remember, I love you. I want you to come to the airport to see me off, will you?"

Francesca didn't know what to make of it. For some strange reason he acted humble and powerless. She didn't like his change of behavior; did he somehow feel threatened by her? Did he suspect something? Francesca couldn't help but wonder. Regardless, it was too late. This time she kissed him goodbye in her usual dutiful wife manner, but she never asked him when he was coming back or begged him to please come back soon. No, she did not want him to come back: she let him go.

Her husband, on the other hand, was puzzled. He shook his head. *Something isn't right with my wife*, he thought, *and she didn't even ask me when I'm coming back.* He had flashbacks of when she hung around his neck begging him to come home soon. He tried to shake it off. *Oh well, she's a woman who knows what she wants.*

Francesca's heart was pounding. She knew their relationship was all a lie. Andrew was the only one she desired and dreamed to be with. After all the affairs he had, how could she be concerned about Angelo's comings and goings? She pushed to seek the right answer; she knew the timing was closing in on her. It wasn't just her, the innocent soul growing daily inside of her was a constant reminder to take responsibility and make the right choice. She needed to think like a mother. Why on earth would she be concerned in pacifying and pleasing her husband when he had been the culprit for her insanity?

Chapter Fifteen

While Francesca was in despair in Sicily, Andrew was in despair in London. It hadn't been easy for him either. His mental state was up and down. He was moody and often slipped into bouts of depression. He missed Francesca and couldn't get her out of his mind. The worst part was not being able to communicate with her. He wanted to call her, but she had forbidden him to do so. He wanted to write to her, but she adamantly protested. He felt all the avenues leading to Francesca were blocked. It would take an army to break her frontier. To fight her husband, would be impossible. He could only hope that she would come to her senses and communicate with him. He knew she loved him. Andrew could only live in hope.

He had sweet, young Fabiana here in London, whom he loved like a daughter. Every time he saw her she made him feel closer to his adorable Francesca. Tonight he planned to take Fabiana out for dinner. Andrew couldn't wait. They usually spoke about school, and her new studies. She wasn't in any of his classes; therefore, it was fine for them to be seen socially. Andrew had become her protector and Fabiana appreciated his kindness and help, especially in her studies.

What Andrew didn't know was that Fabiana was keeping in touch with her aunt regularly and continuously encouraging her to come to London. "Auntie," she begged her, "please come. You can travel by train, the Professor and I will meet you."

She had now rented a place on the northwest side of London. A two bedroom flat newly remodeled and it was very comfortable. It was small, but this was London. The location was perfect. It was only a short walk to the subway and within a few minutes she was at the university.

In one of her conversations with Francesca she asked, "Can I tell the Professor that I know about your love affair? It will make him feel better and he can talk freely about you to me."

"No, Fabiana, you mustn't say anything about us!"

"Auntie, stop being so old fashioned, and start to live, please!"

"Fabiana, I know you're right but it's hard for me to take the leap."

"I won't tell him about the baby, that's your job, but I'd just like to tell him that you confided in me and I'm happy for both of you. If anything, you two deserve to be together."

Francesca knew Fabiana was right, but it was easier said than done.

Lora had been on her case lately as well. She was fretting on her account because time was running short. She called this morning saying, "Francesca, my dear, I would like you to come over for supper. Tonight we will break the news to Anthony, and I will back you up, Francesca, don't worry. I know it's difficult for you, but we will make him understand."

She held her breath, dreading the ordeal, remorsefully hating herself for having shamed the family, especially her older brother.

"Francesca, answer me. Do you want me to send Joseph to pick you up?"

"Lora, okay, I will be there and I will take my own car. Oh, how I hate to break my brother's heart."

"Francesca, we need to do what we have to do."

"I know, Lora. I know."

All day she rehearsed what to say. Was there a gentle way to break the news to him? How would he react? She needed her own family, Fabiana was right. She couldn't go through this alone. Tonight she needed the courage for this next stepping stone. At seven o'clock she arrived at her brother's place.

Anthony happily met her at the door, "Hello, Sis," he kissed her on the cheek. "Where have you been hiding lately? Did you forget about your brother and make yourself scarce?"

"Anthony, what do you worry about? You know you are my favorite brother and the only one."

"Yes, yes, you know we need to see you regularly."

She slapped him in a caressing gesture, kidded with him like old times. She turned to greet Lora and Joseph, proclaiming to be starving.

"Come on you two, sit down. We're having roasted stuffed capon with potatoes and yellow grape peppers. Fresh baked almond biscotti with our coffee for dessert."

Anthony poured his homemade red wine and they cheered for good health. Francesca, speaking up, suggested, "Let's say our prayers and thank the Lord for our abundance of food and to bless our family." She recited her prayer, quietly imploring for courage and forgiveness for the shocking surprise she was about to spring on her brother after the meal.

Lora was nervously chatty during the meal. Francesca on the contrary, was absentminded and not attentively listening. Her mind was concentrating on how tactfully she could handle herself. *Where am I going to begin?* With these unpleasant thoughts going through her mind, sweat started to pour down her spine. Francesca was overcome by that tremendous fear again. This was another shameful ordeal to go through. How was she going to face her brother after she would break his heart?

***

Angelo's life in New York wasn't running smoothly either. He was in the midst of construction with his new hotel. His crew had finally started to move forward after so much red tape. Then, his top man Gestiniano Ambruzio, came into his office alarmed, "We have big problems, Boss. Big problems this time. A scaffold reinforced with wire ties came loose, it tumbled down and brought five men to their deaths from the twenty-fourth floor. The labor department has shut us down; the D.A.'s office is investigating. The union is threatening to sue us. The families need assistance. I tell you, Boss, we are in a big mess. The insurance company is investigating, looking for loopholes."

"Gestiniano, do you suspect there is somebody behind this? What do you think?" asked Angelo.

"Boss, I don't know. You know nobody likes competition; you are beating the other hoteliers with your marketing strategies."

"Nobody is going to stop us; we better start our own investigation."

"You tell me, Boss, where do we go from here?"

"I suggest we start by waking up Lorino Gambera; that big attorney of ours needs to be alert. Plus, I suggest we launch an investigation of our own with a private investigator."

"Boss, I'm here to proceed with your orders."

Angelo extended his hand and tapped at Gestiniano's shoulder in agreement, "You're a good man, Gestiniano."

As soon as his manager left he called his Lula, "Baby, I'm coming home soon, my muscles are in knots, do get ready for me will you?" He knew she would follow his orders and he needed his massage more than ever tonight.

***

Back at the Taverna's residence, supper was over and Lora came out of the kitchen with her aromatic espressos and a plate of biscotti, which would complete her meal.

Joseph was itching to join his friends. It was Friday night. He hesitated to excuse himself from the table. In respect he walked over to Francesca, "Bye, Auntie, it's been nice to have you with us tonight. Should you need anything please call me okay." He kissed her on the cheek, said his goodbyes to his parents and left.

Lora and Francesca looked at each other. Who was going to initiate their unavoidable disturbing dialogue? Francesca nodded her head for Lora to go ahead. Lora watched Anthony sip his last drop of espresso. Then, as gently as she could Lora spoke up, "Anthony," she said to get his attention, "Francesca and I have something serious to tell you."

"Serious! My goodness, what's so serious? Is anything wrong with Fabiana? What is it?"

"No, everything is fine with Fabiana, it's right here. We have a problem."

Anthony was definitely paying attention now.

"Francesca, now you tell him."

Francesca took a deep breath, "Anthony, I don't know how to tell you this…" Tears automatically started to flow down her cheeks.

Alarmed he was holding his breath, "Can somebody tell me what's going on? What's the matter?"

"I am pregnant," there, she had said it.

"For heaven's sakes, Francesca, is that all? You had me really scared. I thought something really bad happened to you or the boys. Not to mention that scumbag of a husband of yours. God forbid, should something go wrong with him."

"Anthony. I'm sorry, but I'm carrying another man's baby."

Anthony was astounded and confused, "What do you mean? You, my sister the saint. Always in church, carrying another man's baby? Were you raped! Who did this to you?"

"No, Anthony, I wasn't raped."

He was stunned and didn't know what he would hear next.

Francesca continued, "Yes, Anthony, me, it's happened. I wish I was dead, Anthony. I'm sorry to bring this shame to the family. I don't know which way to turn."

Her brother got up and brought both hands to his head ruffling his hair, "Francesca, does your husband know?"

"No, of course not."

"You care to tell me who the father is?"

Francesca felt like a troubled teenager interrogated by one of her parents. She didn't answer him. She looked at Lora nodding to her.

Lora took over, "Anthony, you know, and we all know how unhappy Francesca has been, right?"

Anthony listened with a strange glare in his eyes, while wondering what surprise was coming next.

Lora blurted, "Anthony, people do fall in love unexpectedly in life. This is what's happened to Francesca and the Professor, they felt attracted to one another and there you have it."

"What? The Professor! That son of a bitch! You mean he came here to screw my sister and us along with her? I will get a hold of that son of bitch and break his neck!"

Francesca in defense of Andrew spoke up, "Anthony, listen to me, he's not a son of a bitch. He was a perfect gentleman we were both attracted to one another, and it was my fault to receive him."

Anthony walked around the dining room shaking his head, "Let me digest this, Francesca. Sorry, but I never expected that from you."

"I know, Anthony. I know, I was so angry I wasn't thinking rationally anymore. I wanted revenge on my husband and Andrew was there."

"Now what? What do you intend to do?"

Lora intervened, "We're going to put our heads together and come up with the best solution. We need to consider the baby first and foremost."

"Francesca, what does this Professor of yours have to say?" asked Anthony trying to control his anger.

"He doesn't have a clue," she answered.

"What! He doesn't know? Am I hearing right? He's the father and he doesn't know? You haven't told him?"

"Anthony, Andrew begged me to go with him to London. Neither of us knew of this outcome. I totally refused him and told him to forget about me and what had taken place between us."

"Francesca, he needs to know. Or wait a minute, can you attribute this dishonestly to your husband? Is that what you intend to do? Can it be that it's your husband's?"

"No, no it cannot."

"Okay, it cannot. This is absurd. You haven't told the Professor that a baby is on the way; your husband can't pass for the father. So, what is going to happen?"

"This is why I am burdening you with this huge problem, help me, please," she was begging now between her tears.

Anthony hated to see his sister in distress. In a calmer tone he asked, "When is the baby due?"

"In May, I need to go back to the doctor, she will give me the exact date."

"Does our family doctor know?"

"Anthony, I knew better, I went to Agrigento at a woman's medical clinic."

"You're almost six months along. When your husband comes home, how do you plan to hide your pregnancy? This is just too much for me to figure out tonight," he said shaking his head.

"I know, I know, I have made a real mess of my life."

Lora spoke up saying, "We'll all sleep on it, tomorrow is another day, we will figure out the best solution."

They called it a night. Francesca knew in her heart she was now no longer alone in her big dilemma. As much as she knew her family would stand by her, she still felt demoralized. Back home and alone in her king size bed, she tossed and turned all night long and prayed for a better tomorrow.

The morning sun awoke her as it shone through the window. It must be late. In a groggy state, she tried to pull herself out of bed. Letizia must have arrived and would be serving breakfast soon. The ordeal of the previous night soon came to her mind again. Oh, how life had turned so terribly wrong. She needed to go back to the doctor; her visit was overdue. This was another nagging thought on her mind. She dreaded going.

Over the following few days, Anthony called on her daily. Last night on the phone he had said, "Sis, go see the doctor and then we will sit down and decide where we go from here."

She sensed the compassion in her brother's voice and felt relieved, "Thanks, Anthony. I'm so sorry for causing you pain."

He had assured her that they would work it out although he didn't have an answer for his sister right now. He thought of his brother-in-law. He deserved what he got; deep down he could not really blame Francesca. After all, she had lived a widow's life even though she was married. He hated to think what the outcome would be once Angelo got wind of his wife's infidelity. He was known to have a violent temper and anyone blemishing his honor was surely going to pay for it. He knew his kind. Who would know his reaction? *Professor Robertson doesn't realize who he's dealing with*, thought Anthony. He himself had never cared for Angelo. But his sister had been stubborn and fallen for his charismatic personality. Then, his parents were also to blame, they encouraged the marriage because his family was wealthy.

His father kept saying, "She will be well taken care of."

This was how his father had married his sister off; it was all about material values. His mother had gone along with it reluctantly.

***

Francesca couldn't put off the visit to the doctor any longer. As she walked into the clinic, her stomach hurt. She patted her stomach to gain relief. Maybe the doctor would suggest something to alleviate this awful burning at the pit of her stomach that started to occur every day of late. She didn't have to wait long in the reception area, Doctor Filiberta's nurse called her in quickly.

She proceeded with weighing her and got all the other necessary information. When the doctor came in, she was quite cheerful.

While scrutinizing the chart in her hand she asked, "How are we doing?"

Francesca related the acidity problem and the doctor suggested she take some light antacids. She proceeded to check out her tummy attentively. Francesca focused on her facial expressions, holding her breath and watching the doctor's every move.

"Mrs. Frarano, your baby has a good heartbeat. You seem to be doing well, except for your weight, you are going to have a small baby."

"Oh!" Francesca mumbled a confused answer.

"Your weight," she continued. "You haven't gained enough for being six months pregnant. Are you conscious about gaining weight?"

"No, not really," answered a dishonest Francesca.

"The baby's nutrition is important. You need to eat a little more; don't forget there are two of you now to feed."

"I understand, I will," she responded in a daze. "Tell me, doctor, when exactly is the baby due?"

"By the thirtieth of May I would say, one never knows sometimes, but that should be about right."

Francesca thanked her and the doctor left. Once she got home Lora had promptly called her, inquiring of her well-being. Francesca reassured her that all was well. She would go and have coffee with her in the morning.

"Yes, Francesca, do come. We need to call Fabiana, and you know Anthony has been doing a lot of thinking the last few days. We need to sit down again and discuss how we move forward."

"Fine, Lora, I'm tired from the trip, I'll see you tomorrow."

Her normal clothes were definitely not fitting her any more, she resorted to wearing just three outfits she had designed and sewn herself. Now the doctor wanted her to increase her diet. She already felt uncomfortably overweight.

Going forward was going to be a real challenge. *Thank God for my brother and sister-in-law. We need to make a decision and it cannot wait.* She walked to the house library, picked up Andrew's book, gently turned the pages and held his note in her hand for the longest time.

It was all spelled out for her; she could get in touch with him right now. All she needed to do was dial those numbers and he would be on the other end of the receiver. She would be able to hear his voice and she could share her secret with him. He could be her savior. She had never known a man so gentle and kind. Why was she denying him the offspring of their love affair? Francesca suddenly realized she was being selfish.

Her pain and suffering was about saving the family's honor and avoiding a scandal in her congregation and the community at large. She knew once Letizia found out, the whole town would know. Well, tomorrow she would decide what to do. As for Angelo, she wasn't so worried about him anymore.

Her brain was exhausted from thinking. Her body drained. When the boys came to mind, she felt a stab in her heart. But they knew how their father behaved and she had been so unhappy all these years. Now the devil had gotten a hold of her. She figured this was her cross to carry, and it must have happened for some uncontrollable reason. Lora had reassured her by saying, "Francesca, don't you ever consider yourself alone."

A strong movement in her tummy reminded her to walk into the kitchen to see what Letizia had cooked. The doctor had warned her that she needed to eat for two. No sooner had she sat down when the phone rang.

It was Fabiana, "Auntie, how are you doing? The Professor wanted me to give you his regards."

"Oh, when did you see him," she asked.

"After school, we were talking about you, Mom, Dad, Joseph. I miss you guys, and the Professor does too. He said that he is fond of you. Of course he doesn't know what I know."

"Fabiana, I miss you too, and the Professor, believe it or not. It's miserable here without you. Fabiana, I told your parents."

"Good, it's about time. Please come here, Auntie, we will find a solution. I will help you and when the Professor finds out I am sure he will be so happy."

"Fabiana, you make things sound so easy. I'm meeting with your mom and dad tomorrow; they're going to help me. I will let you know what we decide together. Give my regards to Andrew."

"Auntie, please allow me to tell him. I know he loves to talk about you, but he is on guard and afraid to do so."

"Fabiana, I will get back to you, soon. I need to go now and have something to eat. Doctor's orders. Bye-bye, love you."

"Love you, too, I will wait for your call, bye for now."

***

Back at the household of Miliano Cardone, fate had taken its course. Miliano's heart had ceased beating and he died. A week after the funeral Fausto was summoned by his sister Miliano's wife, to help clear some of the files in her husband's office. She wasn't familiar with her husband's affairs, so she needed him. Fausto and Miliano had carried through some assignments together; therefore, she knew he would be familiar with his work.

Fausto was diligently going over files. His brother-in-law's files were in order. He had to admit, Miliano was good at what he did. Every account was well recorded and his notes precise and detailed. Fausto shook his head in dismay and thought he must have really liked spying on people. He couldn't say he shared the same enthusiasm.

He thought of Angelo Frarano's case; it was another boring subject and a total waste of time, but he needed to feed his wife and kids. Every night he added another entry in his diary, it was boring and monotonous. By early evening he had had enough for the day. He was tired of checking names and records of people he didn't even know. He promised to return in the next few days and eventually finish going through all the drawers.

In the meantime, Angelo was in New York and dealing with the chaos in his business. Since leaving Sicily his stress levels had escalated. Even Lula's hands seemed to have lost that magic touch; his body wasn't vibrating with excitement anymore. Instead, he was feeling sensations of remorse and guilt. Strangely he thought, *Francesca, my sweet, Francesca. Yes, you are the only real good thing in my life.*

The next morning he called his manager into his office, "Gestiniano, you know you are my number one man. I knew your father Mr. Ambruzio."

"Yes, Boss, I know," his manager consented with a nod.

"Your father was a hard worker and a noble man. He took his responsibilities seriously and that brought results. I expect you to be just as capable."

"Boss, you should know me by now. Is there something that you are not pleased with?"

"No, no, it's me, nothing to do with you. You know, after my last visit home, I've had a change of heart. That brother-in-law of mine has always insulted me with his remarks. He's always accused me of not being a good husband to his sister."

"Boss, Boss, don't let that get to you, we have big business to look after here."

"I know, I know. This is why I called you in here. My intentions are to promote you as the CEO, and transfer a block of my shares so you will be a shareholder of the New York holdings."

"Boss, I appreciate your confidence in me, but right now, we are in deep trouble until some of these issues are resolved."

"Who's giving you trouble?"

"We have so many lawsuits against us and they need to be sorted out one by one. The families of the victims, the labor board, you name it… I won't get into them all. Let me handle them. The lawyers are dragging their feet. I have given them an ultimatum."

"Gestiniano, be firm with them and don't let anybody push us around. These lawyers if they don't act fast in our favor, replace them."

"Boss, believe me, I have taken steps already."

"You know, Gestiniano, I'm getting older now, I would like to spend more time with my wife. I need to make sure the business is in capable hands."

With that Gestiniano extended his hand, "*Parola di onore,* Boss, I give you my word of honor."

Angelo answered, "I know I can count on you, my man." With that he shook his hand and patted his employee on the shoulder with his left hand as his sign to seal the deal.

Then he thought of his boys. "My boys, they need to finish school and when they're ready, you and I will show them the ropes. Now, my intention is to spend more time in *Sicilia.*"

Gestiniano was a man of action. Standing at six feet two inches, he held an aura of authority. He had slicked-back black hair, big brown eyes and a protruding big nose. Angelo Frarano was in the habit of picking only the best. The staff respected Gestiniano; his orders were promptly executed and respectfully brought to completion.

Gestiniano left, contemplating his promotion while Angelo sat quietly thinking of Francesca. He had watched her every move on his last visit home. A strange feeling had come over him; his wife wasn't the same. She used to beam when he returned and normally she shed tears when he left. He expected to be loved. He didn't appreciate anyone ever abandoning him. His boys and his wife were obligated to love and obey him. With these troubling thoughts churning in his head, he fell asleep in the chair.

Sukee Lee, the new masseuse, was waiting anxiously for his call. Disappointed, she decided she would still charge him. She wasn't about to lose money due to his negligence. She prepared a big fat invoice and mailed it to him. Next time she promised herself she wouldn't commit to spending time with Mr. Frarano without a retainer.

Angelo had remained fast asleep in his chair, until midnight. He looked at his watch, in Sicily it was six o'clock in the morning. Anthony was ready to go to work, Francesca was walking in her garden and Fausto Tarantano was preparing his espresso before heading to his sister's place to finish up with his brother-in-law's files.

He had been there for a week now. It was time to move on. He never should have agreed to be Angelo Frarano's watchdog. Not with cleaning up Miliano's files. Some of the work his brother-in-law was involved with made his hair stand up. He preferred not to know. He planned on burning all the paperwork. He wanted out of working for Angelo. Fausto decided he would go and ask Anthony Taverna for work. Maybe he would have a place for him on one of his farms.

That evening Anthony, Francesca, and Lora were getting together to decide her fate. Anthony now had been overcome by tremendous fear for his sister and he felt responsible to protect her. He wanted to guide her with the right decision.

Francesca had become somewhat docile with knowing Lora and Anthony were on her side, but time was running out. Anthony was right. They had to make a decision; they had reached the turning point.

Andrew, completely oblivious to everything going on, was going through his days like a robot. He taught his classes; worked out at the fitness center; had the occasional dinner with Fabiana; and daydreamed of Francesca. The minute he hit his flat two glasses of Merlot helped him cope.

Anthony spent that day fretting and trying to expedite his loaded trucks to deliver earlier than scheduled. He wanted to get back to Palermo to have a private visit with Father Charles Don Carlo, the priest at the cathedral in the piazza. He needed to seek his advice. He honestly didn't know how to guide his sister under the circumstances. He arrived at the cathedral at four-thirty in the afternoon.

The church was empty; they casually sat at the back of the church. Father Charles knew Anthony was a devout Catholic and a good supporter of the church.

"Anthony, how can I help you, my brother?" the priest asked.

"Father, I wish it was a simple matter, but it's complicated."

"When we can't solve our problems, we turn to our almighty God. He, in His power, can lead us. I'm here to listen, my brother, and we can pray together."

"Father… my sister Francesca has committed adultery. Abortion was never considered, as it's beyond us. This child is coming to life. How do we handle it?"

"The child's father, is he willing to assume responsibility?"

"I don't know at this point, from what I'm told, this child is the result of a love affair."

"Yes, my brother, but what is the father willing to do?"

"We need to tell him and find out."

"He has a right to know, or is your sister willing to give the baby up for adoption?" asked the priest.

"Father, I don't think so. My concern is my sister's husband will go ballistic and I hate to think what he is capable of doing."

"The first thing here is to get in touch with the biological father, to see if he can be of help and alleviate the worry. This innocent child doesn't have one parent, but two."

"You're right, Father, it should have been done already."

"I will pray for all of you. Go now in God's peace."

Anthony walked out of the church with his head down. Who knew what path to take? One thing for sure, Andrew Robertson needed to know that his sister Francesca was carrying his child.

Chapter Sixteen

∙∙∙

Lora was at home waiting for her husband's return and Francesca was due to arrive soon too. It was necessary to send their staff away as they needed privacy. It was hard to have privacy around this busy house. Francesca arrived like a bird with broken wings, the look on her face told Lora she was counting on them to be rescued.

Lora, with her usual chatty personality, tried to lighten up the thick atmosphere in the room. She was happy to cater to both her husband and sister-in-law.

Francesca, deep down still feared her older brother. After all, he had replaced her father. She wasn't too hungry but slowly nibbled at her plate of food.

Finally Anthony said, "Francesca, I saw Father Charles on my way home."

"You did? Now the parish in Palermo knows of my situation?" she asked.

"Francesca, you know your secret is safe with him. I needed to make sure that I'm advising you right. You are my only sister and you know I would kill for you."

"Anthony, please, spare me the drama. I know how much you care for me and likewise I feel the same for you. Again, please forgive me for what I have done. Tell me, what did he say and where do we go from here?"

"You know, Francesca, I must admit he's right. He feels the father of the child is entitled to know. We have no right to keep this major event from him."

Francesca listened with her heart in her throat.

Anthony continued, "I agree with him. We should have told the Professor already."

Lora nodded in agreement, "Yes, Francesca, the Professor needs to know."

"Okay, well how are we going to break the news to him?" she asked.

"Francesca, I have given this a lot of thought and believe me, I haven't slept well since you told me."

"Anthony, whatever you say, I'll follow your advice."

"I suggest the three of us go to London to tell him; this isn't something you announce over the phone. We will be beside you. We need to make an appointment with the Professor."

"Okay, fine, how are we going to get there?"

"I guess we have no choice with you being afraid of flying, we'll go by train."

Lora asked, "Francesca, do you have his phone number or address, otherwise we certainly do, or Fabiana will gladly provide it."

"You know, he begged me to go with him. He slipped his phone number and address in a book he gave to me in case I ever changed my mind."

Lora said, "Francesca, you have been crazy to keep this to yourself, husband or no husband."

Anthony intervened, "Lora, my sister committed a mortal sin and you know that."

"Anthony, how can you make your sister feel guilty? After all, what kind of a husband has she got?"

Francesca intervened, "You two, stop arguing over me. I know I've done wrong."

Anthony said, "I'll call Fabiana in the morning and will relate our intentions. She'll be happy to know we are going. As you know, she's rented a two-bedroom flat and will be able to accommodate us."

"Yes, Fabiana will be delighted and I think I'll call the Professor to inform him of our visit."

"*Sis!*" Anthony roared, "where do your telephone bills go? Do you want a record of a conversation with the Professor? You know how suspicious your husband always is."

"You're right, it's best you phone Fabiana and she can inform the Professor," she agreed.

"I will get my secretary to book us on the Eurostar high speed rail next week and we will see this through. Francesca, there will be five of us doing the thinking, not you alone."

With that she hugged and kissed her brother in appreciation. "Thanks, Anthony, what would I do without you?"

"Our father's last words on his death bed were, 'Look after your sister, don't forget' so, this is what I'm doing."

The next morning Anthony called his daughter in London, "Fabiana! It's me, Dad."

"Dad, what's up? Where's Mom? How come you're calling? Tell me, how is everything at home?"

"Good, good, other than your aunt's situation everything else is fine."

Fabiana held her breath, happy that the news had progressed to her parents, now she wasn't alone with that weighing on her conscience. "Oh, Dad, I am so glad you know. I can imagine… try not to be hard on Auntie, I know how much she has been suffering."

"I know, I know… Fabiana, we're coming to London, the three of us."

"Really! When? I don't believe it."

Anthony could sense the excitement in his daughter's voice. "We're due to arrive next Friday. I would like you to inform the Professor of our arrival. We need to talk to him."

"Oh, Dad, He will be so happy. Ever since he came back he looks like a lost man."

"Well save me a call to him and tell him that we're coming and would like a meeting with him."

"Dad, will do, I will knock on his door to give him the news. I can't wait for you guys to get here."

Fabiana could not wait to get to the university and pass on the news to Andrew. She knew in her heart that he was suffering. As luck would have it, just as she jumped into the elevator there he was, Professor Robertson, holding the button for her to get in.

She was all smiles, "Professor, I've got some good news to share with you."

She could detect a sparkle in his eyes, "What news, Fabiana?"

"You're not going to believe this, my Aunt Francesca and my parents are coming next week. They'll be here on Friday."

She was right; he couldn't believe what he heard. Andrew's ears leaped. He tried to compose himself, but before he knew it the elevator doors sprang open, "Hold it, hold it here for a moment, Fabiana. They're arriving Friday? That's wonderful news! You know how fond I am of your family."

Fabiana thought to herself, *yeah yeah, wait until you hear the news, Professor.* She couldn't wait to be able to speak freely and stop this false pretense.

"Yes, Professor, my dad called and he specifically asked me to pass on a message to you, to make yourself available for a meeting with us."

"That sounds serious, I'll be more than happy to spend time with your family. As matter of fact, I feel honored, I look forward to it."

Fabiana did not let on anything and zipped her lips, "I will tell him, Professor."

He looked at his watch; he was due for class in ten minutes, "Fabiana, where would your dad be now? I would like to call him."

"Who knows? You know him and my brother are all over the place. It's hard to track him down."

"What about your aunt? Can I call her? I want them to know how happy I am that they're coming to London."

Fabiana needed to run for her class and the Professor was walking on clouds. He walked to his classroom feeling like a new man. He greeted his students, "*Buongiorno!*"

Today he was happy so he wanted to say hello to everyone. He was ready to give his students the best lesson ever. They looked at him bemused, wondering what had gotten into him this day.

After class Andrew looked for Fabiana but she was nowhere to be found. He wanted to know more; what time were they arriving? Could he go with her to meet them at the train station? Did he need to make a dinner reservation? What was he going to wear?

Then he thought of his flat. How could he even dream of inviting these people to that dump? Mr. Taverna would raise his eyebrows in disgust and not to mention Francesca, who was used to so much luxury. He panicked as he compared their living situations. What would he do? Maybe he should rent a suite at one of the best hotels in the center of London. But then, where was he going to get the money? These thoughts hampered his happiness at seeing Francesca. He tried to erase them gently from his mind and indulge only the pleasant ones.

***

Francesca wished her husband would never come back. In her mixed up life she was hoping that somehow, someway, fate would work in her favor and she would be with Andrew.

A couple of days later, Anthony stopped by to check on her well-being. He said to her, "You know, Sis, I'll have a good talk with the Professor and feel him out. But I think if we can manage to keep your husband away until the middle of June, you should be fine."

"What do you mean I will be fine? You know, Anthony, I don't feel anything for him anymore. Scandal or no scandal. I want out of this marriage." There, she had said it. She had spoken her truth.

"Sis, do you realize what you are saying? There is no out for you."

"I will get out of my farce of a marriage. No one can stop me."

"Oh, really! Have you forgotten those goons your husband is associated with?"

"I'm not afraid of anybody anymore. I've done a lot of thinking and my anger is turning into retaliation."

Anthony shook his head, "I need to go now, and we'll talk some more later." He hugged his sister and left for another day's work, silently impressed with his sister's resilience.

Anthony wasn't the only one running to catch up with his chores. Fausto Tarantano was also fast at work trying to clean up his brother-in-law's files. He was anxious to get out of there and move on to other tasks. He opened one last drawer at the bottom of the filing cabinet and pulled out a bunch of large gray envelopes, well secured with a thick elastic band to keep them together. He opened the first file. Large developed pictures showed a gentleman he didn't know or recognize. Dates were written on the back and he figured they were before his time. He safely replaced them in the envelope and opened the next one. The date read August, so he took a second look and noticed it was Angelo Frarano's wife with someone. He dug further now looking for more and thought, *perhaps this day will be productive* he mumbled to himself.

He couldn't believe what he was seeing: Angelo's wife in bed with another man. Then he found a recording device in the same envelope and stopped to take the time to listen to the conversation. Who was this guy with her? This is absurd. The information and pictures he was looking at were the ones Miliano had taken in Cefalù. They were very incriminating… double proof for Angelo, both pictures and audio. "Oh my God! Lord Jesus," Fausto exclaimed to himself as he swept back his hair with one hand. "I was fooled. I guess her husband knew more than I did." He was talking to himself. Suddenly it occurred to him, "I should check to see what's on Miliano's camera." Miliano had his own darkroom and he was private with his findings. But, he had to report to her husband. Whenever he had placed his phone call it had been always the same, "Nothing to report, Boss, you have a good wife."

Strangely enough he sensed Angelo's happiness with his good reports. Now, he had to give him this unpleasant news about his wife being unfaithful to him. He wasn't made of the same cloth as his brother-in-law. He didn't want to give people bad news. He knew no one liked bad news. He decided to sleep on his new discovery. In the morning he would return to check Miliano's camera that had miraculously stayed with him during his ordeal and his wife had retrieved from the hospital. Yes, there were probably photos in that camera too but he also knew Angelo's reputation and wasn't sure if he wanted to get involved. He did not sleep well all night.

Early the following morning, he let himself in with his own key to the back door, as quietly as possible without waking up his sister. He located the camera and made his way through the digital photos. The pictures were taken by a water lagoon. There was the same gentleman, Fabiana and Francesca in certain photos, but nothing strange. These photos were not damaging. He was relieved. The worst were the pictures and the tape recording from the hotel in Cefalù. From the conversation on the tape he sounded British, he must be someone from out of town or a visiting tourist. Regardless, he knew he had to make a report to Angelo. He would wait for the weekend and make the call then. Fausto was in no hurry and definitely not plotting blackmail like Miliano was. He knew his brother-in-law was a hard person, always plotting in his favor and driven by his greed for money.

Francesca had been totally oblivious to this man's evil plan. She never knew him. His death and accident worked in her favor; fate had stopped him from bringing his action into play. Fausto thought, whatever little evidence he had collected, was enough to send her husband into a rage and hang her and the fellow. He would have made it his business to find out more about the man with her, whoever that man was.

Completely oblivious to Fausto's discovery, Francesca couldn't help but get excited. She had already carefully packed her suitcase. The weather would be unpredictable this time of year. Anthony's secretary had made all the travel arrangements. The trio were ready to leave Palermo Friday morning. While a ray of sunshine seemed to appear in Francesca's life to lift the miserable darkness that had governed her for the past seven months, Angelo's life in New York was turning into a horrendous nightmare.

Gestiniano Ambruzio had come into his office pale as a ghost, "Boss, we're in deep trouble. The district attorney's office is relentless. I tried to strike a deal with them. They threatened to put me behind bars for obstructing justice."

"What do you mean?"

"Boss, you can't buy off these people, they will not drop the charges." Signs of stress were showing on his forehead. He was looking for answers.

"We have five lawsuits on our hands. The company is being sued, and even you personally. Plus they are laying criminal charges against us."

"How dare they do this to us; who do we need to call? Find out and act upon it."

"Boss, you know the labor department had warned us about the safety conditions for our workers, we didn't abide by their orders fast enough. The fact is, we did nothing to improve their work situation, nor did we take any precautions."

"Gestiniano, I don't care what you have to do, but do it. I want results not panic."

"Boss, I slapped money on their table, they will not budge."

"Did you get a hold of Eddie Burnbaum? He can play hard ball with them."

"Boss, he doesn't want to take our case, he refuses to talk to us."

Angelo's anger was rising by the minute. He was definitely not used to refusals. He thought his money was power.

"Gestiniano, do I need to replace you? Bring me results not excuses!"

Gestiniano put his head down, "Yes, Boss. I'll see who I can contact."

Each one of the victim's families had launched a lawsuit against the company, plus the principal of the company: Angelo Frarano himself. He was liable for negligence. The labor department wanted to nail him because he was known to make his own rules. The defendant's attorney was adamant. Harry Burnstein was vehemently studying his case trying to approach it from every angle. He was a big man and a smart litigator with a revengeful vendetta against Angelo Frarano himself. Not to mention the boys from law enforcement – they had enough evidence this time and they wanted to get him convicted and put behind bars.

His attorney Joe Malcom, called Angelo in his office, "Look, I have received a deposition here. I'm to advise you not to leave the country. This deposition is coming up soon and you have to be here."

Angelo listened in disgust; no one ever controlled him. These guys were eventually going to pay for detaining him. Joe, his attorney, was a big powerful man, who had graduated at Harvard Law School with distinction.

Angelo protested, "I'm going to do what I choose to do."

Joe Malcolm responded, "Angelo, I am warning you. You're in regulatory criminal charges and you're ordered to attend personally. Should you try anything funny you will be taken in – in handcuffs."

"What! You mean I can't move from New York because they say so? What the hell are you telling me?"

"I'm advising you according to the law. My hands are tied. Angelo, I am warning you, don't make things more difficult than they are."

Angelo felt like a lion in a cage. He was going to get even with these guys. He was going to recruit some young fresh blood and whoever stood in his way was going to pay for it. No one but no one was going to stand in his way.

In the meantime, he ordered his attorney to launch a lawsuit against the insurance company for not assuming full responsibility. Yes, he strongly felt the insurance company was responsible for his problems. He was fighting the district attorney. He was pressuring Gestiniano. Angelo felt everyone was against him. The people he had around were draining him of his energy. He felt as though they were trying with all their might to make him surrender in defeat. But he wasn't giving up that easily. Step by step he would get rid of whoever didn't please him.

He had gotten rid of Lula. She wasn't pleasing him anymore therefore he had no use for her. He had hired this new Asian girl, she seemed sweet. She was twenty-one, while he was over fifty. He felt her disgust when she worked on his fat belly and genitals. Then his thoughts returned to his lovely Francesca, thank goodness she was in his life. Along with his sons, she was the only decent thing in his life. He hoped to clear this mess soon and spend more time with her.

He had planned to retire in Sicily. He was sure Diego would take his place once he graduated while Daniele pursued his degree. Angelo was grateful for that. The boys could work together. Angelo never doubted that his sons might want to choose a different route in life. They would have to oblige. He considered himself very fortunate. Francesca and the boys were his security nest. When he checked on her the other night she said she was taking a trip to London with her brother and sister-in-law to visit Fabiana. Her parents wanted Francesca along for company. Plus, Fabiana was having some health issues and wanted her aunt to be there. He hadn't objected, besides with the mess he was in it was better to leave Francesca occupied.

Back in Palermo, Fausto had sorted through all the pictures. He hated to do what he had to do. He wouldn't engage in a phone conversation. He would mail the pictures and the recording and leave it at that.

In England, the sun was shining and Londoners were out and about in abundance. The air was crisp and invigorating. Andrew was making his way to work. Tomorrow he would see his beloved Francesca. He and Fabiana were going to travel together. They had both been busy making plans to receive their guests. They checked restaurants for dinner reservations and they were going to the theatre. Fabiana knew what they liked. Andrew wanted to impress Francesca so he was hoping she would consider leaving her husband for him. To think that she had taken the initiative to come here, he figured was a good sign. *Now I can only hope for her to come to her senses and make the decision to get a divorce.*

After a smooth trip Francesca, Lora, and Anthony all arrived safe and sound. Anthony leaned over to Francesca, "You know, Sis, it was a good idea for us to take this route; we have crossed the sea and land and gone through underground tunnels. It sure is a change from traveling by plane. You see, that tells you; where there is a will there is a way."

"You're right, Anthony, but I would still like to get over my fear of flying," Francesca said.

"You know, Sis, if you try, I am sure you can do it. Especially, if you want to see the people you love the most. Love conquers all and flying is the fastest."

She smiled at her brother, and kissed him lovingly on the cheek. She was so grateful for his support. Francesca had elected to wear a royal blue shift dress with paler blue matching shoes with a wide mid-high heel, which added stature to her height. Her black hair cascaded in gentle waves onto her shoulders. She was a picture perfect model of a seven-month pregnant woman.

Lora and Anthony were both well groomed, in proper traveling attire. One could recognize their outfits were a signature of distinction.

Strangely enough, the traveling had taken her mind off her troubles and she glowed radiantly, happy that she would soon see Andrew. They arrived at the London terminal station and stepped into the outstretched arms of Fabiana.

"Mom, I am so glad to have you here," Fabiana hugged and kissed her mom. "Dad! How nice, you make me so happy for being here."

Francesca stood aside waiting for her greetings. "Auntie! Look at you!" Fabiana opened her arms to embrace her. "You can walk the runway as a top model. Let me give you a big hug."

Fabiana was ecstatic to see her family.

Andrew stood aside and watched the happy family reunion, revealing their deep emotions without reservations. He did not know what to expect from Francesca. He was pleased to get cordial embraces from Lora and Anthony. And then finally, there she stood in front of him.

"Francesca! You are here in London, can I believe my eyes, welcome, welcome, how wonderful of you to come." He held her tight briefly in control… kissing her on both cheeks, while his heart desired so much more. Oh how he wanted to take her in his arms and hold her forever. But they were not alone. Therefore, he bravely controlled his emotions and behaved like a polite English gentleman.

He noticed she had gained a little weight, but he would never mention it to her. She was as beautiful as ever. After the cheerful greetings and laughter they headed in a taxi for the Waldorf Hilton in the heart of London, where they would go for dinner.

The traffic was horrendous, but Fabiana's chitchat distracted them. Andrew never took his eyes off Francesca. He watched her every move. The strangest feeling came over him. Was it intuition or was it a universal message. He suspected that something wasn't the same with Francesca.

At dinner, the conversation was pleasant. Everyone was being polite and courteous. After dinner, Anthony privately called Andrew to the side, "Professor, we made this trip for a good reason. It's important that we get together tomorrow. We need to discuss a very serious matter concerning you and Francesca."

Andrew felt guilty. He didn't know what to think, but he was worried. "Why don't we discuss it now? Please give me some idea of what is going on."

"Professor, we will sleep on it for tonight. We're all tired. We can meet for lunch tomorrow." They shook hands, said their goodbyes and Andrew stood waiting for tomorrow to come.

The next morning they were surprised to find Andrew in the hotel lobby waiting for them. He wanted to join them for mass at St. Paul's Cathedral. Andrew never dreamed of going to church on Saturday mornings, but since he had been in Sicily and noticed how devoted these people were, especially Francesca, he thought it would be a good idea to go. Besides, as long as he could be with Francesca he was willing to submit himself to anything.

After the service was over Andrew suggested that they go to L'Auberge for lunch. They were escorted to a table in the corner. After they placed their order, Andrew could hardly wait for them to settle and be informed of whatever it was Anthony had on his mind. His anxiety was high and hard to control.

Andrew tried to eat but was not really enjoying his food. Everyone was polite and lingering in small talk.

Finally, Anthony called out to him, "Professor, of course we came to visit Fabiana in London, but what brought us here is mainly a serious matter concerning you and Francesca." With that he looked at his sister, and said, "Francesca, it's time you tell the Professor the situation you are in."

Fabiana stopped eating. She carefully watched the Professor's reaction.

Francesca took a deep breath and spoke, "Andrew, I'm expecting your baby."

"Oh! My Lord! Really?" He almost choked on his saliva. He wasn't sure if he could hug Francesca with her family present or what was acceptable.

Everyone was relieved when Anthony finally broke his spell, "Professor, we need to decide what will be our next step."

"Of course, of course. I had no idea, when did you find out, Francesca? Why didn't you call me? I would have come for you? Oh, my lovey."

Francesca slowly related the facts of her ordeal to him. Andrew felt so much tenderness towards her.

"Oh, my lovey. It must have been such a shock and to handle it all on your own." Turning to Anthony he asked, "Can I hug her? Is that okay? Sorry, Anthony. I love Francesca immensely."

Anthony gestured in concession and then quickly spoke, "Professor, I'm glad you love my sister and I wish the situation was that of two people having fallen in love who could create a new life together. But there is a problem here. Francesca is married and once you're married in Sicily divorce is unheard of, especially in our family. Besides, not to mention her husband's definite retaliation, she will also face excommunication by our church."

"I'm prepared to go to any length for Francesca. I love her. And now even more, to think that I will have a child of my own from the woman I adore is the best thing a man like me could wish for."

Anthony interrupted him, "Professor, I've done a lot of thinking. I think we have no choice right now. Francesca needs to stay here until the baby is born. Then, after the baby is born, the baby will stay with you and my sister will return to Sicily to resume her life."

Andrew looked at Francesca and with pitiful eyes, "Francesca, what do you want? What do you desire to do? Why can't we ignore everyone and be together? I want to look after you and the baby, my love."

Francesca looked at him with the same passion, "I'm willing. But I know my husband is the biggest problem."

"He will just have to accept it. People fall in and out of love."

"Yes, that sounds reasonable in your thinking, but not for someone like Angelo Frarano. He will not forgive a woman walking out on him."

Lora and Fabiana looked at each other understanding the difficult situation Francesca and the Professor were in. Fabiana promptly said, "I'll be more than happy to help you and the Professor with the baby."

Lora confirmed Fabiana's offer, "Yes, Fabiana can be of much help to both of you with the baby. She could assume responsibility."

"Sis," said Anthony, "you need to come back to Sicily after the baby is born. It will be hard, but Lora is right. Fabiana can help in taking care of the baby until the smoke settles down."

Francesca listened to everyone, she knew deep down what she wanted, but the reality was that there were big obstacles to overcome. She knew the road ahead was a difficult one. How was she going to manage these two months should her husband return to find her big and very pregnant? She needed to find a good excuse and an alibi for her prolonged stay in London. In time, she figured with the help of Andrew and Fabiana, they would come up with a solution as long as her husband stayed away.

In the meantime, Anthony came out with a statement that troubled Andrew greatly, "I hate to tell you this, but I know how this needs to be handled. Francesca has no choice but to leave the baby with you, Professor. Fabiana can help a lot and may have to assume maternal care. Francesca has to pretend this never took place and come home to continue to be who she was. You see, I doubt very much that my brother-in-law, if he finds out what has taken place, will leave my sister free. I don't want to be pessimistic and I can't guarantee you that it won't happen. You have to understand the gravity of the situation."

Andrew's body was overcome by a tremendous fear. He didn't want to lose his Francesca and more so given the fact that she was carrying his baby.

The days that followed were spent in a false sense of existence. Together they went sightseeing around London, while trying their best to let the dark cloud fade away. To Andrew, Francesca looked even more beautiful now. He wanted her in his arms even more. The plan was to stay at the Hilton until Anthony and Lora returned to Sicily. Afterwards she would move in with Fabiana. Andrew had stopped worrying about his shabby place as his mind had been invaded by more important concerns. He was about to become a father. It was something he had never expected.

Fabiana was thrilled to have her family and Francesca in London. She suggested they meet after school every day to stroll around and shop. They were mostly looking at baby clothes and the classic cashmere suits Francesca hoped she would be able to get back into after she gave birth. Lora often remained behind at the hotel; she preferred to rest. After all, she had been in London so many times and she wanted Fabiana and Francesca to do their own thing.

Every day Andrew couldn't wait until his classes were over. They met for dinner every evening. Although his money was scarce he felt duty bound to pick up the bill on some evenings. Fabiana knew it must have been hard for him and said, "Professor, let my dad pick up the tab, he doesn't mind it and he can well afford it."

"Fabiana, I feel obliged to do so because you people have been so kind to me. Thank God for credit cards, I will pay it eventually." Chuckling happily he added, "Don't forget, I'm going to be a father. I really need to increase my income as I will provide for the baby. If only Francesca will allow me and of course I would be delighted if she remains here. I would finally have a real family of my own."

"Professor, don't let my father worry you. You and I are going to work on it. I know my aunt would love that too. I think you two are meant for each other and should be together. I know my aunt's eyes gleam when she looks at you."

"You think so? I hope you are right, Fabiana. If Francesca can get a divorce and become my wife, I will take her and the baby to America to show her off to my brother's family. My brother never believed I'd be capable of having a family of my own."

"Professor, I will certainly encourage my aunt on your regard, but don't count on traveling to America, you know she's terrified of flying."

"I'll find her a counselor and try my best to help her overcome her fear. With great counseling you can conquer any fear. I'm surprised that her husband never thought of it or suggested…"

She interrupted, "Professor, has it not occurred to you that that's the way he prefers it? He doesn't want her there. She is supposed to be his safety net at home where she belongs."

Francesca joined them after getting herself together to go to dinner, "Are you two talking about me? I thought I heard my name mentioned."

"Yes, my lovey, I was telling Fabiana that I can't wait to show you off to my brother, as soon as you decide to become my wife."

"Andrew, I can pray for it to happen. God knows I need you and my family, especially you, Fabiana. Well let's hope for the best. Only time will tell."

Chapter Seventeen

Fausto had gone over the photos a number of times. He put them in a padded envelope along with the recording. Yes, the most damaging evidence was from Cefalù. He recognized the location and the hotel.

He wondered if Angelo knew his wife's lover. He himself certainly didn't. He must be someone from out of town. It's a shame, but here's the proof. He decided to mail it all to him and resign from the job. He preferred to earn his living working on a farm or on a cattle ranch. He scribbled a short note listing his intentions and apologizing for the news he was giving him in regards to his wife. According to him, a beautiful woman like that shouldn't be left alone.

Fausto realized that his brother-in-law died while working on this assignment. Otherwise, there may have been many more incriminating pictures.

***

At this particular time, Angelo's life in New York seemed to be totally out of control. As much as he ordered people around and demanded them to take action and bring him results, his situation didn't ease up. His protesting had turned against him and placed him in deeper trouble. Savagely, he struggled to have his way. But no one was listening to him. Even his newly appointed CEO, Gestiniano Ambruzio, wasn't getting anywhere.

Gestiniano asked for a meeting with Angelo and brought two assistants with him.

"Boss," he started, "these guys can tell you, we can't talk ourselves out of court. All these court cases are going to drain our bank accounts. I wanted Joe Malcolm our lawyer to call Harry Burnstein the opponent's lawyer to settle out of court. So far, they refuse."

"I don't want to hear any more laments from you! Take care of business. This is what I am paying you for. Hire whoever you need to hire, get me out of this bind. If Joe Malcolm is not capable, then fire him, and get another attorney, someone like Howard Silverstein who can influence these guys."

"Boss, are you aware of how much he charges? Plus the retainer? Besides, no one wants to take our cases; we're lucky that Joe Malcom is still on the job. He has been threatening to resign."

"I have had enough of this already. The construction of the hotel has come to a halt. There is no date in place to resume the work. We are losing the best men we imported from Chile. They were to carry on with the front façade of the architecture. This was to be the building of my dream. Now all I'm watching is every stage being red tagged."

"Boss, you're right, leave it with us. Now you go home and try to relax, something has to give soon."

They shook hands once more and Angelo took a deep breath to fill his lungs. He was becoming less and less powerful. He pressed the intercom on his desk and told his receptionist Agada that he was going to call it a day.

"Cancel any appointments I have for the rest of the afternoon."

"As you wish, Mr. Frarano. Mr. Malcolm has called twice. Would you like to return his calls?"

"No, not today. You call him back and find an excuse. I don't want to talk to anybody."

"As you say, Mr. Frarano, consider it done."

Angelo decided to retreat to his penthouse apartment and call Francesca. He needed to hear her voice today. He suddenly realized how much he needed and missed her in these troubling times.

He arrived home feeling edgy. His fearless personality was somehow failing him and he didn't like it. He was going to do some serious thinking and reclaim his audacity. He had just made himself comfortable on the couch when the buzzer startled him.

He thought, *Can't I have some peace and quiet around here? Who can be bothering me now? I don't want to answer it.* But the buzzer kept going so he opened the door. A security man was standing there with a delivery.

"Mr. Frarano, we have a special delivery for you. We had to sign for it. It's our duty to make sure it's delivered to you personally. Would you please sign this receipt?"

Angelo signed the delivery sheet and looked at this well embedded cushiony gray envelope. He was jittery, with all his bad luck these days what else was in the cards for him? He gave a quick glance to scrutinize the sender. Oh, Fausto Tarantano. He had called to say he was mailing some information. On noticing his name, he was somewhat relieved, at least he was getting news from back home, nothing from those goons in New York that have been hunting him lately like a wild animal. He slumped his body on the couch again and with a sharp opener started to open the envelope. It was pretty heavy. The recorder fell out first, he ignored it and dug for more. "Pictures, don't tell me he has gone to all this trouble to send me some of Sicily's pictures." Then he took a second look. His heart started beating faster and the shock sent him into a tailspin.

"No, no! I don't believe this! Am I hallucinating? My wife, this is my wife in bed with this… holy shit, the visitor from England,

don't tell me!" He felt faint. He put his hands on his chest and tried to calm his heartbeat. Was he going to have a heart attack? He got up and walked around like a madman. He wasn't sure what to do next. He was alone and those ugly pictures were staring at him. Should he call the boys? Should he show them these pictures? Should he scream from the top of his lungs, and tell them, your mother is a whore, she's disgraced us. *Our family honor is destroyed.*

Did he want to listen to the recorder? He wasn't sure. *Maybe later,* the pictures had done enough damage to his vision, his soul, and his heart. Why, why now? *The Professor,* he thought, *he sure picked the wrong woman. Just too bad for him. He is as good as dead.*

In that moment, Angelo Frarano thought all the problems he had in New York were nothing in comparison to this family matter. There was no way in hell the Professor was going to get away with this. And Francesca was definitely going to pay for it. He decided to place a call to Fausto Tarantano. He checked his watch but the timing didn't seem right as they were hours ahead, so he needed to wait until morning.

He went to the bar and poured himself a strong brandy, hoping the drink would dull his brain; he just didn't want to think anymore.

He picked up the recorder and pushed the play button. Their playful conversation combined with their moaning lovemaking was well recorded. Angelo had a sleepless night. He tossed and turned and was glad to see daylight appear. He moved from room to room thinking and searching for answers. He had grabbed Francesca's picture and slapped it face down on his dresser. He was going to place a call to Fausto and hear what he had to say. Now she was in London, with her lover. Was her family in on this? He knew his brother-in-law hated his guts. He would seek revenge, however, how many people did he have to consider in this plot? It would now be one o'clock in Sicily. He placed a call to Fausto Tarantano.

"Pronto."

"Fausto, hello, it's Angelo here, how are you?"

"Oh, Boss, I'm fine. How about yourself?"

"After what you've sent me… how do you expect me to be? You kept saying I had a good wife, she was a saint of a woman, you see now how she has deceived me."

"Boss, Boss, listen to me, I have never seen anything. Those pictures were taken by Miliano before he died, I have never seen this man with your wife."

"Fausto, think. You have not seen him because he went back to England, dummy. She has fooled you and me."

"Boss, I'm sorry, I didn't want to give you that kind of news, believe me. If I may say so you have a beautiful wife. Why have you left her unattended?"

He raised his voice in anger, "Look, I didn't call you for you to tell me what I should or shouldn't do. We need to take action here. The Professor isn't going to ever walk again and, as for my wife, she will pay too."

"Angelo, what are you saying? Do you want to harm these people?"

"Fausto, harm is not the word. I want them both eliminated."

"Boss, please. I know you are mad now, but in time you will calm down and get used to the idea, these things happen. Your wife has been alone too long."

"Look, Fausto, are you working for me or are you working for my wife? All I need to know is, are you willing to carry through my orders? Another question, the Tavernas, especially Anthony – do you think he is in on this?"

"Angelo, what can I tell you? I repeat, personally, I haven't seen anything unusual. As for Anthony, you can't find a better man than him."

"Answer my question. Regardless, the Professor and my wife need to pay. Are you going to do it?"

"Angelo, I should have never taken this job, it's not for me. Originally it was just to watch for the safety of your wife and family, which was fine. But bringing harm to people is not for me. I think you better think it over."

"Here we go again; are you willing or not?"

"No, I resign."

"I should have known better. I thought you had guts, apparently, I was wrong. No use continuing this conversation. I have nothing more to say to you. Goodbye."

Before Fausto could reply Angelo slammed the phone down. He knew he needed to recruit someone hungry for money. He would assign the chore to Gestiniano Ambruzio. Angelo shook his head in disbelief. He had so much bad luck lately. He felt as though the devils were erupting up from Mount Etna to shake him up. *No one is going to destroy me. I will take care of them, one by one.*

Francesca had become his number one despised person. His head was full of revenge. In time, he would handle the matter and put everyone in their place. But right now he was totally drained. He stayed home all day. He didn't want to face the world. He called his secretary to say he would take the day off. He was in despair. Angelo looked down on the busy streets of Manhattan and the world seemed to go on freely out there, yet he felt so troubled. The hours slowly went by. He watched the sunset and before he realized it, dusk settled in. He sat in the dark holding his head in his hands. He had lost his stamina.

Looking at those pictures and listening to the tape over and over again drove him insane. He felt alone and abandoned. He reminisced about the early days with Francesca. Stubborn as he was, there was no way he considered himself at fault for her misbehavior. He sat there idle for hours before he made his way to the bedroom. Angelo's inner power was diminishing, but his anxiety was the driving force behind his actions.

When he awoke the following morning he was instantly reminded of events from the previous day, wishing it had been nothing other than a bad dream. He couldn't understand why his wife would decide to deceive him after all these years.

In his somber mood, he went to the office and summoned Gestiniano Ambruzio.

"I need to see you immediately. We have another big agenda on our cards, so get here as soon as you can."

Gestiniano's raw nerves were getting the best of him. He resented always having to oblige such orders. But on the other hand he reminded himself that he was paid well. Therefore, he thought it better to bite his tongue and not to mess around with his boss. He knew only too well that these new guys who had joined the company were eager to advance.

He politely responded, "Yes, Boss, I have a meeting with Joe Malcolm right now, I will be there as soon as I'm finished. Or would you like to be present at our meeting? Your presence might just motivate his aggressiveness."

Angelo's mind now was more disturbed than ever. Due to his new discovery, all his previous problems had become secondary now. "No, no. I have some planning to do. I prefer to wait for you here. You tell him what we expect from him."

"Okay, Boss, see you later."

Both Angelo and Gestiniano were under a lot of pressure. By the time Gestiniano arrived at Angelo's office it was noon. His stomach was growling for something to eat. He hoped they would go for lunch; with a full stomach he could handle things a little more calmly.

As he entered his boss's office, he knew something was terribly wrong. His hair was disheveled, his tie was sloppy and he hadn't shaved. "What in the heck has happened to you, Boss? Have you had a bad night? You look like you just came out of a gutter!"

He was sitting behind his desk; Gestiniano hadn't noticed the pictures sprawled out in front of him.

He lifted up his hands and said through his tears, "Take a look at these pictures."

Gestiniano had never seen his boss so humble. He looked like a beaten up old dog. He picked up some of the pictures and recognized Francesca. He had never met her in person. But Angelo had shown pictures of his wife many times and they were around his place. From time to time Angelo did talk about his wife in Sicily. Many times he had remarked, "A good woman, this is what you do, you find yourself a good woman, and keep her in reserve for your old age."

Gestiniano knew this was not the case here in America. But if that was what his boss thought, he wasn't going to voice his opinion. In the meantime, he quickly figured out what must have taken place. He didn't know what to say.

Angelo was shaking his head, "Gestiniano, she should have never done that to me. I don't care if I have to remortgage my hotels. Right now, this is my biggest problem."

"Boss, what do you mean?" Gestiniano asked, while the acidity in his empty stomach was burning. He knew from the look of things there was no chance of a good Italian lunch today.

"I have it all figured out what has to happen." He picked up a picture and pointed out Andrew. "You see this Romeo, I want his legs broken, after his legs are broken, I want a couple of plumber's tweezers and squeeze his genitals and his penis until he turns black and blue and begs for mercy."

"Boss, you are too upset now, you are not being rational. Digest it, in few days you will get over it. Why don't we go grab something to eat? You will feel better."

"Me, get over it? Oh no, as for that *puttana*, I want that whore eliminated. Yes, she is as good as dead. I want her crushed like a bug. Make it look like an accident."

Gestiniano was alarmed to hear Angelo's evil actions of revenge. "Boss, calm down. You're so mad you're not making sense right now." He didn't know how to distract him from focusing on his wife and her lover. To change the subject he said, "What about your Lula girl? I thought you were in love with her. You used to comment on how much she pleased you."

"That Lula girl, what are you talking about? That was just passing time; after all, I am a man. My wife was my idol. I cherished her like a preserved special fruit."

"Boss, I think you need to redirect your thinking."

His answer seemed to trigger Angelo into a mad rage. All of a sudden he started to give Gestiniano orders on what steps to take. "I want you to recruit someone capable to carry this through. I don't want to hear excuses. That stupid Fausto from Sicily is out, he resigned from the job. You need to find someone in London."

"Boss, let's talk about this again in a couple of days when you have had time to cool off. If you still feel determined about the situation, I will instruct one of our new guys to follow orders, I promise."

"Gestiniano, they underestimated my power; those two are walking on borrowed time and I want to shorten it as soon as possible."

Chapter Eighteen

....

Back in London, Anthony and Lora prepared to leave for home, content to leave Francesca in London with Fabiana and Andrew. Teary-eyed, Lora hugged Fabiana and Francesca while Anthony looked on seeming serene, but deep down he was troubled. He was gravely concerned for his sister's well-being. He knew the old customs and how the consciousness of those times still prevailed in Sicily. God only knew how his brother-in-law would react; it was just a matter of time. Therefore, he silently feared for his sister. He gave a big hug to Francesca and held her in his arms for a long time. He looked straight into her eyes and whispered, "Sis, look after yourself, will you?"

"Anthony, go peacefully, I'm in good hands and I'll be fine. Please don't worry about me."

"You're the only sister I have. You know I promised Papa to look after you. I'm leaving you here, assure me you will take care of yourself."

"Anthony, stop it. You're treating me like a child. You forget I will be a mother of three pretty soon and not just your little sister anymore."

"I will miss you."

"Cheer up, and have a safe trip back. I will call you every day if it makes you feel better. My God Anthony, you are worse than our father, goodbye."

After their long goodbyes, Andrew couldn't wait to have Francesca to himself. He wanted to rejoice in this unbelievable event that had taken place in his life. Fabiana was anxious to return to her studies. She was also aware of how much her aunt and her professor must have wanted some time to themselves.

"Listen you two, should you want to go on your own tonight it's perfectly fine with me. I know you lovebirds need to talk. I need to get to my research if I don't want to fall behind. How about you do your thing tonight and I will see you tomorrow, Auntie?"

Andrew and Francesca looked at each other; Fabiana must have read their minds. Andrew could hardly wait to take Francesca in his arms. "Francesca, my love, this is like a dream come true. I want you to put your right hand on my heart and feel my heartbeat. Do you have any idea how happy you have made me? And the miracle of a life growing inside you being my very own child. My darling, it's the most precious gift I could ever imagine to receive." He sealed her lips, taking her breath away. Francesca had never known such tenderness. Her own heart melted for Andrew. She looked at him, passionately, thinking that after so many long years of misery, he was a godsend to her.

"Andrew, my darling, let's stay here at the hotel and pretend we're on our honeymoon. Let's not waste any time and live every moment to the fullest. I know Fabiana wants us to be together. We'll go to your place tomorrow night."

"Yes, my love, as you wish."

***

Andrew gently undressed her and carried her to bed. The burning desire inside him was out of control. But he reminded himself to be cautious; he had never made love to a pregnant woman before.

It was obvious Fabiana wanted them to be happy together. She wasn't something for them to worry about.

The next day, as planned, they went to his flat. He had instructed Mrs. Brooks to provide him a cleaning lady and supervise her to make sure his place was tidy. Mrs. Brooks was more than happy to oblige. It gave her something to do. She admired the Professor and thought of him as her adopted young lad. Once they arrived at Bethnow, Andrew wasn't nervous about Francesca's acceptance of his place. He knew in his heart she was a kind woman that truly loved him and wouldn't judge his housing arrangements.

As they entered his place he proceeded to excuse himself for his humble abode, yet Francesca glided through the apartment with her arms outstretched she turned to hug him, "Andrew, you're heaven and earth for me, as long as I have you everything else is meaningless."

"Lovey, do you really mean that? After I came home from Sicily, I must confess, I thought how foolish of me to hope for you to come here and be with me after seeing your luxurious lifestyle."

"Andrew, you underestimated me. My darling, you were so wrong to think that way. In my opinion material things don't hold any happiness."

"Agreed," he said, "but they sure make one's life more comfortable."

"Maybe, but the comfort without love is invalid. I know I can be happy with you in a cave. Our electrifying chemistry fulfills all the wants in the world."

Andrew looked at his precious Francesca glowing in happiness. He was so pleased with her response. No wonder he had felt so attracted to her since the moment he had laid eyes on her. They spent another night in splendor holding each other and fulfilled with their lovemaking.

Francesca discarded any thoughts of her husband that came to her mind. Yes, she had been in denial since she arrived in London and reunited with Andrew. In a blurred fog she thought of her boys, how was she going to explain? Would they understand and forgive her? Would they condemn her? The movement in her abdomen was more constant these days and it continued to bring her back to face reality. Only when she was with Andrew she felt safe, loved and protected.

As much as he wanted to, Andrew was afraid to bring up the divorce. He decided to take everything one day at a time and let fate take its course. He told himself luck had brought Francesca to him and in some strange way he trusted that in time things would fall into place.

After a couple of days Fabiana helped her aunt move from the Hilton to her flat. This would make it legitimate that she was staying with her. "Auntie, you feel free to be with the Professor whenever you like. I know you should. Should you receive a call from America, I will protect you."

"Fabiana, you're such a darling, I am so blessed to have you. But I think it's important that I call the boys tonight, I want to hear their voices. As for my husband, I will wait until he calls me."

As the two women were chatting away the phone rang and sure enough it was Diego. "How are you, cousin?"

"Couldn't be better, as you know I had my parents visiting and now Auntie is staying with me for a while. It's been fabulous."

"I'm glad, it's great for Mom to be there, she should do it more often, make sure she has a good time."

Francesca was beside Fabiana smiling and anxiously waiting to speak with her son.

"Here, I will pass you to your mom, talk to her."

"Diego," Francesca said, "I'm so glad you called. I was planning on calling you and Daniele tonight. How are you doing, dear? How is school?"

"Mom, I'm so happy to know you are in London. It's about time you decided to travel. We're up to our eyeballs in studies, preparing for our term exams and hitting the books until the late hours."

"I understand, where is Daniele now? Can I talk to him?"

"He's not back yet, he should be here soon. He can call you later."

"Okay, you look after yourselves, be good, love you, dear."

"Mom, are you enjoying yourself? Make sure you see as much as you can, and have a good time with Fabiana, you promise. I love you too, Mom."

"Don't be concerned about me, you take care, and hug your brother for me. Talk to you again, my love. Bye-bye."

Francesca's emotions had been stirred by hearing her son's voice. Suddenly guilt set in once more. She felt she had done her two boys wrong. She had failed them as a mother. Fabiana noticed Francesca's change of mood by the sadness in her eyes and the creases on her forehead. "Auntie, how about checking the theater tonight. Can we go just the two of us?"

"Andrew needed to mark some papers and I told him I would spend the evening with you."

"What do you say? Should we go out and live it up?"

"Fabiana, I prefer to rest for tonight, we will plan for another evening if you don't mind."

She sank into her deep thoughts again from her husband to her boys… the baby… and Andrew. Her husband hadn't called lately. In their last telephone conversation he had mentioned his affairs were in trouble, but he never went into the details with her. He always said, "No use burdening you with business, you wouldn't understand." She had accepted that for years and kept out of his business world.

Time away from Andrew was giving her a chance to concentrate on her family. She thought of Anthony, Lora, Letizia, and Maurizio. For a moment she missed her home and her brother and sister-in-law.

She shook her head and turned her thoughts to Andrew. Going through this with Fabiana was a big relief. She tried to focus on making plans for the baby, after all the delivery date wasn't far away. It was now April, and once into May the days would roll along quickly.

Anthony wanted her to go home after giving birth. Francesca knew that was the right thing to do, to pretend nothing had ever taken place. She would resume her life in false pretenses worse than before. Fabiana would be finished school for the year, she would remain for a while until other arrangements were made for the baby. Francesca's head was spinning, she needed to discuss everything seriously with Andrew. Everything seemed so complicated. How was she going to leave the baby once it was born? She loved this baby and it was going to break her heart.

Chapter Nineteen

Angelo was pacing the floor in his office. He was waiting for Gestiniano to come back with his latest report. He wondered how long it was going to take to get him to recruit a hungry dog to follow his orders. He had put off calling his wife. He had no desire to talk to her. Now he had nothing good to say about her, only swear words. In time he would inform his two boys, he couldn't do it now.

The phone rang and it was Gestiniano, "Boss, I've found the right person for you. I would like you to meet him."

"Gestiniano, are you a man, or are you a mouse. Why would I want to waste my time with some Joe Schmoe? What have I got you for? I expect you to use your judgment and pick the right candidate to carry out my orders."

"Yes, Boss, I understand, I was just asking in case you were interested."

"I'm telling you I'm not. You're my man. You execute what I am telling you to do."

"Okay, Boss, as you say. I will meet you at two o'clock and we will discuss the contract."

"Now we're talking, see you then."

Angelo hung up the phone, sat behind his desk and planned the fate of Francesca and Andrew. If his brother- in-law had anything to do with it he would get his share also. He knew Anthony always detested him. Angelo didn't realize he wasn't being rational. He was attributing blame to everyone except himself. *Yes*, he thought, they had planned for this English Professor to visit, or encouraged this liaison at his expense.

Patiently he waited for Gestiniano. He had lost his appetite these days. He had no intention of stepping outside of his office. He buzzed his secretary to bring him a decaffeinated coffee and a double toasted bagel with cream cheese. A knock on the door distracted him from his thoughts. Gestiniano didn't need to be announced by his secretary. He was glad to see him.

"Gestiniano, it took you long enough. I thought these guys were a dime a dozen out there. What took you so long?"

"Boss, I needed to make sure I got the proper element. Then it took some negotiation and it was more entailed than I anticipated. And getting the job done in London is more complicated."

"Okay, okay, skip the ceremony, just tell me who you have hired?"

"Boss, this guy is perfect, they call him Scarface. He has a deep scar on the side of his head. His name is Vladimiro Swarzovisky. He's Russian. He has carried out other jobs in London."

"You know it has to look like an accident, for that whore of mine, but as for the Professor, I want him without legs for a while. Afterwards we will finish him off."

"How do you want the accident to occur?"

"Again, you ask me again, Gestiniano? You kill me sometimes. Run her over with a car. As for him, as long as his legs are broken I don't care how they do it, they have the experience not me."

Gestiniano noticed Angelo had lost weight and was looking older. As far as he was concerned, these things happened every day and Angelo hadn't been faithful. But maybe the combination of the issues at work and this information about his wife had driven him over the edge. He hadn't ever been a soft person, but these days it wasn't pleasant to be in his company.

"Boss, this guy wants an accomplice; I had to give out more money. I had to give him one-third in advance, and he wants another third after he has acquainted himself with the area. He gets the final payment when the job is complete."

"How much is this going to cost us?"

"He has to take care of two people so he wanted no less than one hundred and fifty thousand dollars in U.S. funds – each."

"Can we spare it?"

"We have to. I assume that you'll want surveillance reports until the job is done?"

"Yes, I will and the payment plan is fine."

Gestiniano wished he had the courage to say, *what if your wife received pictures of you and all the bimbos you've been with?* How would she feel towards him? But he knew he wouldn't walk out of the room alive if he did.

They shook hands and Gestiniano went on his way. Now he could give this Vladimiro guy the go ahead and soon *Operation Twelve* would begin.

Vladimiro Swarzovisky stood six feet five tall with broad shoulders and sharp ears. He was a professional killer without mercy or remorse. Most of the fellows that knew him, feared him, and they didn't dare cross him in any way. He was unforgiving. He grew up in Singapore, having survived the youth gangs, and raised by a single mother. His father, who had been an alcoholic, was hit by a train while attempting to cross a railroad track. He was used to his father coming home drunk, causing chaos, beating up his mother and slapping him around. He had grown up in an abusive home, he hated his mother due to her sexually catering to the strange men she would bring home, one after the other. Finally, at the age of fourteen he left home.

On the streets, he had learned to fend for himself the only way he knew how: retaliate in violence. He had been in jail a few times, but was always released due to lack of evidence. Rumors circulated that he had carried out jobs all over the globe. The underworld kept him employed. Concurrently, he was a hunted man, but the law hadn't tried and committed him yet. He wasn't married; therefore, he didn't have any ties. This enabled him to travel to wherever he needed to go.

Swarzovisky booked a flight and was scheduled to arrive in London early the next morning. Gestiniano had provided him with all the necessary addresses: Fabiana Taverna, the Hilton, the university, and Andrew Robertson's residence. He had also provided photographs for easy identification.

Vladimiro knew what he had to do. First he would check out Francesca and familiarize himself with her daily moves. Later, he would follow the Professor. He was going to get in touch with Skinnyboy from Birmingham, to assist him once he was rested. He got off at Gatwick, made his way to Victoria Station, and then headed for a cheap hotel. He woke up late afternoon, had a fresh shower so he could think better, and called Skinnyboy, "Hello, hello, Skinny, how are you doing? Vladimiro here."

"Vladimiro, is it really you? I'm fine, what about you? Where on earth are you? Where are you calling from?"

"I'm here in London, I have a job assignment here. Are you willing to give me a hand?"

"You're kidding me? You are here in London? Scarface, you know you can count on me, tell me when and what I need to do."

"I just got here, I will have to do some research first. I will call you again and set up a date to meet. I need to plan the hunt precisely, make sure it's all clean. You know how I work."

"No shit. Yes, of course. Keep me posted and I'll be glad to help. How much money are we talking this time though? You son of a bitch, you short-changed me the last time."

"Okay, okay I will make it up to you. This guy is loaded, let me see how much is involved and then I'll know, I can always press for more."

"All right, buddy. I'll wait to hear from you."

Vladimiro did not want to waste too much time in London. At the airport he had picked up a map of the city and in red ink he circled the areas he had to check out. He was familiar with

London, it wouldn't be difficult for him to find his way around. He stopped at an Italian restaurant for a hearty supper and tomorrow he would start his job.

Meanwhile, Francesca, Fabiana, and Andrew met that day after class. They had made early dinner plans and wanted to catch a movie afterwards. Andrew thought Fabiana and Francesca would enjoy it. Although Francesca was getting much bigger these days, she felt like a new bride expecting her first child. The misery she had felt in Sicily had gone away. She knew it was all because of her dear Andrew. Oh, how she loved him.

That morning she had said to Fabiana, "I'm so grateful to you, Fabiana. It's because of you my days have turned into sunshine. Yes, it's been you that has brought Andrew into my life."

Fabiana hugged her aunt and kissed her on both cheeks, "I am delighted for you, Auntie. I need to find myself a young lad, someone who is just like the Professor."

"You will, Fabiana my dear, you will, just follow your heart and when the time is right it will happen."

"I'll meet you and Andrew at five. Okay? Have a good day." She ran out the door.

Francesca had gotten into the habit of taking public transportation to Piccadilly Square and roaming around the many shops. She just admired the beautiful styles. The window displays were fabulous. She would take a break occasionally and treat herself to a cup of coffee and an English scone with marmalade. She looked at her belly getting way out of proportion, but she thought, *Why not indulge now?* After all, with her sons she had never had a weight problem, she knew her body would go back to normal. It had gotten to be a joke with Andrew and Fabiana, they would ask, "Okay, Francesca, how many scones did you have today?"

Bursting into hearty laughter she would shrug her shoulders, and teasingly answer, "Until my heart's content!"

"Good for you, my love, whatever makes you happy and that baby of ours." Andrew would put his arm around her bulging waist and pull her close to him. On the weekends, Andrew was doing a great job showing her a good time and taking her to the best parts of London.

"Andrew, you're spoiling me too much. I love these days with you, I don't know how I am going to manage going back to Sicily."

"Exactly, my love. I don't want you to go back to Sicily. We found each other and we need to be together, regardless…"

Francesca gave Andrew a kiss. She had been in denial these days. When her husband entered her mind she dismissed him quickly. She didn't want to think about it now, but she knew that one of these days soon she would hear from him. Maybe she would have enough strength and anger in her to burst out at him and let it all out. She had buried so much for so long. At this point in her life she didn't care about what he thought. All she knew, was that since she had come to London, she was living. She felt alive, she looked forward to each day. She had a reason for living.

This morning was no different, she got dressed, and instead of looking for anything in particular she would look for a few things for their baby. After all, she was going to deliver in the next four weeks. She went to Fortnum and Mason's department store and afterwards she went to Jermyn Street. She wanted to get some presents for her two favorite people: Andrew, some fancy shirts, and for Fabiana a package of Yardley English perfumes. Francesca was having fun. She had never felt this relaxed in months. The salespeople were pleasant and helpful. Francesca communicated well with an obvious accent, and she enjoyed responding to all the questions. The sales girls sincerely seemed to be interested in her pregnancy, the arrival of the baby and the naming and so on and so forth. Francesca seemed to be living in a dream. For that afternoon she loved being pregnant and sharing the news safely with strangers.

Vladimiro had been following her from a distance; watching, taking notes and pictures. He was pretending to be a tourist. He was surprised to see the obvious protruding bump on her belly. *No!*, he thought. *I need to make a phone call to Gestiniano.*

He decided to wait to go back to the hotel and place his call from there. He was angry. *Why wasn't I told? I bet he's trying to cheat me out of my money.* He was pissed off. He decided he would continue with his surveillance; however, they would have to cough up more money.

He had found Francesca without any trouble and she led him straight to the man in question. The young girl with them wasn't an issue, but she needed to be kept at bay if she was stuck with these people. So far she was not part of the deal. Vladimiro thought he better not rack his brain with plans until further notice.

At three o'clock the following day he placed a call to Gestiniano. It was nine o'clock in New York. Gestiniano was in his office, and he picked up fast after his secretary announced the phone call was from London.

"Hello."

"Hello, it's me, Vladimiro."

"What's up?"

"You double crosser, maybe I should break *your* legs."

"What are you talking about? What's going on?"

"Why weren't you honest with me?"

"Vladimiro, what in the hell are you talking about? I was fair with you."

He raised his voice, "You rat, you want me to get rid of three people and pay me for two."

"Vladimiro, why three people? There are only two"

"How do you count a pregnant woman, as one or two?"

"A pregnant woman? I don't know of a pregnant woman, no one told me. Are you sure you got the right person?"

"Are you underestimating my intelligence now?"

"I didn't know, no one told me. I swear over my grandmother's grave I didn't know."

"Well, this Francesca lady is very much pregnant. Your price has gone up. I need a quarter of a million dollars, and consider it a bargain buddy. Otherwise no deal."

Gestiniano listened carefully. He couldn't take it upon himself to pay out another one hundred thousand without Angelo's permission. *Darn Angelo Frarano, why hasn't he told me?* He needed to talk to him and get back to Vladimiro.

"Fine, I need to talk to my boss, you know I'm only following orders."

"I don't give a shit what you are doing or what you have to do. You don't call me; I will call you tomorrow. You better have an answer. Otherwise I keep the deposit and you look elsewhere." Vladimiro hung up, brushed his hand through his hair and muttered, "I have executed many jobs in my life, but a pregnant woman, on her last term, I must admit it takes guts."

If there is supposed to be some good in every human being, then Vladimiro's conscience must have been touched. He sat in his hotel room and thought of his mother, big and pregnant. Late at night when his father would come home drunk he would pull her out of bed and beat her up until she lay helpless on the floor. He had witnessed her aborting in a pool of blood. As a young boy he had to clean the mess and aid his mother. It seemed violence had been his constant companion in his life.

In New York, Gestiniano rang his boss. "I need to see you, Boss, it's important. I can't make this decision without your permission."

"All right, I'll wait for you. I was going to take a flight to Boston and take the boys out for dinner. I haven't seen them for a while. This won't take long I hope."

"No boss, I'm on my way."

In no time Gestiniano was at Angelo's door. As he entered his office he noticed his boss looked worse than ever.

"Okay, Gestiniano, tell me, have you been able to strike a deal with those lawyers? Can you imagine? I can't leave New York. I had to ask permission to go see my sons." With that much anger in his voice, he looked disturbed and manic.

"Boss, I'm not here to talk about the troubles we have here, I'm here to talk about the matter of your wife."

"Yeah, what about her?"

"Boss, why you didn't tell me she is pregnant? You know this guy I hired isn't a character to play with; he threatened to break my legs because I cheated him in bargaining the price down. He wants another hundred thousand otherwise he walks."

Angelo remained perplexed, speechless, and paralyzed. "What, my wife pregnant? What are you saying? Are you sure?"

"Boss, I'm not sure. I don't know anything. I have never met your wife in person. I have only seen her in pictures and I only know whatever you have told me about her. Sorry, Boss, you should know. Is she pregnant? This guy tells me she is close to giving birth."

Angelo's head was spinning, he was trying to recollect his past. *When was the last time me and my wife… ?*

"Wait a minute." He brought his hands to his head. "Let me think for a minute. No, I can't be the father. I haven't slept with my wife for a long time; she always had excuses when I went home. Come to think of it, I was home for such a short time and I was tired."

"Boss, I don't want to get involved in your private intimate life. I'm only here to take your orders. Can we give this guy another hundred thousand? Do you want to go ahead with this? Or should I cancel the whole thing? Tell me it's off. Boss, why don't you sleep on it? Digest the news, let me know tomorrow, okay?"

Angelo slammed his fist repetitively on his desk in retaliation, harder and harder in rage like a madman, yelling like a ferocious animal ready to attack. He jerked his body around tightening his fists. "No, I don't need to sleep on this. Regardless of what you think, I loved and cherished my wife. She should have never done this to me. After I worked my ass off to provide for her and the boys this is how she repays me? Oh, no. She will pay for it, pregnant or not pregnant. She has made a fool out of me."

"Boss, you are upset now, calm down."

"You call this guy and pay him whatever you need to pay him and tell him to proceed, the sooner the better."

Gestiniano wished he would change his mind, but now he seemed more adamant than ever. His ego had been wounded and there seemed to be no reasoning or forgiveness. "Okay, Boss, but I'm asking you for the last time, won't you reconsider? This could get us into a lot more trouble than we already have. How about giving it some thought, eh?"

He slammed his fist down one more time. "Look at me, is fool written on my forehead? Tell me. That whore…" He called his wife names and mumbled uncontrollably.

Gestiniano shook his head in dismay, knowing that he better not argue with him any longer. He was an opinionated, stubborn man. "Okay, okay I will make the call, on your orders only."

He walked out with a heavy weight on his chest. These kind of orders had never been part of his job description. He didn't like it. Angelo had promoted him to be the shareholder of his companies. His new position tied him to Angelo, but he didn't expect these deals as part of the bargain. Now he was getting involved in operations he didn't like.

The next morning he made the call to London. He tried to ignore what Vladimiro was hired to do.

Vladimiro promptly started talking money. "I have to give the fifty grand to my buddy here, I can't pull this off alone, and I expect the balance on my return to New York in cold cash."

"Fine, I'll have it ready for you."

The phone went dead. Vladimiro had some figuring out to do. He couldn't help this poor woman if her husband wanted her dead. He called Skinny. "Hello. Skinny, get yourself here; the sooner we get this job done the sooner I am out of here."

"I'll get to London tomorrow, around eleven; where do I meet you?"

"I have taken a cheap motel on the outskirts just before you enter the highway. On 34 Westside Street, the first one to the right, after the service station as you enter the city. I will wait and watch for you. I'll give you the phone number here just in case you need it. I prefer you not to call though."

He had watched Francesca for few days now. She would take the transit to the shopping district and then meet her companions between four and five o'clock. He needed to corner her when she was alone, that would make things easier. Skinny would have to be at the wheel, he was only going to coach him from the passenger seat while rehearsing. His job now was to familiarize Skinny with the route at a high traffic and pedestrian time. As for the car, they needed to steal one – hot-wiring was a breeze for them – and ditch it afterwards, switching into another for their getaway. He would be waiting a distance away around the next street. The public transit in London via subway or bus was easy and accessible.

Francesca was totally oblivious to what was happening around her. She had been living in a dream world. She couldn't wait to show Fabiana and Andrew her purchases, it was nearly time to meet them. She waved when she saw them walking towards her from a distance.

Andrew was all smiles as he saw her, "My love, do you know how energized I feel to know that here you are waiting for me?" He didn't care about the crowd, he kissed and hugged her as though they were the only ones on earth.

Fabiana said, "You two, forget I'm here? Okay, okay I understand, you're in love."

Fabiana thought she had never seen two older mature people so drawn to one another. It was beautiful to admire them. "Auntie, more shopping? What did you find today?"

"I found more things for the baby. I'm only buying white and yellow colors, pajamas, blankets, and diapers."

Andrew cut in, "This baby is going to get so spoiled and sure deserves to be!"

Fabiana chuckling with them asked, "What do you think the baby will be, a girl or a boy?"

Francesca said, "I know I'm being selfish, but I sure hope it's a girl this time."

"My darling, I will love this baby regardless of gender, you know that."

"Oh, Andrew, I know you will."

Fabiana, asked, "Have you thought of a name yet?"

"Actually, I think we should think about that tonight, what do you say, love?"

"Yes, we should."

They went to Mamma Leon's for dinner and took turns choosing potential names.

Francesca exclaimed, "If the baby is a girl we'll name her Gracy Rosalia, if it's a boy… Andrew, I think it should be totally up to you."

"Oh, my love, thanks for your confidence in me. I guess it will be Oliver Sean Robertson. How does that sound?"

"Great, it has a musical sound to it, darling."

"Your turn, Fabiana."

"You guys are doing fine. I like Gracy Rosalia because Saint Rosalia is the patron saint of our mountain in Palermo. Good choice, Auntie. The boy's name is great also."

The thought of leaving the baby with Andrew and going back to her old life in Sicily suddenly made Francesca feel sad. She frowned and shook that thought away. *I will only live one day at the time.* Their happy evening ended with Andrew having to travel alone to the east side. Fabiana and Francesca headed for the subway to travel to her place in the west end. As soon as the women had settled in their seats, a disheveled middle-aged man sat down beside Fabiana. He struck up a conversation using the usual tourist approach, "Are you girls enjoying London? Where are you from?"

Fabiana was just about to answer him, when Francesca nudged her in the side with her arm. She spoke in Sicilian dialect, "*No respondere.*" She had noticed him sizing them up and didn't like this character, he gave her a strange feeling. Fabiana was taken aback and pretended not to hear him.

It was Skinny. He had put on a dark navy beret, big glasses, a trench coat and wore a fake mustache. He was tall and slim with a soft voice. He was trying to find out information that may serve his purpose. The ride had served fruitless but he was a skilled man, laughing under his mustache. "I will get to you, lady, one way or another," he mumbled. He didn't understand what she had said to the young lady, but he figured she had instructed her to ignore him.

Chapter Twenty

....

Every now and then Francesca would wonder about her husband. She had not heard from him, which was a blessing. He had mentioned how busy he was, she figured sooner or later he would surface. The silence had worked to her advantage. She could pretend he did not exist especially for now being in London.

Francesca was getting used to her daily routine. London offered so much to see and do. Her days were spent discovering new things. Today she promised herself to get on the double-decker red bus and sightsee throughout the city until mid-afternoon. Then she would stop at the grocery store not far from the university and poke around there for a while. Andrew was coming home to Fabiana's place tonight; they were going to meet as usual after school and ride back together. She wanted to create a fun evening of cooking. She would have to find the ingredients to make Andrew and Fabiana a delicious Sicilian meal. Andrew would love a home-cooked meal.

In the morning she hugged Fabiana, "I'll be waiting at the same place at the same time."

"See you after class," she answered.

Once alone, her thoughts again flashed back to her husband. *It's a blessing*, she thought, *I have not heard from him for a while.*

But I wonder what's happening in New York? It's good if he is busy.
She was getting so used to this new life and her adorable Andrew
that she couldn't think rationally. Strangely enough, she noticed
the guilt had left her. Wishing she was dead no longer entered
her mind. She felt energetic and happy. She couldn't wait for
tonight.

Francesca put on her favorite outfit and comfy shoes. She
stood in front of the mirror and didn't like her bulging stomach
and put on her loose trench coat. She decided she better grab an
umbrella, just in case it started to rain and out she went.

It was Friday and she was excited about Saturday, because
Andrew was taking her to the Columbia Flower Market in the
east end of London. Then they would stop at one of the coffee
shops for their favorite pastries, tea or coffee. Although the
crowd was a struggle, as long as her Andrew held her hand, she
felt blessed and protected.

She glanced at her watch, the time was going by fast, maybe
because of all her planned excursions. She walked with more
bags full of groceries than she had intended to. They were going
to make manicotti, with ricotta cheese, parsley, cilantro, and
spinach. She would broil blood oranges for dessert, and then
cut them in half, served with almond brioches, drizzled with
marsala, and *limoncello*. She was loaded.

She noticed the sky had now opened up and the clouds were
about to release a relentless downpour. She didn't have far to
walk, she would make it to meet Fabiana and Andrew and they
would help her carry her bags. Francesca was so happy with her
findings, that she didn't mind carrying the weight in the rain.
In quick steps she reached the square to wait for her two favorite people.

The traffic was horrendous as usual. She was trying to cross
the street carefully when the lights started flashing. Suddenly,
on her left hand side a gray car came swerving totally out of
control and sent her flying with her bags, the groceries splatter-
ing everywhere. The car arrived like lightning and disappeared

in a flash before anyone realized what had happened. Francesca lay unconscious on the cement. The fretting pedestrians screamed for help. No one really knew or had seen what had taken place. This lady had bounced off the car and flew up in the air. Passersby realized an accident had occurred, but no car had stopped at the scene. Someone had summoned for help. The paramedics and police were approaching. They got her into the ambulance and couldn't get a pulse. In the confusion Andrew and Fabiana were looking for Francesca. The ambulance sped away while the police remained at the scene trying to control the traffic and the pedestrians so they could investigate. No one could give the officers a definite answer. They saw the woman hit the pavement head first without noticing the car that hit her. Fabiana, in total shock she remained perplexed as one of the officers was holding a purse. She recognized it. It was her aunt's purse.

"Oh, *no! No!*" She started to scream from the top of her lungs.

Andrew was confused in the chaos and the police were trying to keep the people back. The crowd was pushing through, bags of groceries were scattered on the ground amongst the broken bottles. Fabiana was frantically screaming. At first Andrew couldn't understand what had hit her. The officers thought they had another incident on their hands. She pointed to the purse and asked, "Where did you get that purse?"

"From the lady involved in the accident, do you know her?"

"Yes, it's my aunt's. She was to meet us at the coffee shop just across from here."

The officers were desperately looking for clues and any information to shed some light on the horrific accident. They scribbled down as much information as they could gather from the people around. Then they turned quickly to interrogate Fabiana while Andrew stood stunned at her side, trying frantically to control his composure and understand what had taken place.

Fabiana shivered in the rain as she spoke with police. The officers gently tried to calm her down, checking her identity and verifying Fabiana's declarations.

"We're her family here. We must get to her, where has she been taken?"

"Yes, get in our car, we will find out, and we will get you there as fast as we can."

Frantic, Andrew said, "Officer, I am her friend, she is eight months pregnant. I need to get to her, please!"

The officer put on his sirens and headed for the East Central Hospital where the ambulance had taken Francesca. It seemed an eternity for Andrew and Fabiana with their escalating fear and anxiety. But in a few minutes the officer delivered them to the emergency entrance and escorted them to Admitting. The nurses in attendance were relieved to see them. They paged Dr. Blue who had been asking and searching to contact the next of kin, he wanted to talk to them.

Fabiana, needed to call her parents, "Professor, we must call Mom and Dad, they must get here."

"Yes, we must."

Once they dialed the number, Ersilia came on the line, "Ersilia, Fabiana here, I need to talk to my mom or dad or Joseph, are they home?"

"No, they went to Messina today; they might be back late, that's what your mom said this morning."

"I will call again later, Ersilia, bye." She turned to Andrew: "Professor, we are on our own to handle things until I get a hold of my parents.

Dr. Blue, came out on the nurse's request. But he had not much time for them, he barely answered their questions.

Andrew asked, "Doctor, is she okay? Can we see her? Where is she? We are her only family here, she is from Italy."

The doctor shook his head, "I'm afraid not at this time, sorry, she is badly injured. We need to perform some emergency surgery to stop the bleeding. Her skull is badly fractured. We will try our best. We might be able to save the baby. We detected a good heartbeat, we need to do a caesarian immediately in order to save the baby otherwise we will lose both of them."

Andrew couldn't believe this turn of events. In disbelief his perfect world had suddenly turned into a nightmare.

"Yes, doctor, please, do whatever is necessary."

The nurse brought some papers for them to sign, in a blur Fabiana signed consent, while the doctor in a hurry disappeared behind folding doors, there was no time to waste. The nurse said the hospital probably would need her health insurance number, but right now they would be concerned with the urgency of saving her life.

"You wait in this room," the nurse indicated, "Dr. Blue will see you after surgery."

Teary eyed and shivering they held each other in support. Every passing moment seeming an eternity. Andrew started to pace the floor with his nerves getting out of control. His heart was beating quickly as the clock was ticking and he kept glancing up at it. "How long has it been, Fabiana?" He had to restrain himself. "Fabiana, we need to call your parents. You want to try again?"

Fabiana placed another call; no one answered this time. "They are not home."

"Should we get the authorities to contact them?"

"No, Andrew, we will see what happens. I don't want to cause my father a heart attack."

Andrew needed Anthony for reassurance. He was so distracted from the strong desire to get behind those doors and see for himself what was going on with his beloved Francesca. Finally, Dr. Blue emerged, while taking off his gloves and head cap.

Fabiana and Andrew jumped up, "Doctor," they said in unison.

Andrew continued, "Please, tell us, did things go well?"

"I have some good news, we saved the baby. As for the mother…" Dr. Blue's face was obscured. "We did everything we could. There wasn't any hope that we could save her with her severe injuries. But we had to try, her heart failed, she was bleeding profusely from her head. So, sorry." Dr. Blue chose his words carefully. He did not want to tell them that her skull was shattered.

Andrew broke down in total despair while the doctor continued, "We have a perfect little baby girl, six pounds seven ounces, and nineteen inches long. Pretty healthy for an eight-month delivery, her lungs are a little weak but she will be fine with a little boost of oxygen for a few days. You can go in and see the baby."

Andrew was not sure of anything any more. It was Fabiana who responded for both of them, "Yes, we would like to." She was trying to come to grips with everything submerging from this unexpected hell.

The doctor continued, "As for Mrs. Frarano, we will make a report of her injuries for the police. They are investigating. She will be kept under observation and scrutiny at the hospital morgue, the investigation might be lengthy. They want to speak to you and you must be in contact with them in regards to claiming the body and for funeral arrangements. You need advice as to the proper procedure in London to remove the body. We will issue the death certificate while the coroner will do his investigation report. The authorities will advise you."

The nurse came out and escorted them to the nursery. There, they were allowed to view the baby through a glass window. A small bundle in a pink bonnet and white fluffy blankets was resting while hooked up to a respirator.

The nurse said, "She is a healthy baby, a little fatigued right now from the trauma, but she will be perfectly fine. You will be able to hold her in a couple of days. And she will be all yours in a couple of weeks or as soon as her lungs can breathe freely."

Andrew had never had the privilege to observe a newborn. He reminded himself this little bundle was his flesh and blood. He must feel something, but at this moment he was numb. The new baby now distracted Fabiana's thoughts. She was over-whelmed with admiration, her cousin had an adorable face. And the nurse showed them two perfect hands and feet. Such a tiny body, but feisty, as she was stretching out. While being completely absorbed with the baby Fabiana almost forgot the ugliness behind the birth.

Fabiana shook her head. How could the world turn upside down so fast? My poor aunt, a suspicious doubt surfaced in her mind. She kept it to herself. She forced herself to be stronger than Andrew, so now it was her responsibility to take matters over into her own hands. Where would she start?

She would have to break her father's heart with the horrible news, then the boys in Boston. But first she needed to find her dad and he would take over from there. This was just too much for her right now. Andrew was in a bad state of mind and they had the baby to worry about. The need for her mother aroused deep inside her. Involuntarily, she cried out to Andrew. "Why? Why did this have to happen just when things were going so well! Auntie was starting to accept her new life."

As soon as she got home she placed a call to Sicily one more time. Joseph picked up.

"Oh, Joseph, finally, where have you been?"

"Fabiana, you are screaming in my ear… what's the matter?"

Just as well, she thought it was easier to talk to Joseph first then her dad.

"Joseph, there has been an accident, it's Auntie."

"What? How is she?"

"I have some bad news, you will have to break it to Dad."

"What are you talking about? What's happened?"

"Joseph, it's Auntie, she was in an accident. She is no longer with us."

"Sis, what are you saying? Are you serious?"

"Joseph, it's no joke, she was run over by a car and she is dead."

"Oh my God. Dad has gone to bed, but Mom is still up. I will break the news to them. Fabiana, how are you holding on? We will fly out on the first flight, you poor thing."

"Don't worry about me, the Professor has been with me and I'm as well as one can expect under the circumstances."

"Joseph, who is calling at this time of night?" asked his mom.

"Mom, we must get Dad, there has been an accident. Aunt Francesca is dead."

Anthony heard Lora's screams. He jumped out of bed in terror, running downstairs to check. He found Joseph holding and comforting his mother. Joseph felt for his sister, but now how was he going to break the news to the rest of the family.

"Joseph, Lora, what's going on? What's happened?"

"Dad, I cannot break the news to you in any other way. Fabiana called… it's bad news."

"Oh! Don't tell me, it's Francesca."

"There has been an accident."

Anthony interrupted, "What? An accident, when? Where? How is she?"

"Dad, she is dead."

Anthony brought his hands to his chest, grasping for breath, "Oh no, it cannot be." Like a crazy man he was pacing the floor in several different directions. "I knew it, it's my fault, I should have never left her there. The hell with my brother-in-law."

"Dad, there's no reason to put blame on anyone. It was an accident, we need to call the rest of the family and get ourselves to London. Fabiana needs us."

Joseph watched his father breaking down in sobs, weak, and helpless. He knew he needed to be strong. It was his job to take over. The overseas calls were placed and shortly after they were on a flight to London. The boys were in shock. Angelo was going along pretending to be the broken-hearted husband.

He needed a letter of permission from the court to leave New York. As much as he hated to go, he had to be there to save face.

His sons were important to him. His brother-in-law better not give him a hard time otherwise he would have to take care of him too.

As usual, he summoned Gestiniano so that he could give him his orders. "Do what you need to do to get me to this funeral, the sooner it's over the better." After all, he felt she got what she deserved.

"Consider it done, Boss, where am I booking you for Sicily or London?"

"Sicily," he answered. "Let her brother handle London's red tape. I am the *cornuto* – the horned one – don't forget. As for the boys, as much as possible, I want to spare them any anguish. They don't have to go through any more than they have to. Going to the funeral in Sicily is plenty upsetting for them."

The Taverna family had arrived in London. After making a few phone calls to gather as much information as possible on how to proceed according to the rules of the UK, Anthony went off immediately to meet with the investigating officers. They had contacted him by phone and were expecting him. Anthony wanted to talk to them to find out exactly what had taken place. He was anxious to understand what had happened. How had his sister been run over? He had a lot of questions going through his mind… and doubts.

He was received with care and sympathy by the London investigative department. Mr. Benjamin Tayler was the head of the investigation. After escorting him into his office and extending his condolences, he asked, "Mr. Taverna, I understand you are the brother of the victim, right?"

"Yes, I am."

"She is married and has two sons. What about her husband, why isn't he here?"

"Mr. Benjamin, I am glad he is not here."

"We have notified him."

"Mr. Benjamin, they are married, but distant from one another. I usually look after my sister's well-being."

He seemed stern in his questioning, but professional and direct. "I see, I see. Her two sons, why are they not here?"

"The sons, they are two fine young men. They are abroad attending school. They are devastated with the news and wanted to fly here. I wanted to spare them, there is nothing they can do for their mother here. I suggested they fly back to Sicily for the funeral service."

"I understand, the coroner has his report for you. You know you need to go through all the legalities before the body is released."

"Yes, I have been told by the Italian consulate and the coroner. I guess I have a lot of work ahead of me."

"We are ruling your sister's death as an accident. The fact that it was raining heavily during rush hour traffic, and with all the pedestrians, unfortunately the likelihood of such accidents is quite high under these circumstances. It could have very well been totally unexpected.

However, we are dealing with a hit and run accident. So far not one of the witnesses can tell us anything specific and no one has come forward. It could very well be the person in the vehicle was not aware, or not willing to come forward. We have not been able to trace anything so far. Believe me the investigation is still going to continue."

"I see, I cannot understand if she was among so many people, how it can be possible that no one saw anything."

"Mr. Taverna, Friday night at five o'clock, everyone is in a hurry, and with the rain their heads were stuck under their umbrellas, and concentrating on their footing especially at a crossing, so unfortunately, no one saw the driver. We have plenty of reports as to how the victim hit the ground."

"I will leave it for you to find out soon I hope, and it will be a big relief to know for sure it was an accident." Anthony could not say anything at this time. He felt it was better to keep his thoughts to himself.

After a week of legalities, Francesca's casket was placed in a cargo plane bound for Palermo.

Anthony with the help of Joseph handled everything the best they could. Andrew was with them only in shadow, he was numb while they arranged to transport the body. Father and son, with Francesca's body in cargo, they flew back to Palermo. Fabiana, her mother, and Andrew followed the next day. Lora had insisted on seeing the baby in the hospital, however, because of the turmoil, Anthony was unable to as he needed to get back to Sicily and start the funeral arrangements. The rest of the Frarano family would be arriving soon. Despite his anger and suspicions toward Angelo, he clenched his teeth. He could not let his emotions of hatred get in the way now.

God! Let me get through this, he thought. He knew his nephews needed to be respected, as for Angelo, *God forgive me for the hatred I have toward that man*. He went ahead with her death announcement. To keep with tradition, he had notices plastered on the walls of public places so everyone in the city would read it and would be aware.

One person who saw the notice stopped in disbelief. Fausto Tarantano was stunned. "My Lord, don't tell me Angelo went ahead with his crazy idea? Oh, Saint Rosalia don't let it be!"

It is a Sicilian custom to turn always to the Saint of the Mount for help and protection. Now Fausto's conscience was troubled, but he also needed to keep things to himself for now while he pondered what to do, and the possible consequences. Should he reveal the truth?

Angelo and the boys arrived for the funeral. One could see how Diego and Daniele were barely holding up; they grieved for their mother. Anthony embraced them, "Diego, Daniele, your mother's love will always be with you, regardless of where you are, don't ever forget that."

Angelo, to save his face, had put on a sad face of a widower in distress. He went over to shake hands with Anthony and burst out crying, "I will miss her so, how am I going to come home to an empty house from now on?"

Anthony had a hard time pretending. At the same time, he could not reveal how much he detested his brother-in-law as it would only add to the distress of everyone around. "I know, Angelo, I know. We will miss her terribly." He was proud of how his anger turned into being amicable.

When Angelo saw Andrew, if only his eyes could have shot him dead, he would have. He took a deep breath and swore quietly to himself, "You son of a bitch. I have to look at your face." He gave a wild scream in anger. People turned to console him, thinking he was having an attack of grief for his wife. Once left alone he muttered, "You are not going to escape me, you scum of the earth with your fine English accent. Your funeral will be next."

Andrew felt uncomfortable on seeing Angelo, the guilt turned his stomach upside down. He reluctantly made his way to him, to offer his condolences. He extended his hand holding back, "Angelo, I am so sorry." He could not bring to say much more to him. Because he knew how much he would miss her. He could not tell him that his wife had given him back his life. Now it was taken away forever. Of course Andrew in his good nature, would never attribute the mishap to Angelo as much as he resented him for Francesca's mistreatment.

The boys were with Fabiana in a strong embrace crying together. Fabiana cried, "Diego, Daniele. Your mother was so happy these days, why did this have to happen? I don't understand. I lose faith sometimes."

The boys were torn and stressed with sorrow. When the Professor came over to Fabiana they excused themselves and went to stand beside their father.

Standing next to their father, the boys said, "Dad, Dad, I know it's hard, get hold of yourself." Then Daniele, put an arm on his shoulder and said, "Dad, you will always have us, we love you always."

Angelo, shook himself and looked at his boys. Teary eyed he said, "I know, guys, I am so lucky to have you, too. Oh, how much your mother loved you both." He retrieved a white hanky to wipe the tears running down his cheeks.

His personality was fickle and genuine at times. One could actually be fooled and feel sorry for him. The boys turned to their father for support.

Francesca was well respected. Her funeral was well attended by all the townsfolk who paid their last respects and condolences to her family. She was laid to rest in the family mausoleum beside her parents with all the honors of sacraments of the high mass from the church of Saint Rosalia.

Chapter Twenty-One

Daniele and Diego did not want to remain in Sicily longer than they had to. The void of their mother around their house was felt tremendously. They said their goodbyes to their aunt, uncle and cousins and returned to school. Angelo played his part well. After the funeral, he went to Anthony inquiring about the findings in London and what the police had to report as to the investigation of Francesca's death. "I have been told it was an accident, and no one has been charged."

Perturbed, Anthony did not care to discuss much with him regarding his sister. Especially with the birth of her daughter, who was now left behind.

"Yes, apparently it was raining at that crucial time. What can I say? Nothing will bring my sister back now. I would rather not talk about it for now."

"You are right, Anthony, what can we do? Do you know if they need to talk to me, or anything?"

"Angelo, I am not going to stand in the way of the police, they know what to do with their investigation. If they need to question you I am sure they will contact you. As you know, I am their number one contact. Francesca always resorted to me as her next of kin."

"I know, Anthony, you have always been her protector, and she adored you for it."

"Angelo, do me a favor will you? Right now spare me your ceremonies, okay? Go back to New York and attend to your affairs. You've got two boys without a mother to love, don't forget that. Double duty for you from now on."

"Anthony, do you think I am not going to miss my wife? Regardless of what you're thinking, I loved your sister."

"Look, Angelo, I don't care anymore. Do you understand? You will be gone, at the other side of the world. I have been here. I am here now, how am I going to pass by your house and my beautiful sister is not there anymore because some scum of the earth crushed her with his car? Tell me, Angelo, how am I going to accept that?"

At Anthony's remarks Angelo was touched. Had he not played the part right as the disconsolate widower?

He questioned himself. Or did that louse brother-in-law of his break him with regrets. *The hell with him. I will be gone in a few days and he can rot here in Sicily with his duties as the noble Sicilian.*

Andrew's world had collapsed. The abyss in front of him was immeasurable. Now he had a baby girl waiting for him in London. He needed to take it up with Lora and Fabiana, he definitely needed their help and he found comfort with them.

Where will I begin? He wanted to get back to London. This place brought back happy memories and now he was alone. The morning after the funeral Andrew was up early and the others were already having a cup of coffee. Anthony suggested they step into the library for complete privacy.

Lora was the first to speak, "We all know that the baby is our secret. Angelo Frarano must never know. We need to keep it that way. Now, Andrew, we can assume full responsibility should it be difficult for you to do it alone."

"Oh, no, no. I need your help, but she is my child and I want to take full responsibility."

Fabiana intervened, "We all need to get back to London. As soon as they release the baby, she needs to be baptized. Auntie had asked me to be the godmother."

"Of course, of course, she told me too, Fabiana."

"Mom, I will take care of her until further arrangements are made. Maybe you can get a nanny for the first few years."

With a look of pain on his face, Anthony said, "We'll do whatever it takes to look after the well-being of my sister's child. You can be rest assured, Andrew."

"Thank you, thank you, I'm so grateful and I know I can count on you."

Once back in London their first stop was a visit to baby Gracy. The nurse cheerfully gave them a general report of her progress, "You need to speak to the doctor."

Andrew was relieved to hear the good news, now he needed to familiarize himself with being a father. This little bundle needed him. She was almost ready to be released and soon after Lora would take charge of taking care of her niece.

Despite having a hard time concentrating at work, Andrew looked forward to stopping over to see his little daughter every night. He never missed a night before returning home. Her progress was amazing. The three of them were watching with a keen eye. The baptism was scheduled to take place as soon as possible. When Anthony arrived, Fabiana had already purchased the complete white outfit. She dressed Gracy like a white dove and she received the sacrament of the baptism at St. Paul's Cathedral.

To celebrate, Lora opened a bottle of special champagne and made a toast to Gracy's good health, "Cheers, we all know her mom is up above watching over her, and she will guide us in raising her." Gracy was the centerpiece and the four adults smiled over her in admiration. Andrew knew how lucky he was to have this family on his side. He raised his glass, "I vow for our Gracy to be brought up with love and affection and I promise to make sure she knows the love of our beloved Francesca."

Now, Andrew was going to rearrange his life to accommodate his daughter. He seriously thought about moving closer to Fabiana. This would make things easier and more convenient for both of them. So far they had all agreed on everything in regards to the baby's well-being.

Chapter Twenty-Two

....

The London police investigators were beside themselves. They hadn't had a break on the case. It was frustrating. Constable Benjamin Tayler had relentlessly continued his investigation since he had been assigned to the case. He was a stern officer and very focused on his work. He well deserved his many medals on his uniform. He wanted to have the satisfaction of informing the family of any new leads. He had mentioned to one of his colleagues. "A fine chap that Mr. Taverna, and his friend. I would like to give them some hope in solving this case."

***

On the day of the accident Skinny had successfully abandoned his stolen vehicle on a secondary street. Vladimiro drove by with a getaway car. He had been sitting there waiting for him to arrive in his rented vehicle. On a secluded street Skinny jumped in the passenger seat. He laughed and raised his hand to give him a high five and Vladimiro sped away as fast as he could. Once they were out of the city limits, Skinny extended his hand, "My dough, partner. Mission accomplished."

"How do I know she's really dead? I need proof."

"Are you serious? Have you ever known me to miss! When I hit, I hit and without leaving a trace. Don't play games with me."

"Okay, okay, but what about the guy? Have you forgotten his order?"

"For heaven's sake, Vladimiro. You are a relentless skunk! Take it easy. Wow, wow, one at a time. He is going to get his biscuit soon."

"How much did I promise you for half a job? Refresh my memory."

"Vladimiro, stop the jokes. Look," Skinny was getting irritated, "I just killed a beautiful pregnant woman. You owe me fifty thousand U.S. dollars; you cough up thirty-five for now and the rest when I do the other job."

By now Vladimiro had reached Birmingham. He had driven one hundred and nineteen miles. A good enough distance he thought. He pulled into a gas station and gave him his share of the deal.

"How long will it take for you to do the guy?"

"I'm keeping my eyes open. As soon as the waters calm down I'll do what I need to do. Don't worry. Trust me."

"I want to fly to Moscow as soon as this is over. I can't wait for too long."

"Well then, give me the money up front. I will deliver. You don't trust me?"

"Oh no, I don't pay in advance. When the job is done, the money will be in your hands."

"Whatever you say. It's your call, but I act only when the time is right."

"Fine, I cannot wait around forever. There are other jobs if you are interested."

"Scarface, do you want a professional job, or a botched up one? You know I don't want to end up behind bars."

"I'll leave it to you. In the meantime I need to get back to New York for few days. You keep me posted. All you need to do is leave me one message. Say, 'RESOLVED'. Then, on my way to Moscow, I'll make a stopover and pay you."

"Okay, leave it to Skinny."

With that they parted. Vladimiro was getting older, every time a request came in he was going to abandon the darn job. It was getting to him. Lately he had resorted to subcontracting his jobs. He was still the culprit and an accomplice. The money lured him, and his soul was possessed by the devil.

Andrew had no idea what was in store for him. He was just trying hard to adjust to his new life. He was rejoicing with Gracy's development and Lora had gotten into the habit of greeting him with her lovely meals at the end of every day.

At the same time, someone else was having sleepless nights in Palermo. Fausto Tarantano was heavy with deep remorse. He couldn't erase the image of that beautiful woman. That crazy husband had asked him to kill her. Now she was dead, he had no peace. Did she die in an accident or was the accident caused on purpose?

That fellow, the Englishman, he wanted him harmed too. Yes, he was to pay for having had the affair with his wife. My God, he is a madman. *I think I need to go for confession and have a meeting with Anthony Taverna.* With good intentions, Fausto planned to visit Anthony at his home.

It was late afternoon and Anthony had just gotten back from a hard day's work from Catania. He missed Lora's greetings lately, but he knew in his heart that she needed to be in London. He was about to fall asleep on his leather couch in the family room. Ersilia would soon be serving his dinner. He didn't have an appetite these days. He was surprised when Ersilia announced that a gentleman was at the door wishing to see him.

"Who is the gentleman?"

"He said his name is Fausto Tarantano and it's very important that he talks to you."

"Show him in."

"My apologies for this intrusion, Mr. Taverna. I'm Fausto Tarantano," he said as he extended his hand. "I feel a strong obligation to talk to you."

Anthony was puzzled. *What now?* What could this man want? A nervous humble man, he noticed. Was he seeking employment? They always made it sound like such an emergency. The man didn't respect the appropriate timing, but he detected a nervous urgency in his voice.

"What can I do for you? Please sit down."

He looked around towards the door, almost reluctant to speak, afraid of being overheard. "Can we talk privately? What I have to say is serious and confidential."

Now Anthony's hair stood up. Immediately he knew this guy had bad news.

"Please come in the library and we will shut the door. In the meantime, allow me to advise my housekeeper not to serve dinner until our meeting is over."

"Mr. Taverna, believe me, I haven't had any peace since I saw your sister's *Manifesti* – death notice."

Anthony held his breath, "Go on, what do you know about my sister?"

"My brother-in-law Miliano Cardone, was a private investigator. Apparently he had been hired by your sister's husband to keep tabs on her and report to him. Well he passed away and his wife needed some help going through all his files. In the meantime, Angelo had asked me to replace him. Once I took the job, I had nothing to report to him. I kept telling him that he was wasting his money. His wife was a good woman. He insisted I be on his payroll. I didn't like it, but I needed the money. I have a family to feed. But then one day after Miliano's death, when I was sorting through his files, I found some pictures. They were taken in Cefalù with a recording tape and the works. There they were, his wife and this Englishman. I sent it to him in New York. I thought it was my duty, after all, I was being paid. When I came on duty I never saw anything wrong. I guess when Frarano received the pictures he went ballistic. He called me to order his wife killed."

Anthony put a hand on his heart. "Oh my God, you… please, I can't hear any more."

"Mr. Taverna, please listen to me. I refused him cold turkey and I quit. I told him I didn't want his paycheck anymore and I was finished with him. There is more. The Englishman, he requested to have his legs broken, for him to be tortured and killed afterwards."

Anthony felt sick to his stomach; he was about to pass out.

"Mr. Taverna, I thought he was just mad and blinded by jealousy to talk so revengefully. I never believed he would carry it through. Now I'm telling you this. Maybe it was an accident with your sister. But I don't think so, I'm warning you for the gentleman. Plus, he also mentioned yourself, he wanted to know if you badmouthed him. If you did, then you would be next."

Anthony's head was full. He knew Angelo was a monster and he never liked the local hoodlums he associated with. He had a bad feeling in his gut about him. He always suspected that his poor sister was in danger with that criminal.

"Now, Mr. Taverna, I'm here to warn you, this is to be confidential. I took a big risk by coming here. I don't know who his stool pigeons are. I could be their next target for talking to you."

"Thanks, thanks. I appreciate your warning. If only we would have known, but I must admit I feared it."

"Now, I have no knowledge as to your sister in London, if she died of an accident or if it was done intentionally."

Anthony got up and so did Fausto. Their meeting was over; they were both instilled with fear.

Fausto said goodbye and reminded Anthony, "Remember this is strictly between the two of us. My lips are sealed. We never spoke."

"Let me ask you one more thing. Did he ever mention any threats towards my daughter?"

"No, no, he never mentioned her. His targets were the two lovers and a strong dislike for you."

Anthony's stomach churned with disgust. Trickles of sweat ran down his spine. "Whatever he is planning is sick. I need to take some action immediately to protect myself and what's left of my family. You want this kept confidential, but it's my obligation to warn the Professor. Are you willing to repeat what you told me to the authorities?"

"Absolutely not. I will be as good as dead."

"Okay, leave it with me. I know what I need to do."

With that Fausto left, hoping he could still salvage some peace.

Anthony was restless now. He searched hard for answers. *What about Gracy? What if that monster got wind of her existence?* He couldn't afford to fail her. He had an obligation to take care of his sister's child. Anthony had never anticipated that Angelo Frarano had learned of Francesca's pregnancy. Now, as far as Angelo gathered, his wife had been killed including her unborn baby. That is exactly the way he had wanted it.

Joseph took over everything related to their business. The following day Anthony took the first flight out to London. Lora was thrilled to see him and showered him with food and drinks. Anthony was more interested in admiring the baby. He wondered how he was going to tell them his new findings.

Andrew arrived, shortly followed by Fabiana. They were both overjoyed to find Anthony waiting for them. Anthony, as usual, took time to initiate the family meeting.

"Andrew – I will call you Andrew now as you were dear to my sister – I came here for a serious matter. I had a visitor last night. He gave me reason to believe that Francesca was murdered."

Lora and Fabiana gasped. "Oh, *Santa Rosalia Benedetta* – blessed Saint Rosalia. By whom?"

Andrew didn't flinch. "Don't tell me, let me guess."

"You're guessing right, Andrew, and there is much more."

"You're in danger and I have no clue what that dark soul of his is scheming, or if he knows of Gracy's birth."

They remained stunned.

"Anthony, who was this visitor, how can he help us? We must relate this to Detective Benjamin. Something must be done."

"It's not as easy as that. This fellow fears for his life. It took a lot of courage for him to come and talk to me. He is not willing to talk to anyone. What he told me is strictly confidential, he wanted to warn me."

"Andrew, you're their next target."

He didn't want to shock Fabiana and Lora. Therefore, it was better to leave his own threats out.

"We must go to the police."

"Yes, we need to do something, this is why I rushed here."

"Why don't we call the detective right now and seek his advice?"

"Andrew, we can, but you don't underestimate these killers, they have no mercy."

"We are guessing and working on hunches, we need definite proof and information. Was this fellow for real, or was he bluffing to scare me?"

"He was a scared rabbit himself. He said if anyone had followed him and knew he was talking to me he would be dead meat."

"Let's go to the London police tomorrow. Can you take some time off work?"

"I guess I need to. I will take the afternoon off. I will call detective Benjamin Tayler first thing in the morning."

"Listen this is quite a blow for anyone. I suggest you remain here tonight. Once we talk to the detective, we will see what they suggest."

Andrew didn't want to admit his fear. But he was worried for his safety now. Look what had happened to his poor Francesca. Lora was such a good soul and she started to accommodate Andrew and make him comfortable and safe for the night.

Fabiana didn't want to say anything, but yesterday when she was rummaging through her aunt's belongings she had found her diary. Her stuff was placed in her room since she needed to accommodate her mother with the crib for Gracy. Should she pry into her belongings? Not now, another time. Now hearing this news, she felt an urge to get to it. Maybe it was her aunt's wish. Maybe that's why she found it. There might be something there that she needed to know. Did she know something? Did she suspect anyone? It might shed some light on the mystery of the unexpected death. Tomorrow after school she would get to it. It was her duty to safeguard some of her precious belongings for Gracy. She would appreciate some of her mom's memorabilia later in life. After all, she was her godmother. Her role was to fulfill the same duties as the biological mother should the need arise.

The next day Andrew and Anthony met Detective Constable Benjamin Tayler at two o'clock in the afternoon. They sat privately in a small room.

"Gentlemen," the detective began, "we have offered a reward for any information. We have followed every lead, speculating, and questioning anyone of interest. We have not moved forward."

"I have been told in confidentiality, that my brother-in-law was the mastermind behind it all. This anonymous gentleman also reported to me that Professor Andrew here is next. Plus, there are threats made against myself."

Andrew said, "You never mentioned that last night."

"I know I didn't. I couldn't let Lora and Fabiana know."

Benjamin Tayler's ears perked up. "Tell me everything in full detail."

Anthony slowly and methodically repeated the story told to him by Fausto Tarantano. Afterwards, Constable Tayler stopped the recorder. "This confirms our suspicions. The husbands are often suspected.

"But we need proof, real proof to nab whoever did this. We talked to the New York Police Department and we spoke to the Sicily Police Department. We can't pin anything on this guy. He is in trouble all right, deep trouble with other charges, but we can't pin anything on him for murder, or even the mastermind or an accomplice."

"Constable Tayler, this fellow told me he asked him to carry the job through and he refused."

"How do we know he is telling the truth?"

"Should the police question him he would deny our meeting and besides he's in deep fear for his own life should anyone find out he talked to me."

"You see our hands are tied due to people like this individual. We can't charge anybody. This is why I am frustrated, we know the culprits, but they play cat and mouse with us, they are smart crooks, and they laugh in our faces."

"What do we do now? Don't you think the Professor needs protection?"

Then he turned to Andrew, "Professor, what can you contribute to our investigation that could help us out?"

Andrew shrugged his shoulders, "Other than what I have already told the police… I don't know any more. This is shocking to me."

The constable smiled and after a brief hesitation he continued, "I hate to tell you, Professor, you don't have an affair with a mobster's wife. Bad idea. You're doomed. Guys like that don't forget and don't forgive. What were you thinking? We're short funded and short staffed. Our officers are over-worked. I can't act or promise you much from this information. I will talk to the fellows on the night beat in your area, but I can't promise anything."

"I know it wasn't right Constable, sometimes one cannot dictate to the heart what to do. But now I know, these guys don't fool around. I do fear for my life."

"I suggest you to be super cautious, to look over your shoulders, be aware of your surroundings, and don't stay out late at night. Stay in public places, and try not to be alone. I want to reassure you, from all my years of experience on the force, usually they don't strike soon after the other, and they know we are on to them. In time, who knows… people might cool off with vendettas."

With a shaky voice Andrew offered, "Let's hope you're right."

"Mr. Taverna, I suggest you notify the authorities once you return to your hometown, but I can assure you, their hands are tied as well."

"I will get my own bodyguard in Palermo. As for whoever is causing all this harm to us, he will burn in hell." Then he turned to Andrew, "What about you? Do you feel the need for one, at least until things settle?"

"No, Anthony, it would make me more nervous, and it would look foolish around the university. I prefer to be careful and on alert on my own."

The constable stood up and handed his card to both of them. He turned to Andrew and said, "Good idea, Professor, you can always call us should you see or suspect anything. I will keep in touch and definitely notify you of any new developments."

Anthony and Andrew were disappointed and discouraged. It wasn't what they expected to hear. They knew for sure it wasn't an accident that took Francesca's life. *So what next?*

Andrew did not want to admit it. He was terrified. He had a daughter to raise. It was bad enough she had lost her mother, what was her fate going to be should something happen to him?

Anthony said, "Andrew, don't mention much to the women. Leave it to me to do some thinking, I need to come to some resolution that will work to our advantage. Don't worry, we will find a way."

Lora was all excited about the baby when they got home. She had gotten so many smiles out of Gracy and that had made her day. Lora was truly a devoted aunt, she enjoyed relating her day to the men and Fabiana.

"Enough about me and Gracy," she chuckled, "please, tell me what did those officers have to say?"

Anthony was evasive, "Nothing much, other than knowing that Francesca's death was intentional. And they have offered a monetary reward for any information."

"Anthony, but what about the threat on Andrew?"

"Oh, it's hard to say, this guy could have made it up. He won't admit anything, so they have nothing to go by."

"But the Professor could be in danger."

"Lora, don't worry, he's not a child. He has to watch himself. You need to stop being such a mother hen." He knew the inquisition wouldn't stop.

Andrew felt he needed to behave like a man and resume his life courageously while Anthony needed to get back to Sicily, in his demanding territory. That night Andrew returned to his flat in Bethnow. After treating himself to a glass of brandy, he was fast asleep.

***

Fabiana was drawn to look through her aunt's belongings. Before she knew it there she was opening the diary. She found a pocket behind it holding several small notes, phone numbers, and an unsealed and unaddressed white legal envelope. She removed it and continued to browse through the pages of the diary. Then, her attention turned to the envelope. She recognized Francesca's handwriting. Yes, she needed to read this letter.

March 2, 1983.

Francesca, Taverna, in Frarano.
12359 Via Lago Maggiore,
Palermo,
Italia, 97138.

On this day, with this note I revoke my previous will, and testament.

I am under no one's pressure and sound minded. These are my wishes:

At my demise, I wish my parental inheritance in cash deposit of one billion lire, plus bearing interest, at the post office, which is in my name and trust to be released and distributed periodically as the need may arise, for the care and use of my unborn child; my land in Catania of 300 acres, entitled roll no.39675 on Via Del Ponte to my two boys Diego Frarano and Daniele Frarano in equal parts. Once my third child, stated now as my unborn child, becomes of age twenty-five, I grant my land consisting of 150 acres, currently being a Muscat vineyards, situated on via Della Roccia in Agrigento, roll number 56103 for the sole use and enjoyment. My third child, I assign, my niece Fabiana Taverna, as trustee along with my Brother Anthony Taverna, both residing at 90021 Via Maddelana, Palermo, 4561, Sicily.

I state herein that Andrew Robertson of 3491 Bethnow, London England, 4456 is the biological father of my child. Should the need arise, Fabiana Taverna and Anthony Taverna, can distribute monies to Andrew Robertson, to take care of his child, as the need may arise, providing their discretion is consciously implemented in partial distribution with monitored receipts and expenses, which it should not access its necessary obligations. I revoke any inheritance, belonging to myself from my husband Angelo Frarano. In the sole agreement that it is passed on directly to my two sons, Diego Frarano and Daniele Frarano, residing, part time at Via Lago Maggiore, Palermo, Italy 97138. and 35900 Third Ave, New, York, U.S.A. 1271.

This is my last testament and wishes.

Francesca Taverna, in Frarano.   On this day of March 2, 1983.

Witness: Father, Alfonso di Giacomo.   On this day of March 2, 1983.

Witness: R. Luigi Donatelli.   On this day of March 2, 1983.

Fabiana, knew the witnesses on the signature. *I see she had Father Alfonso sign it, good choice. She had written this before she left for London.* Fabiana put the letter down. *Now I know why I was drawn here. I needed to read this. Poor Auntie, did she anticipate her fate? Did she know?* Tears rolled down her eyes. Suddenly Gracy's shrill cry reached her ears and she ran to her, but Lora was already at her side.

"Mom, Mom, why is she crying so loudly, what is wrong?"

"Fabiana, babies get tummy aches don't forget. A little hugging and rubbing will make her feel better."

Fabiana thought her mom was such a pro at this; what would happen once she was back home? After all she could only stay a bit longer. They couldn't take the baby to Sicily. How would she and Andrew manage without any experience? As much as she loved the baby she needed experienced help. Yes, they would have to hire a nanny.

Anthony was worried about returning to Sicily. He didn't like having his family so spread out, it increased his worry. In the morning Fabiana showed him the letter, he read it, and his heart melted as he imagined Francesca creating this makeshift will alone in her home. Did she anticipate something happening? In a way, he was relieved. This would ensure her family would be taken care of.

"Dad, what about the threats on Andrew's life?"

"Don't worry about it, it won't take place. I will stop at nothing to keep Andrew and the baby safe. Let me get back home, I will contact our police there and I will talk to our lawyer. You take care of yourself and your mother. We need to put our heads together and come to the best solution, especially for the baby."

He tried hard to reassure his daughter by pretending he was the big man to keep things calm and under control. Meanwhile, Anthony's head was full and Andrew felt helpless.

Skinny had gone into hiding in Birmingham. He rented a room in one of the city's industrial areas. The media was relentless in looking for information to find the killer of the hit and run. Now they offered a monetary reward. He needed to cool it for a while and keep out of sight. *Those bastards*, he thought, if they got hold of him he was done. They weren't forgiving. He had plenty of experience of being inside. He had been in and out of jail so many times.

This offer could be tempting for any one of his scum friends on the streets. He didn't want to be caught or discovered, especially charged for murder. He now needed to be careful and chill for a while. He got rid of his scruffy clothes, purchased a new vest, shirt, pants and a sports blazer. He cut his hair short, and shaved off any stubble. Overnight he became a polished gentleman. After taking a good look in the mirror, he liked his reflection.

He decided to call himself Blake Scott. This name sounded more civil. He placed a call to Vladimiro. "Buddy, Skinny here."

On the other side of the line Vladimiro's groggy voice responded, "Who is this?" He didn't appreciate a call in the middle of the night. "Why are you calling me at this time of night? Have you forgotten what time it is here?"

"Partner, this is important."

"How important is it that it can't wait till morning?"

"I don't know how much London news you hear, but the cops have offered a reward for information."

"What do you mean? You knocked her out, don't implicate me. Have you forgotten where I was?"

Skinny was irritated by his answer. "Scarface, don't forget who you're talking to. Don't play games with me, it was your idea."

"Let me get back to sleep will you? Call me in the morning."

"No. You listen to me right now. I'm sitting in the hot seat here, not being able to go to London. I'm one hundred and nineteen miles away, in hiding. The investigation is still going strong. I need to tell you, I have changed my appearance and my name."

"Okay, Okay, can this wait?"

"No, it can't wait. My red hair is black and I cut my hair and shaved."

"Fine, fine, whatever. Why do you need to tell me this crap in the middle of the night?"

"Why? You ask me why?"

"Yeah, have you been drinking? Or are you high or something?"

"No, I'm not high on anything. I want to tell you that my name is now Blake Scott. The next stunt on the Professor will have to wait".

"Why wait? You spoke so big and powerful when I was there. What changed your mind?"

"Cops have been snooping around asking questions. They stopped me on the street, questioning me."

"You're safe aren't you?"

"My street buddies have been promised rewards to sing, they can lie and make up stories, and you know they will say any-thing, for a fix."

"Look Skinny, you do what you need to do and keep me informed."

"I need more money, all this change of ID costs money. I want an extra fifteen thousand."

"Skinny, are you looking for trouble? Don't play games with me or I will blow your brains out." Now he was totally awake, his voice got louder and louder. "Back off, will you?"

He knew Scarface had a violent unforgiving reputation. He decided maybe he should change his tactics. "Scarface, listen, I have put quite some work into this. I know it and you know it. I can't pull off this job successfully on my own. I need a couple of guys here to help me."

"So get whoever . . . and get the darn job finished."

"That's what I want to do. The trouble is right now it can't be done. The police are questioning all the druggies on the street."

"Skinny, you figure it out when the time is right, do it and call me. What more can I say?"

"Yeah, but it's taking much more time. I can't move until this is over. Time is money and the two more guys are going to cost me money. Do you understand?"

"Okay, okay, end of conversation. How much more money do you need?"

Skinny knew he had a long record with the police, this is why the police were asking questions. Now this Vladimiro character was also intimidating with threats.

"Vladimiro, I really need fifteen, but, for you, I will settle with another ten thousand at least."

"Fine, I will give you the extra ten. But get the job done."

"Scarface, believe me I know when it's time to strike."

Vladimiro wasn't being pressed for anything at the moment. He was on the other side of the continent; therefore, free. He hadn't been involved in the actual hit, it would be difficult to charge him. He felt untouchable. He had plenty of money in his pocket. Skinny had given his word that the job would be completed. Now he was getting cold feet. What was it with Skinny asking for help and more money? They had verbally agreed to a deal. He understood about the timing needing to be right. In the meantime, he wasn't going to lose sleep over it all. He would decide later to give him more money or get rid of him completely if he continued to bother him.

***

Recently Gestiniano hadn't been bothered by Angelo. He was overloaded with all their business crises. The depositions, the pre-trials, and discoveries… it was all endless. He was trying hard to save money but the plaintiff's attorneys were aggressive and relentless.

Angelo had become a recluse since he returned from his wife's funeral. He was suffering from painful gout attacks and could hardly walk. Since he wasn't used to pain he was behaving like a lion in a cage. His temper was volatile. He resorted to sitting by his desk in his apartment barking strong orders and demanding unreasonable requests like a madman. Gestiniano was running out of patience with him. He was ready to throw in the towel. But he knew better, he was in deep. How was he going to find a way out of this misery? He wished Angelo would drop dead. His dictatorship was testing everyone's patience. Gestiniano was just about to go for lunch with their accountant, Leonardo Quarantino, when his phone rang.

"Gestiniano. Get your ass over here, I need to talk to you."

"Boss. I'm on my way to a meeting. Can I see you later? I won't be long."

"Gestiniano. Cancel your meeting. I need to talk to you now."

Gestiniano shook his head and clutched his teeth in despair. Mumbling to himself he blessed his boss with the "F" word. "I will see if I can reach Leonardo and cancel out. I will be right there."

Obedient as always, he was there. He opened the door to Angelo's place and before him his boss was shriveled on the sofa like a pitiful man.

"Boss, what's going on? You need to get a hold of yourself."

"I'm finished." His eyes were red from crying. He was still in his housecoat, unshaven, and held a cane. It was past noon.

"What do you mean you're finished? We have so much to look after, Boss. I need your input. Your sons need you. You have to get to a doctor to get you feeling better and be yourself again."

"Oh, Gestiniano, I will never be myself again. I have lost my precious jewel."

"Boss, what are you talking about? You're talking nonsense now."

"Francesca is gone. I loved her you know. She was my everything."

Gestiniano didn't know what to say next. Should he hit him over the head or should he sympathize with him?

What a foolish bastard, he thought.

"Are you forgetting that was what you wanted?"

"I know, I know, she should have never done what she did to me."

"You got your revenge. You took care of that business, get over it, we have so much work to focus on."

"I can't. I'm depressed. I can't sleep at night. I am having a hell of a time."

"We better get you to a doctor, he will prescribe some medication to help you feel better. I will ask the boys to come home and spend some time with you. Once you get a clear head, you'll be better in no time."

"Gestiniano, tell me, if your wife cheated on you, would you kill her?"

"I don't have a wife, Boss. No. I would not kill her. It would depend how much I cared. How hurt I would be. If you want my honest opinion, if that is what she wants to do, there's the road. Good luck to her. You know how many women are out there."

"You fools from the younger generation. No respect for the family, no integrity for the honor. Do you realize what she made out of me? *Cornuto*. She put horns on my forehead."

"Think the way you like. I don't see it that way."

"Tell me, has that fruitcake been taken care of yet?"

"Are you referring to the Professor?"

At his mentioning Angelo seemed to get his powerful anger back, "Yeah, yeah. Who else? Tell me he's not still walking around."

"I'm sure he isn't. The job was well assigned. I haven't talked to Scarface lately and he hasn't collected the full payment. I will check with him soon."

"I need proof. I wish I could have gotten my hands on him myself. It would have given me great pleasure to watch him squirm. How dare he hit on my wife."

"Boss, Boss, stop thinking about it."

"Yeah, how do you stop when your insides are boiling?"

"It's over. Think about getting yourself back on your feet. We have a lot to do. He's history. You can be rest assured." Gestiniano was seeking a way out of this situation. He ruffled his black hair while letting out a deep sigh, "I am calling your doctor and taking you there, or should I ask him to come here?"

Angelo's mood, from being an angry wolf switched back to self-pity. "He better come here, I don't feel like getting dressed. I don't want to go anywhere."

Great. On top of everything else he now needed to nurse his boss. Funny how his sex bunnies hadn't been around lately. They had all flown the coop. Angelo had cut out their funds. No wonder he felt and looked like an old abandoned man.

When Dr. Cornilius arrived he took one look at him and said, "Angelo, I have limitations here. You need to come to my office where I can check you properly. Or if it's necessary, I may need to have you admitted to a hospital. Your kidneys were failing the last time I saw you. You need proper professional care."

"Don't bullshit me, Doc. You know I pay you enough you do as I say. I'm going nowhere. You take care of me right here."

The doctor turned to Gestiniano, "He's so unreasonable these days. Let me check his medication." On checking his medication, he noticed the pills he had been prescribed were sitting in the plastic bottles hardly taken from his last medical checkup.

"Angelo, you are not going to get better if you don't take your medication, I cannot help you without your cooperation."

Gestiniano turned to Angelo, "Boss, why aren't you following the doctor's orders?"

"Ah. You too. Lay off. Don't try my patience."

"If he continues in this state, I'm going to have to give him some tranquillizers."

"You're telling me. He's been a stubborn mule." Then he turned to the doctor and said, "Mr. Frarano has been wasting inside here for almost a month."

"I need to admit you, do some tests and get you back in good health, Angelo," said the doctor.

"Doctor, what is really wrong with him?" asked Gestiniano.

"He has neglected himself. The last time his hemoglobin was down, I ordered him iron pills to boost his blood cells. I see the bottle has hardly been touched. He is weak, his blood pressure low. I need to take more blood tests. When the count is down, his body can shut down, his main organs are crying for blood supply, the heart, kidneys, every other organ is following suit. This is why he has no energy and is sleepy."

"It's serious," said Gestiniano, "I thought it was all mental."

"Your thoughts bring emotions, emotions bring physical damage. I told him that not long ago when I gave him a complete physical. But he ignores my diagnosis. I am sure he has not been eating right to help himself."

"Okay, you guys. You talk as if I'm not here. Why don't you both get out of here and go fly a kite?"

With that he struggled trying to get up, but his legs had no strength and he collapsed on the floor. Dr. Cornilius dialed the emergency dispatcher and an ambulance arrived in minutes. Gestiniano was so relieved. He was up to his eyeballs at the office he didn't have the energy to coddle his boss as well.

Chapter Twenty-Three

··

Andrew kept the cleaning lady Mrs. Brooks had provided for him on a weekly basis, and the spare bedroom had been turned into a nursery. It was time. He needed to assume full responsibility of his daughter. Lora could not remain in London forever and Fabiana was of great help. But he was the biological father and she belonged with him in his place. He hired a professional nanny so he knew she would be well cared for while he was at work.

Three months had passed since Francesca's death. He was grieving deeply inside. A sword seemed to be stuck in the middle of his heart. But he had Gracy and he had to be responsible. Oh, how he loved and cherished his Gracy. She had Francesca's features and jet black hair. At the last visit, the doctor had assured him that she was progressing amazingly well. Her little lungs were breathing normally for a premature baby. Andrew thanked him, if only Francesca could have seen their little bundle of Joy. She would be so proud. As for himself, she was certainly giving him a new lease on his crumbled life.

He told Fabiana, "I must be strong. I have a reason to go on."

"You have to, Professor, she needs you."

His nanny was a middle-aged lady with a nursing background and a degree in child psychology. She was their perfect candidate. Mrs. Sylvia Morrison was more expensive than anyone else they had interviewed. She was also a widow, so she was flexible with Andrew's schedule. Plus, he only wanted the best for his child. Every now and then he treated himself to going home by taxi if he was tired, or worked late. This was going to be eliminated. He preferred to sacrifice himself, saving his money, taking the tube, and walk home the rest of the way instead of riding taxis home. Mrs. Morrison had just finished her long-term assignment with a family with three children. They were all grown up now and didn't need her any longer. Her black hair was pulled back in braids, she had a serious but kind look on her face with piercing brown eyes. For an older woman she held her own and moved with a fast pace.

Andrew liked that she was cheerful and witty. Her upbeat energy was just what they all needed. She had excellent references. During the week she would sleep in a single bed in the baby's bedroom and go home on the weekend. This was perfect for Andrew as he planned to spend as much time as possible with Gracy when he wasn't teaching. His new life was falling into place. Lora, Fabiana, and the new nanny courageously encouraged him to pick up the pieces and begin his role as a new daddy.

Lora returned to Sicily; her heart aching to stay with Gracy. She had bonded with the baby. Fabiana, of course, would remain to continue her studies. Now she could breathe, knowing that such a loving nanny was taking care of her goddaughter. Plus, she knew she would be babysitting from time to time. She loved to hold and cuddle the baby in her arms while singing lullabies in Italian and English. "*Stella, stellina* – star, little star," she would sing in a soft voice as she rocked her in the rocking chair in the nursery. "Night is approaching, the flame flickers, the cow in the barn, the cow and the calf, the ewe and the lamb, the hen with the chick…" Then holding back tears she would complete the song, "*ognuno ha la sua mamma* – everyone has a mother."

Andrew watched these women taking care of his baby. He knew in his heart that from up above, Francesca would be watching with pride.

He had never been religious. Actually, after his parents died he had become an atheist much to Francesca's displeasure. Francesca was such a devoted worshipper. She carried the rosary with her and morning and evenings she would excuse herself to recite her prayers. Andrew had willingly gone along with her worship and even participated in attending mass on the Sunday services. He had to admit, sometimes in his deepest despair a calm did come over him. As for Gracy, he felt some guardian angel was looking after her.

The past few weeks had been so busy. Andrew was exhausted when he went to bed. He also remained vigilant for the baby feeding and diaper change whenever he was at home. This was all so new for him. When he stood there looking at his daughter his tiredness seemed to dissipate. He would whisper to his Gracy, "You're worth it, my little darling."

Sylvia was doing a fantastic job and he assisted like a dutiful good daddy.

"Professor, you need your sleep. Let me take care of everything, believe me, I'm used to this. I will nap when the baby naps."

He got into the habit of rushing home as soon as his classes were over. He often brought work home. The papers needed to be marked and he would manage somehow to get it done before the next day. When it came to Constable Benjamin Tayler's warnings to be aware of his surroundings, and to be vigilant, he had forgotten all about that these days.

The police were still patrolling the neighborhood, it was a part of their daily routine. Since the meeting with Constable Benjamin, he had noticed their presence. He kept his guard on, but he had to admit his nervousness and anxiety had subsided. He just had so many other things going on. He refused to have dark cloudy thoughts enter his mind. On a positive note, he had been blessed with a daughter to go home to. He would not allow himself to indulge in self-pity anymore.

Chapter Twenty-Four

From New York Vladimiro had been pressuring Skinny lately, "What are you doing sitting around? Can we get this job completed and move on?"

"Scarface, you're so clever giving me orders and telling me what to do. Why don't you go fuck yourself? I told you, I will know when the time is right and when it isn't."

"I'm telling you. It's past due; plant the guy and it's over."

"Yeah, and who's going to end up behind bars? Not you, right, smartass?"

"Are you shitting in your pants for a small lousy job like that?"

"No, I don't shit in my pants. I play it smart, my way."

"I'll give you few more days and should you keep stalling, you'll be replaced."

"Look, I have it all set up. I got a couple of winos helping me out."

"Okay, okay, you're waiting for the full moon to disappear. It should be taking place soon, let me know."

With that Vladimiro hung up his phone and dialed Gestiniano.

"Hello," he answered.

"It's me," said Scarface.

"Jesus Christ, don't call me here. I told you I would call you. "

"Okay, okay, make sure you've got the balance of the money ready."

"You scumbag. You know what I need before you get paid off?"

"You will get it done only when the money is in my hands."

The phone went dead.

Vladimiro wasn't a pushover. Business was business. He always carried his powerful weapon. His outer appearance was of a man of distinction, except for the scar on his face. His verbal skills were eloquent. He had accumulated a healthy bank account in Switzerland. All of that gave him power should anyone decide to double cross or shortchange him. After all he was a professional at his work.

Skinny knew the police had been pretty steady in the area where the Professor lived. He certainly couldn't corner the Professor in daylight. It was going to have to be a night job. He had stalked his prey virtually unnoticed. He just needed a combination of circumstances to move in his goons who were always a whistle away.

Andrew was working earnestly these days. Term papers were due and the students were writing their first term exams. He wanted to go home as early as possible, but sometimes he just couldn't.

At times Mrs. Morrison kept Gracy up waiting for him if he wasn't too late. Andrew just melted from the tenderness he felt for his daughter. He'd walk in the door and she was ready to jump out of the Nanny's arms into his. Andrew had never experienced such love and being so wanted by anyone before in his life. Maybe this was how his mum loved him. How sad they were never taught to show their emotions. This child was like a miracle for him.

He complimented Mrs. Morrison, "What an excellent nanny you are."

Lora called often and kept in touch and had nothing but kind words to say. Of course she was genuinely concerned for the baby. Fabiana was faithfully there whenever she could, but she was spending many hours working on her finals.

Anthony in his worries, quite often woke up from nightmares. They were about Angelo. He should have taken serious action. He was always asking himself if there was any way he could bring this man to justice. He would call his nephews every now and then, mainly to check on their well-being.

***

It was a dark and dreary November night in London. The fog was rolling in. A misty chilling rain was slowly pouring down; it was an ugly cold night. Andrew had been attending a meeting. The president had summoned most of the instructors to the boardroom as a new curriculum for the following semester needed to be discussed. It was important for Andrew to be there. Afterwards, they were all going out for supper. Andrew reluctantly joined them and before he realized, it had gotten pretty late. He was watching his money carefully these days, since he needed to pay Mrs. Morrison and provide for Gracy's necessities. He would have preferred a taxi but at this hour it would be costly. He resorted to the subway and he would walk the rest of the way to his flat. He had left the main artery and walked swiftly as the dampness penetrated his bones. What a nasty night. Relieved to be nearly home, he picked up his speed. It must have been way past midnight. The window lights in the neighborhood were all out. The streetlights were dimmed by the fog. Good thing he was familiar with his territory.

Suddenly, four hoodlums surrounded him. He tried to remain calm. What could they want from him? No one spoke, they were wearing balaclavas that covered their faces.

One grabbed his briefcase with tremendous force and sent it twirling in the air. Andrew screamed, "What is this? What do you want from me?" Panic struck. Immediately his thoughts, *Angelo Frarano. This must be it.*

There was no response. He tried to find an opening. He was petrified. He was trapped. They started to bounce him back and forth between them. Suddenly, a strip of tape was tightly slapped over his mouth and eyes. Some strong arms held him in a back fold. Like lightning he felt a big blow to the back of his legs. He buckled and slumped over onto his knees. He fell on the wet cement powerless and in excruciating pain. They weren't finished with him. They started at his genitals kicking and torturing him until he completely passed out.

There, they left him like a wounded animal on the ground.

"There you go, buster," said Skinny. "I have waited long enough for you." Now he was pleased to have completed his assignment and anxious to collect his final fifteen thousand U.S. dollars, plus the extra ten.

He had given his helpers one hundred pounds each to help him rough up Andrew. They willingly participated, making his job much easier.

Afterwards they discarded their balaclavas, and proceeded to the local pub to resume their drinking. It had taken them twenty minutes. They joked among themselves on how they had actually enjoyed doing the job, as always it had been fun for them.

"Oh boy, that must have hurt," one of them chuckled.

"What did he really do anyway?" another asked.

"I heard he had an affair with a mobster's wife."

"Oh, I see."

"Now I understand why the squeezed balls and the tweezing of the penis."

"I will tell you he must have a pretty damaged prick..."

"I bet he will never be able to use that again."

"No, sir, the message there is to stay away from another man's wife."

"He will stay away for sure from now on. He will die in his pool of blood."

One character laughed so hard, he exposed his toothless gums.

Skinny had picked these bums at a local pub. They were drug addicts he knew from the streets and would do anything to support their habits.

Mrs. Morrison had received a phone call from Andrew earlier that evening that he might be late and not to wait up for him. She went to bed tired and did not worry about his absence.

Andrew remained there, passed out. At dawn, the street sweepers came around. The driver discovered Andrew lying in a pool of blood and immediately called for an ambulance. As people slowly gathered and stood over him, Andrew remained motionless and silent.

The paramedics arrived quickly. They felt his pulse, it was slow and faint. He had lost so much blood.

Then they noticed the tibias protruding from the front of his legs. The skin had been pierced. The fibula was also badly damaged and he was just a mess covered in dirt and blood. The first thing the paramedic tried to do was stop the bleeding. They slid him over on a stretcher and rushed him to the same hospital where Francesca had been taken. He arrived at the emergency completely unconscious. The interns and the nurses summoned Dr. Blue. He was the general surgeon on call and well skilled to repair his damaged legs.

Dr. Blue was shocked when he recognized him, "This poor guy must really have bad luck; first his partner gets run over, and now he is badly beaten?"

The nurse replied, "Yes, I remember the pregnant lady. We lost her. The baby we saved."

"This needs to be reported to the authorities, the hospital will deal with that later, and we have no time to be concerned with that right now."

Their number one concern was to stop the bleeding; once the bleeding was under control, his breathing would improve with his heart rate. Andrew's heartbeat was getting weaker. The nurse hooked him up to a monitor and supplied him with oxygen as Andrew began to moan. "He is in critical condition. We will lose him if we don't take him in the operating room. We need to do what we need to do, to save him," ordered Dr. Blue.

"The family needs to be notified, and the police," one of the nurses passed on the message to an assistant.

"Oh yes, I am sure there will be papers to be signed…"

The hospital emergency department made the necessary phone calls.

In no time the police arrived, questioning and trying to get some facts to write down a report. The doctor forbid them to see or talk to Andrew as he was in no condition to be interrogated. Mrs. Morrison hadn't realized that Andrew had not returned home at all the past night. When she received the call from the hospital she was shocked. It was five-thirty in the morning. She couldn't leave the baby.

Immediately she called Fabiana, trying hard to control her shaky voice, "Good morning, dearie, sorry to wake you up dear, there's been an accident. The Professor has been taken to emergency."

"*Oh no! No!* Don't tell me…"

"Yes, dear, they need a family member there. I can't leave the baby."

Fabiana immediately jumped out of her bed, "I will go immediately. Which hospital did they take him to?"

"To the Central East Hospital."

She looked at her watch; it was nearly six in the morning, Sicily time would be eight o'clock.

"How can I give my parents this other horrible news?"

She decided to go check things out first and then make the call. Silently, she prayed feverishly, "Please God, Jesus, spare the Professor. Don't let Gracy be left a complete orphan without a dad too."

Shaking more than ever and totally alone she was waiting again to talk to Dr. Blue. The nurses had informed her that the Professor was in surgery. Dr. Blue would talk to her once surgery was over.

After a long wait the gray doors opened and Dr. Blue finally came to talk to her. He was caring and sympathetic. Her eyes flashed back and forth scrutinizing his face. She did not detect the same look on him as when Francesca had been here... that ugly memory.

"We are waiting for his heart rate to stabilize; he might have suffered a coronary, or a minor stroke. We don't know yet. Without complications, I think he will recover. He has been badly beaten, both his legs are broken and he has some serious damage to his genitals. A nurse is monitoring him closely. The surgery on his legs went well, once we stopped the bleeding."

Dr. Blue put an arm around Fabiana's shoulder in comfort and continued, "You can be reassured, he seems to have a strong constitution, patience and endurance should pull him through. I am told the police are here and would like to ask you some questions."

At the mention of the police Fabiana panicked. Her body started to tremble; this was just too much for her. She needed her parents here. Two police constables came in to ask her some questions. A third officer, in civilian clothes, joined them shortly after. His name was Detective Constable Benjamin Tayler. He quickly produced his badge from his inside jacket pocket to validate himself.

"Can you tell us anything about what may have happened to the Professor?"

"What can I tell you? It's just awful," and she burst into tears.

"Sorry, Miss. I know this must be very upsetting for you." They tried to be gentle with her.

"There is nothing much I can tell you. Except that he was in a meeting at the university, joined some of the other Professors for dinner. He was going home later than usual and from what Mrs. Morrison told me he never made it home."

"Who do you know would want to harm him?"

Detective Benjamin was going according to the previous meeting with Anthony Taverna and the Professor himself.

"No, Detective, there's nothing I can tell you. Maybe the Professor can identify the attackers."

They would have to wait until the doctor allowed them to question the Professor, he had given strict orders for Andrew not to be disturbed. In the meantime they offered to help Fabiana. She wanted to call her parents right away. At this point she appreciated the police being beside her. She was scared and wondered if she was next in line.

The officer helped her to dial the numbers on the public phone. Her shaking hands had messed up three times in a row. The operator quickly offered to help. Finally a familiar voice at the other side gave her courage, "Mom, Mom." She couldn't control her tears.

"Fabiana, what's the matter? What's happened? Is it the baby?"

"No, Mom, where is Dad? Get Dad on the phone."

"He's here having his espresso, I'll pass him on."

"Yes *tesoro* – my treasure, what's up?"

"Dad, Daddy, you are not going to believe this. The Professor is at the emergency in critical condition. He was badly beaten last night on his way home. Dad, you and Mom must get here."

"Oh, my Lord. We'll catch the first flight out… where are you now?"

"At the hospital."

"Who is with you?"

"Detective Benjamin and two other officers."

"Put him on the phone," he said with urgency.

"Detective Benjamin, Anthony Taverna here, please stay with my daughter. I am catching the first flight there. See you soon." And he hung up the phone.

"Lora go get dressed, we're leaving for London. Andrew is in critical condition at the hospital, they got to him."

"Oh, Saint Rosalia." She made the sign of the cross and followed her husband's orders.

Later that afternoon they arrived at the hospital. Fabiana was somewhat encouraged with her parents by her side. Detective Benjamin was still with her.

"Sorry about the Professor, Mr. Taverna," Detective Benjamin greeted with a handshake.

"Anything… any clue, as to who might have done this to him?"

"Not yet, but we are investigating. I have some clever guys on the case. I am sure they will come up with something sooner or later."

Anthony and Lora's priority was to check on Andrew's condition. They proceeded to look for Dr. Blue. They anxiously waited for him to give them hope. The beads in Lora's hands were moving frantically along with her whispering lips.

Anthony's mind was far away. *That monster is relentless*, he thought. *He's hiding cleverly behind all this, who knows when he will stop.*

After they anxiously waited, Dr. Blue came out. He shook hands with them, and tried to reassure them the best he could. He explained, "He is heavily sedated to alleviate the pain, but he should come around soon. The surgery was lengthy, the repairs to his legs went well. As to the genitals, much more challenging. Let's keep our fingers crossed and hope for no complications. The stroke has been minor, the damage to the brain can recover itself, providing no other strokes occurs. A nurse is by his side on constant surveillance, he should be fine, let's give him some time."

When Dr. Blue noticed the rosary beads in Lora's hands he said, "Continue with what you're doing, he can use your prayers."

Anthony intervened, "Doctor, do you think we could see him?"

"No, not now, as I said the nurse is with him. Maybe tomorrow if things improve. I suggest you go home and get some rest."

Anthony's eyes were tired, but far from wanting to sleep. He had plenty on his mind. Lora wanted to check the baby. He sent

Lora and Fabiana to Andrew's house while he remained behind to talk to detective Benjamin and his assistants.

"I want to know exactly what happened to him," he questioned them.

The following day Anthony had a meeting with Detective Benjamin Tayler, but he couldn't relate much to him, other than what little he knew. There weren't any witnesses, no one had heard anything in the neighborhood, yet, he wasn't far from his home. They needed to question Andrew himself, but with his injuries being severe they hadn't been able to. They had to put off their questioning until the doctor gave them the green light.

Tayler said, "I can understand your frustration. Believe me, we would like to get our hands on these criminals."

"You know, if he's been hurt this badly it took more than one person."

"We suspect that, but we won't know until we question our victim."

"Officer, remember what I told you at our previous meeting?"

"Yes, yes, I understand. Again, we need evidence and witnesses."

"The proof is, a man was beaten and is now fighting for his life."

"Yes, but who did it? Proof, proof."

"Did you notify the police in New York, Francesca's husband?"

"Yes, we have checked that part. The guy is in the hospital, quite ill I am told. We can hardly pin a crime on him committed in London, can we? Both crimes as a matter of fact, he comes clean when it comes to murder charges. But, we are far from done."

Anthony felt there was going to be no help from these guys, he knew better. He needed to figure out what to do himself if Andrew survived. Guys like Angelo and his gang wouldn't give up until the job was complete. Besides Andrew, the baby would be in great danger.

The waiting period was agony. Finally after three days Dr. Blue allowed each of them to see Andrew for five minutes at a time.

Lora and Anthony questioned the doctor, he had given them hope, "I think he is turning around, his heartbeat is better. His injuries will take a long time to heal. He will need rehabilitation therapy for walking, and his genitals will be a slow recovery. Once his bladder functions on his own to urinate without the catheter he will be on his way. It will be slow progress, but healing takes time. He sure is a lucky man, I tell you."

The Taverna family was relieved. Lora wanted to concentrate on Gracy. She needed to be loved and nurtured so much and without parental affection it worried Lora. Mrs. Morrison was doing a great job with her and she was progressing well, but she couldn't help herself. She had been such a mother hen with her own children. She felt for Gracy. She went shopping with Fabiana for fresh outfits and they showered the baby with love. Mrs. Morrison felt they loved the baby from the heart. Gracy was lucky to have these people as members of her family.

A couple of weeks passed. Anthony in deep thoughts looked out the window from Fabiana's flat. The air was crisp and the sun was shining. Maybe today the doctor was going to give them good news and the police could finally talk to Andrew. Every morning they visited the hospital, but Andrew's progress had been slow and discouraging. Maybe, just maybe, this morning things were going to be more promising. They were there by ten o'clock. When they asked to talk to the doctor, he came to meet them with a smile on his face.

"I have good news. We can move the Professor out of intensive care and to a private room. Not that he is out of danger, but he is progressing well and you will be able to visit with him. He'll like that. No more than fifteen minutes. We cannot tire him out. He needs all the strength he can get."

As soon as the nurse said they could go in they immediately followed her to Andrew's bedside. This was the first time it really registered in his mind that Lora and Anthony were there. You could see the pupils in his eyes light up at seeing them.

Anthony smiled, "What is this? What are you doing here? Are you trying to scare us out of our wits?"

He smiled back, "Sorry, sorry, guys. I don't recall what happened."

"You don't. Maybe it's a good thing. How do you feel anyway?"

"I am not bad except my legs are heavy, and they've got me hooked up to all these tubes. I don't know what's really wrong with me."

"Keep it that way for now. You'll be fine. We only have a short time to visit. All is well at home; Gracy is fine, and Fabiana sends you her good wishes. We will be in London until you get better."

"Thanks, thanks, you are such fine folks, I'm so lucky."

Lora finally spoke, "Professor, hush, hush, you shouldn't talk too much."

"Yeah, we must go now. We'll see you later this afternoon."

They shook his hand and left. He had actually talked to them. Yes, things were promising. Anthony was so worried. But he couldn't tell everything he had on his mind to Lora.

Andrew was totally oblivious of what he was up against. He was too innocent and trusting. Detective Tayler had told Anthony that Andrew had gone home late that night. He had been warned of the danger. Why hadn't he taken a taxi? That had been foolish of Andrew to walk that time of night. I guess it didn't sink in. Or he didn't believe him or take him seriously. Furthermore, did he realize what would happen to his daughter if that gangster knew of her existence? Andrew preferred denial.

Andrew had been afraid since Francesca's death and after continuously reliving the nightmare, he forced himself to discard bad thoughts. It was hell to live in constant fear.

Anthony couldn't confide in Lora for the moment. He would have a meeting with Fabiana and the two of them would plot and plan. Who knew how long Andrew was going to take to be on his feet. *If that gangster knows that Andrew survived, he will not relent until he finishes him off. Oh God, please help him,* Anthony prayed.

Then there was Gracy. Anthony knew he couldn't hide her in Sicily. She needed to live a normal life. *How is she ever going to live a normal life when there is a price on her father's head and probably her own too. She is a beautiful baby for heaven's sake.* Anthony was distraught by his assessment of all of this. He thought, *Andrew has been so naive of our ways. He thinks all is heavenly and paradise. Although, he has aged since my sister died. Now this. We need to talk to the doctor and Benjamin Tayler. I know I am anxious, but knowing what I know, anyone's heart would be racing.*

Anthony and Fabiana encouraged Lora to spend time with Mrs. Morrison and the baby and they met after school. He shared his fears with her and they set out to speak to Detective Tayler after checking on Andrew's well-being.

And she agreed with him, "Dad, we need to do something. How can these horrible things happen and no one gets caught?"

"Because they are professional killers, without a trace."

Shortly after, at the constabulary, they met with Detective Tayler. He promised to listen to any suggestions they might have.

Anthony asked, "Detective, from what has happened to my friend, I'm seriously worried. I think he's still in danger, and furthermore, he has a baby girl and whoever is after him will want to get to his little girl also."

"What makes you say that? You are just getting carried away with your imagination. Andrew was walking home very late at night, and whatever happened to him, it could very well be unrelated."

Raising his voice, "Listen, Mr. Tayler, listen to me." Anthony was getting angry and frustrated.

"Dad, calm down," Fabiana pleaded.

"I know what I am talking about, those hoodlums that attacked him were hired!"

"Listen, Mr. Taverna, we are not overlooking anything. We go on proof and facts. You are assuming and going on a hunch.

That character that confided in you needs to come forward. Mr. Taverna, do you know how many stories like that we hear that amount to nothing?"

Anthony got up to leave, "This is no use; we're wasting time here."

"Mr. Taverna, where the Professor was walking is a bad area and drug addicts will do anything for a fix; he was at the wrong place at the wrong time. They took his wallet."

In the meantime the detective knew deep inside him Mr. Taverna was right. Unfortunately, however, this is what they faced in their line of work. They suspected and they knew better, but this was the snag of the law.

"Tell me, any lead on my sister's killers?"

"The case is under heavy investigation, and we are checking every lead. We will keep you informed."

They left without answers. Anthony was more convinced that they had to protect Andrew.

"Fabiana, the main thing now is to get him well again and then we need to come up with a solution."

"You're so right, Dad, I will help you as much as I can. You can count on me for whatever…"

"Okay, we need to consult a lawyer. Get that letter of intent in the diary. It needs to be brought to him and checked out. How that will be kept a secret from Angelo Frarano is beyond my knowledge. Once he gets wind of it, all hell will break loose. Andrew has no chance whatsoever. Once Gracy surfaces on Angelo's radar I hate to think of what's next.

Chapter Twenty-Five

In the meantime, Andrew tried to move his legs and the pain shot right through his stomach. His groin felt mutilated. The anesthetic was slowly wearing off. If the nurse did not give him a painkiller or a needle he was ready to scream. He had been surviving comfortably on morphine or fentanyl injected intravenously. Now it had been removed. He had never been one to tolerate pain easily.

He relentlessly kept buzzing the nurses, they promptly attended to him.

A young nurse in her thirties was assigned to him on the morning shift. She did not seem sympathetic, "Mr. Robertson, the doctor has only ordered three of this medication. I will ask if I can increase the dose. Your body needs to heal on its own, to feel a little pain is a good sign of healing."

Andrew had always been a passive, patient man; however, in pain, his patience was short. He yelled at the nurse. "Look, I don't care what the doctor says, just get me out of this misery. I cannot tolerate this pain, do you understand?"

"I am just following orders, Professor. I will have to speak to Dr. Blue."

When the Tavernas went to visit him Andrew was in a miserable mood. Anthony wanted to talk to the doctor and find out the facts of his recovery. After talking to the doctor, he was assured that Andrew was out of danger.

"The recovery is going to take a long time and there is going to be a lot of pain involved. The rehabilitation will be tough. It will be hard work. Everyone recovers differently, it depends on how much he's willing to put into it."

"Doctor, as you know he has a daughter that needs him. He has to get well."

"He's lucky to be alive. The way he arrived at the emergency, believe me, I didn't think he was going to come around. He is a fighter all right. Keep encouraging him. It's a good idea to let him see the baby… that will help him."

"Thanks, Doctor, will do."

Mrs. Morrison brought Gracy to visit and on seeing her father, she jumped up and down reaching for him. She had missed her daddy. Seeing her, his paternal love emerged and warmed his heart.

With Gracy snuggling him with her messy kisses he wasn't worried about her hurting him. She brought him so much joy.

He turned to Lora, Anthony, Fabiana, and Mrs. Morrison all present there. "Look what a great gift Francesca has given me. I have to get better for her sake."

"You sure have to, Andrew, she needs you." They all agreed encouraging him.

It seemed to take forever for Andrew to get better. He was making good progress as time passed. Four months had passed. Now Andrew was sent home, he had lot of rehabilitation ahead of him. He needed to go to therapy three times a week. He was happy being at home, that gave him more time with Gracy. She was crying after him when he left the house for therapy and she would be jumping for joy when he returned. The bond between them was immeasurable. He had taken a year off teaching and was surviving on disability payments. He managed to do some editing to supplement his income and modestly provide for his daughter.

Anthony and Lora had returned to Sicily. Their concern never ceased. Anthony was confiding with Fabiana via phone. They needed to help Andrew with his daughter, before Angelo found out about Gracy. Anthony feared everyday that another mishap or bad news would surface. He had the letter his sister had left. The trouble was how could they pass the money and the inheritance to Andrew? "We know they need the money," he had told Fabiana.

"Dad, I'm with you, all the way."

"We need to talk to the authorities once more."

"What else do you suggest, Dad?"

"I seriously think Andrew and Gracy need to go in hiding. Get out of London. He needs to change his identity, both him and Gracy if he wants to survive and raise his daughter. They need to get lost somewhere in the universe, live incognito."

"Yes, Dad, I agree. It's not over. I know and you know that the danger for the Professor is far from over."

"I need to talk to Andrew, I have been putting it off, and I don't want to scare him. I know he is working hard to get better, but I can't sleep at night. I'm so worried about their safety."

"Dad, I think you better warn Andrew. He should be the one to decide where he would like to go."

"He doesn't realize that he is living on borrowed time. Once you tell him, he can help us in deciding."

Anthony was terrified just thinking about those hoodlums. He asked himself if he should make another trip to London and talk seriously with Andrew and look him straight in his eyes. He wasn't kidding. It was time to act and move on, if Andrew wanted to.

***

After being in the hospital Angelo Frarano returned to his luxurious penthouse apartment. While he had been in the hospital, he had gotten on sweet with one of the nurses. In no time she had moved in with him, to play nurse of course… Angelo as usual had no trouble with women. He impressed her with his gifts and fancy dinners. His motto was, "money conquers all."

Helen was young, tall and blonde. Angelo was impressed with his new conquest. Now he was back behaving like a young boy with a new toy. She was from England. She had emigrated to the U.S. a couple of years since and she purposely sought out an older wealthy man like him to show her a good time and it came in handy.

Helen didn't have any family in New York and it felt comfortable to have someone to rely on. Besides, Angelo was a charming and attentive companion with his girlfriends. He was much older than her, but it didn't bother her. She had noticed this woman's picture by his night table and saw a big portrait of her in the hallway before the entrance to the library. It hung majestically erected above a console with three red candles below. They were lit up electrically day and night. She wondered about the lady in the picture, but didn't ask questions. The candles gave her the creeps though. He had told her he was widowed. She assumed this lady must have been his wife. She noticed Angelo made the sign of the cross every morning and night when he passed by her. He had never mentioned anything about the beautiful lady with long black hair and a perfect face. She had left it at that. After all, who was she to pry into his past.

Gestiniano was glad that his boss had found a new interest. He seemed happier and wasn't pestering him as much lately. He had paid Scarface the last installment. Vladimiro had shown him the Englishman's picture shriveled up motionless on the street. For now Angelo hadn't been asking questions and Gestiniano liked it that way. Gestiniano wondered if he was manic or schizophrenic. This was his behavior, sweet as honey at one time and totally unpredictable, and without mercy another. God help him. Maybe this nurse will be good for him.

He was so deeply involved now with Angelo and his affairs; with no way out. The court cases they were involved in, ordering the assignations, putting up with his shouting and demands made him feel so worthless. *My lips have to be sealed. I have no choice. I better take it for what it's worth and enjoy the good provisions that come along with it.*

In Palermo, Anthony had consulted his lawyer Gennaro Scarpone. He was a man of good humor and most of all held a reputation of fairness.

"I have a real dilemma on my hands, Gennaro." He spent the next half-hour, starting at the beginning and explained the whole situation. Then, he handed him his sister's letter of intent and the revoking of her last will. He gave him a moment to read it and said, "How on earth are we going to handle this? She excluded her husband out of the inheritance and the funds need to be passed on to people that he thinks are dead or he doesn't even know exist."

"Nothing is easy in life, there are always crossroads to overcome. This is why we are here. We need to go through all the legalities of family law."

"Fine, I understand, how long will it take to clear the red tape? The funds are badly needed here for survival."

"Anthony, you do realize this is going to trigger a turf war, if not worse?"

"I know, I know. It's been hell already. My sister has paid with her life. Now we must save her daughter and she needs her father. How are we going to keep him alive with his daughter?"

"Well, I'm not sure how long this will take. I wouldn't wait for this paperwork to be sorted out. Anthony, seriously, you are a man of means. I suggest you get the money out of your own bank account and get these two poor souls to safety. Don't waste any time, if you really care for them."

"Gennaro, I haven't had any peace since my sister died. Of course I want to help anyway I can. How am I going to do it? I can't bring them here. He is a very sick man right now, he needs to be in London where his home is and his daughter belongs with him."

Anthony's blood pressure was rising, he could feel it. He was so angry. If he could only get his hands on that heartless Angelo Frarano. He had caused his family enough grief. *Someone needs to stop him.*

"Anthony, they need police protection, father and daughter. They need to assume a new identity and find refuge somewhere else on the globe, sheltered from harm, where they can't be found."

"Gennaro, don't tell me about police protection, what good did it do? We went to the London police. I related to them everything I knew. Again, no witness, no proof. They can't act on hunches, you know that. Look, my sister got murdered and to date no one has been arrested, even with offering a reward."

"You're right, sometimes the law is a pain in the ass and dealing with guys like Angelo is no joke."

Anthony left, not feeling a whole lot better, but if nothing else, Gennaro had confirmed the urgency to get Andrew and Gracy into hiding and he did not know how Andrew was going to take that. The more he thought about it the more complicated it seemed. His sleepless nights were exhausting. The best thing he could do was to get himself back to London and talk to Andrew. He needed to convince him to leave his nest and move to some foreign country. Also, he needed to have another meeting with Detective Benjamin Tayler. Together they could stress the great danger he and his daughter were in.

The next day Anthony was in London at Andrew's apartment. Andrew was so happy to see him and embraced him like a long lost brother. Anthony was moved by his spontaneous affection and wanted to do even more to help him.

Mrs. Morrison walked in with Gracy in her arms. "Gracy, Gracy, look who is here, Uncle Anthony!" She knew her family well by now and she bounced with joy every time they showed up.

Anthony never came empty handed. He had picked up a toy at the airport for her and brought along a little outfit Lora had sent. Mrs. Morrison, in good manners, excused herself, and took Gracy out for a walk

"Tell me, Andrew, it's now nine months since the incident, how are you feeling these days? Are you making good progress in reclaiming your legs?"

"Anthony, I'm quite pleased, slow procedure, but I'm coming along, I can't complain. Never you mind about me, tell me, what brings you back to London? I must say, I was surprised to hear you were coming."

"It's always such a joy to see Gracy and Fabiana of course, and you. But, I'll be honest with you, Andrew, I'm here because I am concerned about your safety. Gracy's too of course."

"Anthony, what can I do? I live one day at a time. I am trying hard. I should have never walked home that late at night. You know they stole my wallet, who knows . . . those goons did they really need a fix? Was I at the wrong place at the wrong time? It's hard to swallow, I have my doubts. I would rather not think about it, otherwise I will make myself sicker."

"Look, Andrew, that is hogwash. Wrong place at the wrong time. Let's stop the nonsense. I happen to know more than you do, believe me. You are in danger; that monster I know, will not relent, once he knows you are alive, and with your daughter."

"Anthony, my dear friend, I know you care. I don't want you getting carried away with your bad thoughts now. Let's think positive before we drive ourselves insane."

Anthony grabbed him by the shoulders and turned him to face him.

"Look at me in the eyes. This is no joke. Would I come all the way here if I wasn't worried sick about the two of you? Andrew, I consulted my lawyer, the most brilliant in Palermo. Do you know what he said? Don't waste any time."

"Anthony, you are trying to instill more fear in me? Please, is it that urgent? There isn't much I can do in my condition."

"I will tell you what you need to do. My lawyer suggested you need to get a new identity and get relocated somewhere where no one can find the two of you."

"Oh! How is this supposed to occur? How will I manage financially? And looking after a child alone? We need Mrs. Morrison. Gracy loves Fabiana's visits and her babysitting. It would be doing a great injustice uprooting her. Plus, right now I'm struggling to get better. My job at the university, how do I handle that?"

"Andrew, I know exactly what you are saying and where you are at. But it's absolutely necessary that you make plans. Here is the deal. As you know, my sister has left plenty of cash money for you to take care of Gracy plus when she becomes of age, she inherits the land in Agrigento. This needs to go through the procedure of the legalities of the court with probate. My sister was married, I don't think her husband can be completely excluded. Once this comes out in the open, excuse my language, the shit will hit the fan."

Andrew listened, but couldn't believe someone could be so evil. Therefore, he wasn't convinced. He adamantly continued to refuse Anthony's suggestion.

"It will take a long time for the paperwork to be completed. You have a lot of arrangements to deal with. Let's go talk to detective Benjamin Tayler again. They must have helped someone before in a similar situation like yours. They're aware of the wrath of the mob."

Well they did and Detective Benjamin agreed with Mr. Taverna. "Now that I know the circumstances, if I was in your situation, I would seek refuge under a new identity as soon as possible."

Now Andrew's fear returned. Were these goons still going to come after him? Was Francesca's husband that revengeful to commit murder? He had to admit, too much bloodshed had taken place in the last while. Maybe he should do just what they suggested for Gracy's sake. He would never forgive himself should anything happen to Gracy. She had become his reason for living. He loved her to death.

He spent the night awake tossing and turning. It was almost dawn and his tired eyes had just dosed off when Gracy's shrill cry reached him. He jumped out of bed, trying hard to wobble to her bedroom with pain shooting down his legs. He got there breathless and petrified with fear before Mrs. Morrison returned from the kitchen with the bottle of milk in her hand. "Mr. Robertson, you could have hurt yourself running here without crutches. You know I would get to her."

Andrew shook his head. He didn't want to reveal to the nanny of his frantic panic on hearing Gracy's cry. The days and nights had now become a nightmare. If Anthony was convinced enough he was probably right. It was beyond his imagination what these criminals were capable of. He couldn't put his finger on any of the four hoodlums that appeared out of nowhere. As he relived the incident, which became clearer in his brain, the fear sent shivers down his spine. He started to contemplate – where would they go? To his shocking surprise, he pulled out Francesca's rosary from the drawer of his night table and started to pray just like he had seen Francesca do. He focused with his heart and soul, "Oh, my Jesus. I put my little girl in your protective hands. Please spare her from any harm. Give me direction with your guiding light, help me to make the right decision. Amen."

He was surprised how the recital of his Holy Mary's and Our Father's had quickly returned to his memory in an easy flow. He hadn't done this for decades. But now, in his desperation he felt the need. He fell into a deep sleep and he had a dream. There was this guesthouse in the middle of a large piece of land. One had to drive through a hilly forest with a narrow path that barely had room for a car. The foliage was lush. The scent of eucalyptus hit the nostrils pleasantly. The drive seemed endless. Then finally, he came up to a big open flat piece of land. A two-storey home was set off the side of the road. There were animals scattered all around, from chickens to pigs, big and small. The ponies, were nibbling away at some hay. There weren't any people in sight. From a distance he could see a white stucco, one floor building. The sun was shining and the surroundings looked placid and isolated. The horizon was circular and the world seemed to be in completion right there. This place gave an aura of peace.

He woke up, realizing it was just a dream, but it had felt so real. The vision was so vivid in his recollection. That morning he picked up the world globe from his bookshelf. After twirling it around few times, his attention seemed to be concentrating on the Southern Hemisphere. *How much further than that can we get?* Its interest got the best of him, and he seriously started to consider Australia as his salvation and hideout. He knew there was a lot of paperwork and red tape to go through, especially with a change of identity and a baby. It was going to be a challenge. But he had no choice. He knew he could count on Anthony's help and he also needed the authorities. Detective Tayler had been sympathetic and had been checking on him from time to time.

Anthony was glad that Andrew had finally come to his senses. The two of them were convinced to hire a private agent for protection. He would see that they got to their destination safely. Since he had never lived outside of London, many times he was overcome with debilitating emotions that got the best of him. Somehow he got the strength to overcome them and move on with his plans. It took a lot of paperwork and red tape. Mr. Tayler was great help. After an extensive search, they had found a place on a farm way out in the country, in Jellico, Australia. Now the difficult part was the emotional goodbyes. Lora had come to London to help and she did not spare her tears. Mrs. Morrison was apprised of the seriousness of the situation, yet she still agreed to go along for six months. Fabiana was heartbroken for the separation. As much as she knew it had to happen, she would miss them.

Finally, departure day arrived. A Mr. David Nelson, being pushed in a wheelchair by his private bodyguard Michael Struck, took charge of them all. They were traveling with Mr. Nelson's nanny and child. They all boarded a British Airways aircraft, via Los Angeles and connected with Quantas Airlines for Melbourne. After a long flight they finally landed.

Michael was in full charge. They had rented a van and drove for miles to reach their unknown new home. They were curiously taking in their surroundings as they were driving along the endless country roads. Finally, after climbing a steep hill they emerged on this big extension of flat clear land. There it stood. A white two-story home with domestic animals grazing around. It was a sight to see.

Melbourne, Australia

Andrew (now David) said, "This is unbelievable, I saw this place in my dream! It's the same place. Oh, my Lord, I have been led here!"

It was the weekend, they had arrived on a Sunday morning. The front door opened wide and a tall slim man with blue jeans, a plaid shirt, a cowboy hat and a big smile on his face was coming toward them. A lady they assumed to be his wife and five children walked down the driveway to greet them. After the introductions, Farmer John pointed out the guesthouse a little distance away.

"That is our guesthouse where you will be staying, folks."

"I see, a peaceful place you have here," commented David.

The clan followed and in kindness they offered to help with their baggage. Andrew felt a bit reassured. These folks showed warmth and friendliness.

The stretched out stucco building consisted of one floor. As they stepped in, a roomy long open concept living area was light and inviting. The fireplace was centrally placed and already with a crackling wood burning fire going. Farmer John, his wife Liz and their five children showed them around proudly. The place was rustic. It had wood planks on the ceiling, fieldstone on the floor and one large bedroom was nicely arranged with the crib and a bed for their nanny. Liz went on to show them how to use the electric blankets. She explained, "It's winter here now, and it gets quite cold, especially at night."

"The second bedroom is for you, Mr. Nelson," said John.

"Oh, please," Andrew corrected, "call me David."

"For your friend here," referring to the bodyguard, "there is a pull-out sofa in the main room, since I was told it's temporary. He will be comfy as well."

"Thank you, it is mighty kind of you."

"The agent informed us that you will be staying indefinitely with your little girl, your assistant only a few days, and the nanny six months, correct?"

"Yes, John, as I wrote to you, I am a widower, recuperating from an accident, still with some rehab work to consider."

"I am sure we'll be able to guide you in any way. Should you need our assistance or anything, please ask and we will be happy to oblige."

"Thanks, John, you might find me at your door for guidance."

John and Liz, gathered their children, already enamored of Gracy. "Come on… these folks are tired. We must leave them to rest."

He was right. They were all tired from the long flight and drive. Shortly after, they all flopped on their new beds, collapsing from their lost sleep.

Suddenly a strong shrill cry came from Gracy's room. David, wobbling on his feet, Mrs. Morrison, and the bodyguard Michael jumped out of bed and ran immediately to her side. She was crying uncontrollably and scratching her head with both hands.

David picked her up, his heart was in his throat, worried sick, "What is wrong now, lovey? Tell your daddy." But she continued her cries ignoring the three adults.

Mrs. Morrison took over to check her out. She noticed her little fingers going at her head. She took a look, and could not believe what she was seeing.

Her hair was infested with lice. She must have gotten them on the long trip along the way. The men didn't know what to do. Mrs. Morrison managed to calm her down, rubbing her head gently, and singing to her.

"We must find a drugstore first thing in the morning. There is a special shampoo, very effective with the first treatment plus, I will get a tight comb to remove any dead lice." Through her past experiences, Mrs. Morrison had seen it all.

She reassured David, "You folks go back to bed. I will deal with this." Slowly Gracy's sobs turned to a gentle snore. This was their first night in no man's land.

They were awakened on this first morning by the loud chirping of the birds. David had never been in Australia before, and found it to be like no other place he had ever visited.

"That kookaburra bird is relentless. I guess we don't need an alarm clock here that's for sure," said Michael.

"I'll say," agreed David.

Gracy, to their surprise, was still sound asleep. Mrs. Morrison was up and about, busying herself. David was so concerned about his daughter with the lice infestation. He stood over her crib, admiring her as she slept like an angel.

"Oh, lovey, this is all for you, my darling. We must find salvation in this new land," he whispered to her.

Chapter Twenty-Six

· ·

The journey of their new life had begun. The farm was an isolated place, free from the hustle and bustle in London. Liz and Farmer John had shown them how to get to a small town down below. It was within easy reach; driving down the hilly lush road.

As they adventured in finding their bearings, they checked the food stores and the coffee shops. They were loving the food and everything else about this place. David liked it here, he was healing and feeling better. Farmer John and Liz were such helpful folks and furthermore, their five children, (three girls and two boys, from twelve years of age to three years old) were taken with Gracy, and she with them. They often popped over to play with her.

Michael, the bodyguard, announced it was time for him to leave. They days had fast rolled by.

David agreed since he felt safe at the farm in hiding. Michael left after he had made sure David and his daughter were settled in and well accepted in this new place, and feeling there was nothing suspicious. He felt David was now safe.

David knew in his soul he had made the right decision. Anthony was right. He missed them so. They all adjusted well in their new surroundings including Mrs. Morrison, but their arrangement was for six months. She was a widow and her children needed her occasionally. Plus, she wanted to spend the holidays with them; thus, David needed to make new arrangements.

Michael promised to phone from time to time and should David feel suspicious about any threat, he was to call him. A colleague of his in Melbourne would cover for him if need be. David now felt confident, being so far away and in this remote place. He didn't feel threatened. His legs were getting better and slowly he was regaining his strength. He wondered if he would be able to manage on his own, without a nanny. He decided he would take care of Gracy. He knew it would be hard at first, but he was willing to try. After all, he was living on borrowed money from Anthony. His flat was for sale and he knew there was money coming in eventually.

***

Gracy

In no time six months passed and it was time for Mrs. Morrison to return to London.

"We are going to miss you immensely, Mrs. Morrison. It will be hard without you here … a new adjustment indeed."

"Professor, it won't be easy for me either. I will miss Gracy especially, and you have been such a fine chap to work for, I must say."

Mrs. Morrison tried hard to control her emotions, this was the hard part of being a nanny. One got attached – to the little ones especially. It was always hard to leave. Without looking back she made up her mind to shed no tears and keep her head up high.

David and Gracy drove her to Melbourne Airport and said their goodbyes to Mrs. Morrison, watching her until she disappeared. Here they were now, just the two of them. The days that followed were difficult for Gracy and her daddy. She didn't want to eat what he cooked and was throwing temper tantrums. David didn't know what to do. Thanks to Liz, she made sure Gracy was among her children. They kept her distracted and occupied. When she was home with her daddy, he was being challenged by this little precious girl, who he adored.

***

Time passed quickly while the tranquility of the place grew on David. His new name started to feel familiar. Gracy was growing in leaps and bounds, she was now three years old. She was getting around this safe place with no worries, and the children from the main house had become her best friends. All the animals around the farm were her main attraction. She often chased the chickens around. Liz and John encouraged her to have fun with their children. David had started to take nature walks, by descending down the hill on foot holding Gracy's hand. Should she get tired he would gently carry her on his back.

They turned their walks into a discovery game. With a bag of chocolates in his knapsack he would call out, "Whoever discovers a koala, or a cuckoo bird, or an animal living in the woods, first, gets a treat. Okay, here we go."

She would get all excited. The variety of trees was mind-boggling. Flocks of birds flying around with their exquisitely colored feathers. Their singing was music. David had tracked his path, by tying a red ribbon on the trunk of some trees along the way, so as to retrace his footsteps going back. They would not be lost in the darkness of the trees and foliage. He preferred to do their excursion first thing in the morning.

Since his attack, he had become paranoid of the night. He feared the dark, yet he refused the thought of having to look over his shoulder for the rest of his life. He was healing. Through Michael he kept in touch with the Taverna family, in a very discreet manner. His mail went through Farmer John. He loved when a fat beige envelope arrived with updates from all of them.

From the walk in the morning and the errands to run, by the time evening rolled around at night he was tired. Being a single dad, with all the housekeeping duties, left him exhausted. After all his legs were still weak, and often he needed to sit with a cup of tea to catch his breath. He was starting to teach Gracy the alphabet and reading. They were making it a teaching period at her level just for her. David had created a special curriculum, to read and write, and his efforts were rewarding. She proved to be a super intelligent little girl. Of course, at her tender age, her brain and her eyes absorbed like a sponge, and she had the best teacher of all.

David's routine was to relax in front of the fireplace on his comfortable chair every night with one of his favorite books, after he had settled Gracy into bed. One particular evening, his eyelids were drooping into sleep when Gracy's calls alerted him, "Daddy, Daddy, come and see. Something is happening to me."

Immediately David jumped up, wide awake he ran beside her bed.

"What is it? Let daddy take a look."

She was red and blotchy, first her face and then her tummy, and the rash was moving on.

"Oh, Daddy, it is so itchy, I feel awful."

"No, no dear, leave it alone, let me see what I can do to make you more comfortable."

She was sweaty and feverish; uncontrollably agitated. He saw her skin covered with a rash, multiplying all over her body. He was alarmed. He had educated himself in reading books on children's development and diseases. This was to be expected. She was diagnosed with the measles the next morning by the local doctor. David patiently followed procedures and they survived that episode. Then came the mumps, he handled them too, efficiently one by one. David was getting to be a pro at nurturing and playing a double role. As always thanks to Liz, as she was only few steps away, ready and willing to help.

***

Years later, when, the computer era hit the globe David had acquired a new computer and became connected to the Internet. It was much easier for David to write and communicate. He created a website and acquired a good editing clientele. This allowed him to earn extra money, which provided for their needs. It made him feel more worthy of himself since he had not been teaching.

Chapter Twenty-Seven

New York: Angelo had been notified of his wife's newfound will. Once he had found out the baby had survived, he was infuriated. Plus, the thought of her lover just triggered his anger all over again. *He is actually alive somewhere with his offspring. The imbecile that has ruined my honor and made a fool of me.* Immediately he summoned Gestiniano.

"What kind of a loused up job did those guys do? Tell me! Is this what we paid money for? Read this letter by my wife's lawyer."

"Boss, I was told they were done in. You went to your wife's funeral. As for him, they told me they followed your exact procedures and left him dead on the ground."

"Well, he is sure alive somewhere and with his daughter, inheriting my boy's money. You better get in touch with this Scarface you hired and order him to finish his job. You hear me?" He was screaming like an uncontrollable madman.

Gestiniano got out of there and dialed Vladimiro's number, no response.

He was now worried, *"Where am I going to find this devil? God knows where on Earth he could be,"* he mumbled to himself.

He dialed three different numbers. Finally, he got an answer. "Hello."

"Scarface, it's me Gestiniano Ambruzio."

"Yeah, what can I do for you?"

"You have put me in a hell of a situation here."

"What do you mean?"

"You know that professor in London and the pregnant woman?"

"Yeah, yeah, they're history."

"History! Not likely. Apparently the professor and his daughter are very much alive."

"You're kidding me."

"No, I'm not, my boss is threatening me. You better get on your tail and finish the job, like you were supposed to."

"You must be joking."

"I am dead serious, you better complete your job or there will be a lot of trouble. We paid you four hundred thousand dollars."

"Don't get smart with me. We risked our lives, while you and your boss sat in your fancy offices. It was beyond our control if the doctors intervened with the birth."

"What about him?"

"When was the last time you roughed up somebody? Timewise it was lengthy and difficult. The money you paid me, it didn't cover the weeks spent in vigil. We did a job on him. I tell you."

"He is not planted, we wanted him planted. Planted, meaning six feet under!"

"Oh! We will find him for you. And as you request we will plant him. Are you willing to cough up another five hundred thousand?"

"Vladimiro, you can't be serious? We have paid you for an unfinished job!"

"Let's end this conversation, all right, simple as that, no more money, no deal."

The line went dead. Gestiniano didn't know how on earth he was going to inform Angelo that Scarface was looking for another half a million dollars. Angelo had become so difficult again. Nurse Helen was still living with him, yet even she wasn't able to pacify him when he went into his rages. Sometimes she took Gestiniano into her confidence and told him she wanted to leave him. As always, he talked her out of it.

Angelo was capable of being human and kind when things went his way, and his gift giving was addictive. Helen had gotten into the habit of slipping a sleeping pill into his drink when he got to be too much for her. Before he knew it, he was fast asleep.

Sometimes, Helen hated to engage in their lovemaking. His libido had started to fail and that bothered him. His pride seemed to escalate when he got a prescription to help him out in that department. Helen knew he was a fool, should stay away from that stuff. He was stubborn and proud of himself. She decided to leave him alone and let him indulge on what seemed to bring his spirits up.

Angelo continued questioning Gestiniano about Scarface.

"Boss, if you insist on knowing, he gave me some good explanations. He also said, to pursue the matter further, we need to pay more money."

"More money! Is he crazy? How much?"

"Half a million."

"No. He didn't fulfill his contract. You insist, that's strictly my order. He better complete his job or he will end up in his place."

"I will give him another call."

Gestiniano did not appreciate being pressured to deal further with these two dangerous characters. If only there was a way out for him. This wasn't what he had wished to do with his life. Giving orders to kill people; this was insane.

He knew Angelo wouldn't relent, so here he placed another phone call to Vladimiro.

"Hello."

"It's me again. Look, Vladimiro, this is serious. My boss insists that you fulfill your contract. You have been paid, and didn't deliver what you were paid for. I'm warning you. I wouldn't fool around with him."

"You asshole. You listen to me. Tell your boss one more phone call from you with such a suggestion and I'll blow both your brains out."

"Now, now, let's not talk so strong."

"Does your boss realize who he's dealing with here?"

"Fine, I'll pass on the message."

Gestiniano was tired of this charade.

He placed a call to Joe Malcom their lawyer.

"Hello, Malcom and Cohen," answered the receptionist.

"Gestiniano Ambruzio here, I would like to speak to Joe Malcom."

"I will connect you, one moment please."

Relieved, Gestiniano took a deep breath.

"Joe Malcom here."

"Joe, it's me. I need to see you, can you spare me fifteen minutes?"

He looked at the clock on the wall, "I have a client coming in soon. It shouldn't take longer than an hour. See you after that."

"Thank you, I will be there."

He needed to talk to someone before he lost his mind.

Malcom was waiting for him and he was grateful for receiving him.

"Let's move to the boardroom. It will be more private, these walls sometimes aren't soundproof."

"Good, thanks, Joe."

"I detected urgency in your voice, what's troubling you now?"

He let out a sigh and shook his head.

"Let me guess, you have an additional lawsuit?"

"Joe, it is much more serious than that."

He went on to confess what Angelo Frarano had ordered him to do, plus the threat of Vladimiro. He spilled the beans and of course he was well aware, he was an accomplice. He could talk freely to Joe as he knew the protection of client confidentiality.

"Oh, my Lord. This is insane. The lawsuits are nothing in comparison. "

"Joe, I am tormented day and night. I try to keep busy. I avoid Angelo at all costs. I wish the ground would open and I would fall in a hole and hide from this cruel world."

Joe got up and put an arm around him, he didn't wish to be in his shoes.

"What do you want to do, Gestiniano? Should we go to the authorities?"

"I don't know, I just want out of this hell. I don't want to see Angelo Frarano anymore. I don't want to take his orders, deal with his dirty work. I'm tired. I just want out. Help me."

"Gestiniano. It's not easy. You know that. You're a shareholder, which makes you responsible for the lawsuits. To top that, you'll end up in jail for the murders and attempted murder. You are an accomplice. Furthermore, Angelo's associates are not sympathetic. I don't need to tell you your fate."

Gestiniano knew only too well what he was up against.

"You think about it. Should you decide to go to the police, I will contact one of my colleagues from another firm in criminal law to accompany you."

Gestiniano felt a little relief, but he was aware of what he faced. No sooner had he reached his office and Angelo was calling him, but he let the phone ring until it went silent. *I can't handle him right now. Between Vladimiro's threats and Angelo's demands... I have had enough for today.*

Christmas holidays were coming up. Angelo's sons, Diego and Daniele were visiting. Since their mother died they didn't care to go to Sicily to celebrate. Their place now was New York with their father.

Of course they had no idea that he had robbed them of their mother.

Angelo was cheerful these days. Diego was articling for a big law firm in Boston and he would soon graduate. Daniele was an honor student and doing well in his field. He was so proud of his boys. They had to be high achievers, because he wouldn't have it any other way.

The boys were glad he had Helen. They noticed he had aged since their mom died. His health had been failing and they thought that by having a nurse around that was perfect for him. They informed their dad that they needed to return to Boston for New Year's Eve.

"Dad, I hope you don't mind. We have dates and we promised to get back."

Chuckling happily he turned to Helen and winked at her, "That's my boys! Guys, don't break too many hearts."

"Dad, you must meet these girls, you'll like them. The two girls are cousins, their families are of Sicilian origin."

"Oh, I see. You go for your own kind."

"Dad, they are both law students, we are just good friends."

"No problem, as long as you're in good company. Should you get drunk always make sure you get drunk on good wine not on vinegar. You know what I mean boys, eh?"

After the boys left, he got a little depressed. Every time he called Gestiniano he was always too busy to talk to him. He was getting restless. He had told Helen to abandon her work at the hospital, but she insisted on taking shifts and refused to listen to him.

"They need me there. It's my job. I love my work."

Tonight he didn't feel like staying home alone. He decided to go check one of his hotels. He walked into the restaurant and sat at the bar just like he used to. He ordered scotch and water. The bartender was happy to see him and the staff greeted him respectfully. He felt good about himself and powerful, like old times. One of the dancers wearing pink bunny ears came over to him, her boobs were bursting out of her cleavage and one of her legs was rubbing against his groin. That was all he needed to turn his sexual appetite on. He put his arm around her and grabbed her closer to him.

He whispered in her ear, "Let's go to a room upstairs."

She whispered back, "The pleasure is mine, let's go."

Angelo wanted to feel like a twenty-five year old again. He was going to be ready to perform. The miracle pills in his pocket would do the trick. Helen had provided them for him on his insistence.

He led the bunny girl to the best bedroom at the hotel. The night was theirs he told her. They showered together, rolled themselves in fluffy robes with Aloe Vera pile, and wallowed in the soothing scent.

Angelo was having the time of his life and she was an expert in her field. He welcomed her teasing and they playfully made their way onto the bed. The girl obliged his demands bringing him in ecstasy many times. Angelo was proud of himself giving away all he had to prove his masculinity. The girl suddenly felt a strange jolt. His body slumped over her motionless. She stood there breathless for few minutes, thinking he had finally stopped. He must have had enough.

No, something wasn't right. She tried to remove his heavy body from on top of her. His eyes were wide open and his mouth was smeared in white foam. "Don't tell me, he's had a heart attack!" She dialed 911 and hurried to get dressed.

Within ten minutes the paramedics arrived. They detected no pulse, and all efforts on site to revive him were fruitless. They rushed him to the hospital, where Helen was still on duty. He was pronounced dead on arrival. Cause of death: sudden massive cardiac arrest.

The news soon spread. The boys returned to take care of the funeral arrangements and were truly heartbroken. His body would be transported to Sicily, to the family mausoleum. He would be buried beside Francesca.

Gestiniano Ambruzio felt guilty, but deep down in his heart resided a joyful flame.

Anthony and his family, including Fabiana, who had returned from London, went through the motions of the funeral service. They felt sympathy for Francesca's sons, they were completely unaware of their mother's fate.

The Tavernas thought how they could explain to the boys. How could they talk ill of the dead, their father, who had tormented so many people in his life?

A package arrived at Farmer John's mailbox. It was for David. Every time, he received mail from Sicily, he dropped everything to get the news from them. Lora had gotten into the habit of sending gorgeous outfits and treats for Gracy. Today was no different: a sundress, sandals, and white socks with gold stars. They liked to spoil her. Fabiana would do the same. He put the gifts on her bed for when she returned from her gymnastics class.

> *My dear friend, Andrew:*
>
> *I am not sure if this is good news, or happy news, for you and for our family. We have just buried Angelo. He had a heart attack in New York. His body was returned here to Sicily where he was laid to rest beside my beloved sister in the family mausoleum. We gave him a decent burial, with dignity.*
>
> *Now of course, there will be new developments. For now the boys are grieving badly. We sympathize with them. Other than that, all else is well. We wish the same with you and Gracy. Lora sends you both her love, along with Fabiana.*
>
> *My best regards.*
>
> *Anthony Taverna.*
>
> *P.S. I will keep you posted.*

David was shocked. He never expected Angelo Frarano to die a sudden death, but then he thought, *Who are we to predict what's in store for us?* As for the good news, bad news… he didn't know what to make of it. If he had arranged to have Francesca killed and himself left for dead, then, this was good news. To this day no one had come forward with information to claim the hefty reward. He couldn't help wonder who those hoodlums were who had savagely beat him that night.

He was happy here with Gracy. He had never thought of returning to London. This farm was a wholesome place to raise Gracy. They had long survived the separation of Fabiana, Lora, Anthony and Mrs. Morrison. The two of them had bonded well as father and daughter.

***

One year led into the next and time passed quickly. Andrew had gotten so used to being David Nelson. He was happy that he had refused to change Gracy's name. She was Gracy, picked by Francesca, and no one was going to alter her name. There were pictures in the house. He had made sure Gracy knew every one of them and this is how he kept her mother's image alive.

On Gracy's night table was a photo of Francesca. David would tuck her in at night and together they recited a prayer. He repeatedly said to her, "Gracy, we need to pray for your mommy in heaven."

"Why did mommy go to heaven?"

"Because God needed her there I guess."

"How come he doesn't need Liz?"

"Sometimes God chooses certain people when it's the right time."

"Dad, it's not fair, Mark, Jill, Franny, Oliver and Rosy do things with their mommy and I don't."

She was often comparing herself with the other kids. David's heart was torn for her. He tried harder to fill her void.

"My darling, I have told you that your mommy was needed in heaven, but you know, you have a godmother called Fabiana, and she loves you just as much."

"What's a godmother?"

"A godmother is chosen by your mom and daddy when you are baptized. She is there for you in the course of your life, should your mommy not be able to."

"Oh, I see this is why Fabiana sends me all those presents."

"Yes, lovey, she loves you just like your mom would love you."

She seemed content. He would often go through this explanation with her. When he tucked her in bed at night, he would tell her stories of her mom's home in Sicily. He painfully described the beautiful island.

"Dad! Dad! Can we go there?"

"Someday, dear. We'll look into it."

"Dad, promise me. Please, please, Dad."

David's mind flashed back. As much as he wanted to make his daughter happy he knew it was difficult under the circumstances. They were so far away from the Tavernas. Anthony and Lora were complaining about their rheumatic joints. They felt it was impossible to endure such a long flight, Fabiana had written and she was coming to visit. David and Gracy were delighted, they couldn't wait to see her. Plus Gracy needed to spend time with her.

He rented a car and the day had arrived to go and pick up Fabiana at the airport. When she finally arrived there were no words to describe their happiness. Gracy was so hungry for family members, she got a hold of Fabiana at the Melbourne Airport and didn't let go.

"Daddy, Daddy, what do I call Fabiana if she is my godmother? So I call her Mommy?"

"You ask Fabiana. She will tell you what she prefers."

Father and daughter were beaming with joy once Fabiana stepped out on her arrival. "There she is," said David and they both ran to embrace her.

"Fabiana, let me look at you, my precious girl, it's so good to have you here. Finally… we waited so long for this to happen."

"I know, Professor, I have missed you both so much. My stay in London was not the same anymore after you two left.

"You, Gracy, you have grown so much, I cannot believe I am finally seeing you again. Come here and give me a big hug."

Fabiana picked her up and twirled her around squeezing her closer. "Oh, Gracy, Gracy! You are so dear to us all. Yes, you can call me Madrina – godmother – or Mamma Fabiana. I love you as much as your real mommy you know."

Gracy smiled, nodding in agreement.

Back at home, David said, "Fabiana, look at this place. What a contrast to London and to Palermo, what do you think?"

"Oh, Professor, this is a piece of earth all on its own; flat land, and blue sky. It's so, so quiet. Except for the animals, the birds, the rooster, with his hens and the rest of them behind the slope that live in the forest."

"It sure is peaceful. Gracy and I have felt safe here, it's a great place to raise a child, there are children around for her to inter-act with and there's an abundance of nature offerings."

"I see, I see, you told us all about your fine neighbors."

"I can't wait for them to meet you. They are such fine people."

"I have been told how kind and hospitable the people are here and always so eager to offer their help."

As they were talking, Liz waved out the window to them. In no time John and Liz came out radiantly smiling eager to meet and greet Fabiana.

"I am so happy to meet you, Fabiana, we have heard so much about you. We are so happy David and Gracy finally have you here."

"Nice to meet you too, Liz." She turned to John, "And you, John, the Professor has filled us in on your generosity and goodness."

"We are the lucky ones. They brought sunshine to our land; wait till you meet our troops! They are absolutely crazy for Gracy."

"Well folks, we better get our guest in our place before she drops on us after that long voyage."

After giving Fabiana a few days of rest to regain her sleep, David and Gracy promised to show her around and give her a good time.

David said, "Fabiana, it will probably take you three days to get over the jet lag, when you are ready, we will give you a tour and show you this part of Australia. Gracy and I will be your tour guide."

"That is great, it won't take me long to be my old self. A few hours of sleep will do."

She was their first guest and it was her first time in this part of the world. David and Gracy couldn't wait to show her around. They left early in the morning. Their first choice was to drive through Great Ocean Road. The amazing transformation of the rocks and water in the Pacific Ocean was an eye opener. Then, they continued to Phillip Island to observe the incredible penguins at dusk and their human-like behavior. It was mind-boggling. Gracy took both adults' hands. She was full of joy walking along with them.

Great Ocean Road, Australia

"Mamma Fabiana, have you ever seen such rocks? And look at the water going through its openings."

"Professor, this is such a great creation of nature, what a wonderful site for movies. I can just imagine the thrilling scene with the tide rushing in among the carved red rocks."

"Fabiana, now we must take you to Melbourne and to the Victoria Market, we will have lunch there. It is really worth seeing. Then you can compare it to the markets of London and Palermo. It's an eye opener, especially the food section."

"I've got the best tour guide, with Gracy at my side, I am game!"

"Dad, Dad, we should take Mamma Fabiana to our favorite coffee shop."

"Of course, dear. As long as Fabiana is willing. You girls decide. I am only the driver."

The days went by fast and before they knew it Fabiana needed to return to her life in Italy. The goodbyes were sad and Gracy hung tightly around Fabiana's neck, not wanting to let go. David kept his sorrow inside so as not to upset Gracy.

"Fabiana, you know how much your visit has meant to us, come back next year. I don't need to tell you how dear you are."

"Professor, I think you can contemplate coming to Sicily, you know, Mom and Dad are dying to see Gracy and you too."

They stood there watching Fabiana until she disappeared from their sight. Gracy with her Sicilian blood in her veins, let go of her emotions, sobbing, with warm tears trickling down her cheeks.

"Now, now, Gracy, you need to be brave. Every good thing comes to an end. We need to concentrate on the next good thing."

She stopped crying, "Daddy, what is the next good thing?"

"Oh, one never knows, it is always good to wish for what your heart desires, and it might happen."

"Dad, you know what my heart desires?"

"No, don't tell me, it's your secret wish."

Gracy kept quiet; she knew what it was. She wanted to go visit Aunt Lora, Uncle Anthony and most of all be with Mamma Fabiana, and see Sicily.

David not having anyone else, had chosen Anthony to be his executor. At first his place in London had been kept empty. He had mixed feelings about selling. After all, it was his parents' place: the only memory of his family and childhood. After ten years it was time to let go and he put it on the market. One day he got a notice from his realtor, he had a serious offer with no contingencies. If acceptable by him, they would let it go. David took a quick look at the offer, signed it and sent it back without any hesitation. London didn't hold good memories for him, it was best to sell. He didn't know what the future would hold for him here, but he had no intention of returning to London anytime soon.

The funds from the sale of the flat would come in handy. They were living modestly from his income. Plus Anthony insisted on giving him an allowance. He said it was an advancement from Francesca's money he kept saying for Gracy's needs.

Yes, life here, just outside of Jellico was perfect for Professor David. The computer era was advancing rapidly in the nineties. One could function efficiently without having to go out of his comfort zone. He needed time for Gracy, time to read, time to edit. Yes, later when she didn't require so much more of his time he would write. This was his plan. But in his heart, Gracy's happiness was his main concern.

Chapter Twenty-Eight

....

The office occupied by Angelo Frarano had remained untouched and empty. Diego and Daniele would come from time to time knowing eventually they would settle there. Gestiniano Ambruzio didn't miss him. He had paid his respects and gone to Sicily to attend the funeral service. The final eulogy had taken place right beside Francesca's grave. He studied her smiling picture on her tomb and then his eyes switched over to the two grieving boys. Gestiniano was suddenly overcome with a panic attack. He was sweating and he wanted to run and hide, hide from himself. The attack he had suffered at the cemetery was the worst he had ever experienced. That horrible feeling was attacking his entire body daily now. Nearly out of his mind he made a trip to the doctor, He soon provided him with tranquillizers. Prozac did not help.

He felt that if something didn't give soon, he may as well put a bullet to his head himself. After what he participated in, he just couldn't forgive himself. The nights were the worst.

Back in New York he found himself sitting in Joe Malcom's office.

"Gestiniano, what's up? You look like hell, have you been drinking all night? You could use some sleep."

Without answering, he broke down in tears.

"Come on now, I'm here to listen, how can I make you feel better? What can I do for you?"

"Joe, I can't go on like this anymore. I may as well be dead. What did you say your colleague's name is? I need him."

"Are you sure?"

"I am so sure that I don't care what happens to me anymore."

"Gestiniano, we need to go over what you will be facing. You'll be spending the rest of your life in a cell."

"Joe, don't you understand? I don't care. I can't live with my conscience any longer. I should have never let that lunatic push me around."

Joe did not respond, he buzzed his secretary, "Margie. Please get me Aaron Levine will you?"

He was the most dynamic criminal lawyer and Joe knew without a doubt he would go to bat for Gestiniano. He deserved only the best. Joe knew how Frarano worked and this man had been victimized.

In the presence of his lawyer, Joe Malcom, and Aaron Levine, Gestiniano slowly and methodically recounted how he had been called by Angelo Frarano; how he had shown him the pictures of his wife with another man engaged in sex; how he had listened to the tape of the two people in the act of love making; and finally, how Angelo had become a madman and wanted them both killed.

Angelo had instructed him to find and hire the killer. He had done so at his insistence. He explained how Vladimiro had been hired, "I paid him in cash, that was it, and then Angelo found out the fellow had not been finished off. He pressured me every day to continue bugging this dangerous character Vladimiro, who wanted more money and threatened to blow our heads off. I know Angelo is dead now, rest in peace. Between Angelo's pressures, the Russian's threats and what has taken place, plus all the troubles at the office… I cannot live with myself anymore."

With Gestiniano's confession, everything came out in the open.

The London police were immediately informed, Detective Benjamin Tayler had never closed the file. The Italian, Carabinieri Police Force had been informed in Rome and the news traveled fast to Sicily. The hunt was on for Vladimiro Swarzovisky .

Fabiana heard the news immediately. She was not surprised. She was so happy that this associate had decided to come forward. This would confirm their doubt. Anthony and Lora, now that they knew for sure, cried out loud. Anthony blamed himself for taking his sister to London. But she would have been doomed had she stayed in Sicily.

Diego and Daniele were shocked beyond belief. Embarrassed. They refused to talk to the media. Uncle Anthony was concerned as to their emotional well-being. They were young and hopefully strong enough to survive the blow.

Andrew (David Nelson) was the last one to hear about it.

Benjamin Tayler wanted to give him the news himself. He called Andrew at Farmer John's house. He didn't want to wait for the mail.

"Professor Robertson, there's been a big breakthrough in the case."

"Oh, finally. You mean you have proof?"

"We have a written confession and a lie detector confirmation."

Benjamin Tayler went on to explain how the crimes had been committed.

"Unfortunately, it will not bring my beloved back."

"Professor, should you want to come out of hiding, I guess you should be safe now. We have arrested the Russian hit man Vladimiro Swarzovisky. We are told he had an accomplice, who we checked out. He was a street druggie. He died from an overdose a few months ago. His name was Jordano Fontanaros, his street name was Skinny. He had a long record."

"Thank you, it's kind of you to let me know. Yes, it's a big relief indeed. Thanks again, have a sunshine day in London."

After the pleasant goodbyes, the phone went dead. In deep thought he paced the floor with his hand holding his forehead.

Andrew had listened hard. He took it all in. He had to be honest with himself. In London he had felt some fear. He had looked over his shoulders a few times. But here he felt secure and removed from danger. This peaceful place had grown on him more and more. It was nice to know that these mobsters were not pursuing him anymore.

Chapter Twenty-Nine

....

Anthony, Lora, and Fabiana had flown to London to attend Gestiniano Ambruzio's trial. They were there every day. Beside them sat Diego and Daniele. Professor Andrew Robertson had been subpoenaed to be on the witness stand. The Ambruzio's members of the family were also there. Gestiniano was a single man, his parents, sister and brother all sat there with their heads down.

The days of testimonies were lengthy. The boys blanched as their father's tyranny was revealed. The British lawyer Mark Fitzgerald, hired by Levine to defend Gestiniano, questioned them one by one. He desperately wanted to prove to the jury and the court how Gestiniano had been pressured and manipulated into his actions by this maniac Frarano. "He couldn't escape his trap for fear of his own life." He pointed out to the jury. The prosecutor on the contrary was slashing back contradicting him.

The boys heard of their mother's love affair. All the evidence, was presented in court. Before the case began they learned of their half-sister through Fabiana and their uncle. They actually felt sympathy for Gestiniano. It took the courage of a real man to do what he did. Mark Fitzgerald accompanied by Levine had prepared a tremendous case on his behalf with hours and hours of homework. Gestiniano sat there handcuffed; he didn't care any more what his fate was going to be. The judge listened attentively without blinking an eye. One couldn't detect what he was thinking. They would hear him addressing the jury and his recommendations. He stressed, repeatedly, beyond any reasonable doubt to take the victim's consequences into consideration and come to the fair conclusion of their sentence. Gestiniano was not a bad man. He had fallen in the wrong place, with the wrong company, in his life. The final decision was in the hands of the jury.

The jury deliberated for four days and three nights. When the jury came into the court, the clerk of the court asked the foreperson to rise, "Have you reached a verdict?"

"Yes, sir. "The foreman answered and handed the clerk the verdict sheet. The clerk handed it to the judge. The judge remained motionless, took a look, and handed it back to the foreperson.

Then the clerk asked, "How do you find the defendant on Count 1?"

The foreperson answered, "Guilty."

While he stood up to announce the verdict, the foreperson clearly stated after addressing the judge and the court, "We find the defendant Mr. Gestiniano Ambruzio, guilty of first degree murder. On count two, guilty, of attempted murder." Shocked Gestiniano looked at his mother. She gave out a scream of terror, weeping incessantly, his heart was torn to see her in such pain. Then his gaze set on his father, he looked deranged. His family had been there in support, but none of them could help him out of this. He felt so sorry, how could he undo the deep sorrow he was causing them? It was all too late. He put his head down and in total surrender walked with two security officers leading him behind bars.

Later Gestiniano Ambruzio was sentenced to life according to British law, as the murder had taken place in London.

Once the trial was over Andrew said to Anthony, "You were right all along. I didn't want to believe it and preferred to be in denial. I must admit I am a lucky man to be alive."

"Andrew, I feared for my sister and for you too because I know their mentality; they have no mercy."

"Well, my friend, I want to put the ugly hell of the past behind; the best thing waiting for me is my Gracy."

"You are right, you need to get to her."

"Yes, I must, my plane leaves at four. I will say goodbye to Lora, Fabiana and the boys, and I will head for the airport soon."

Lora and Fabiana approached them, "How is Gracy doing?"

"I call her every day and I can't wait to get home."

"You give her a big hug for us, Andrew," said Lora.

Fabiana had a pretty gift bag in her hand, "Here, Professor, she will love this. I found it in one of the boutiques while I was walking to court."

"Fabiana, you spoil her so."

"She is special, wait until Diego and Daniele meet her."

"That will be great, we must make it happen soon."

Anthony suggested they grab a quick bite for lunch together with Francesca's sons. The time had come to go back to their separate lives in separate directions.

Andrew was getting anxious to return to Gracy, she was left behind with John and Liz. The reunion would be joyful for the both of them.

***

Finally, he arrived home to see her again, "I have missed you so much, darling," Andrew said hugging her.

"I have missed you too, Dad. John and Liz asked me to call them Aunt Liz and Uncle John, they made me feel at home."

Meanwhile the Tavernas had arrived back home and resumed their routine in Sicily. Fabiana had taken a position with the news media in Palermo. She was looking forward to her cousins coming from America for their summer break in August. The aura around their household had changed.

Diego had graduated from law school. He was taken under Joe Malcom's wings. He had specialized in corporate law and was a brilliant young lawyer. He was eager to bring in fresh ideas to his father's companies. Joe was happy to mentor him with his skillful experience.

Daniele had followed him, a couple of years later. He had come in with his expertise as the young architect. It was a perfect combination for their family business. For Joe, the best part was that the boys followed the law and rules by the book, contrary to their father. Joe Malcom liked the brothers and did not mind coaching them in an honest way. He had managed to get rid of the lawsuits they were involved with. Yes, he had to pay a lot of money to get rid of the several suits. They were all settled out of court.

The companies were off to a fresh new start. There was no doubt in his mind that the brothers would take the father's business to an even greater success. The two young men weren't done cleaning their father's mess. They needed to take a trip to Italy and settle more financial affairs.

Agrigento, Sicily

Old Gennaro Scarpone was there with his papers for them to make decisions, positive or negative. They told him they hadn't met their half-sister. Diego said, "I feel whatever our mother's last wishes were, they should be executed as such. I have no objection or claim against the money or the land in Agrigento."

"Very well, I will declare your statement in writing and you will sign it. We will move on to release the funds and allocate the land to your half-sister Gracy Robertson."

Daniele nodded, "That goes for me too, sir."

Anthony had provided Gennaro Scarpone with Andrew's address. Now that he wasn't in danger anymore, there was no reason to keep anything secretive about his existence. After the trial, he could have chosen to return to England or moved somewhere else, but he had preferred to remain in Australia.

They had an open invitation to visit Sicily, but he had never made the effort. He had stressed more than once that it would be difficult for him. They stopped urging him to visit over the holidays and left it to his discretion. Lora and Fabiana never ended their phone conversations without saying, "Remember, our home is always open for you and Gracy." To this day he had never come and their hearts ached, as they wanted to see Gracy more often.

The lawyer finished the procedures required by law. The money was being wired in stages as Francesca had requested. The deed of the land had automatically been passed on to Gracy as the beneficiary, with all the stipulations without any claimants.

Chapter Thirty

·····································

The years had quickly passed. Gracy had grown up to be a fine young lady. She had inherited the height of her father and the lustrous black hair of her mother with the facial features that no artist could paint, a real beauty. Gracy had always been intrigued by languages. From her childhood she had heard English and Italian, and her own Australian accent was so different from her father's British English.

"Dad, I am considering studying linguistics. I would like to be a teacher. What do you think?"

"Lovey, whatever makes you happy. You know that."

It was Gracy's eighteenth birthday. She had been accepted to the University of Melbourne in the Faculty of Arts. She had always taken her studies seriously, now even more.

Andrew wanted to appease her desire. He knew how much she had begged him to take her to Europe. She had wanted to see Sicily, and also visit London her place of birth. He visited a travel agency in Melbourne and with mixed emotions purchased tickets to fly to Rome, and from there he would take Gracy on the same route he had done alone so many years ago.

When they arrived in Rome, she was mesmerized, "Oh, Dad. It's been worth the wait."

"Hold your breath, there's so much more for you to see!"

"I can't wait to reach Sicily."

As arranged, the Tavernas had come to pick them up in Messina. As they came off the ferry, there they were: the Tavernas and her two older brothers. Andrew could hardly recognize them. So many years had passed. Fabiana introduced them, "Gracy Rosalia. These are your brothers."

She looked at them. Trying to guess their age. Diego was now thirty-eight and Daniele thirty-six. They were two distinguished young bachelors and perfect gentlemen. She let out a scream of joy and burst into pleasant laughter.

Diego was the first to hug her, "Welcome home, Sis," he held her for the longest time. It was seeing his mother again in the shining beauty of her youth.

"This is Daniele, your brother. "

Daniele came forward with a shy smile, "Welcome to Sicily, Gracy. We have long been waiting to meet you."

She had brothers. She turned to her father after all the salutations and asked, "Dad, why didn't we do this long ago?"

"Darling, I couldn't bring myself to do it. Now here you are, this is your Sicilian family."

No bitterness governed her brother's hearts. On the contrary, after learning what they had endured, they wanted to make it up to them. They promised her a good time, plus a tour of their companies and properties on the other side of the Atlantic.

Andrew had planned to stay three weeks in Sicily and then fly to London for a week. Gracy was fully occupied with the boys. One day Anthony suggested that they take a drive to Agrigento to show Gracy the land she'd inherited.

Anthony turned to Andrew, "You should go along also and make plans with your daughter, since she is still young. She needs your input."

Andrew shook his head and said, "Anthony, what do I know about land? Especially here in Sicily."

He was an educator. He wasn't business minded and he felt unqualified to give his daughter any advice.

He added, "I think that comes from your side of the family. When the time is right, Diego being the eldest can advise her with his expertise."

They drove to the historic city of Agrigento. They visited the *Valle dei Templi,* rising above the River San Biagio, a great place to admire for its temples. It was a sacred place from the Ancient Greek and Byzantine Eras. As they stood above the Montour land overlooking the base of the rivers down below Anthony explained to them how this was Francesca's favorite piece of land. "In the heart of winter, the spectacular almond trees burst with flowers, which cover the valley to create amazing beauty. The people here celebrate the almonds being in flower."

"What is Agrigento's main industry?" asked Gracy.

"Export of almonds, oranges, wine, and education. We have the best schools, and university. We graduate the best pupils and we supply them up on the mainland."

"It's all so interesting," answered Andrew.

"Dad, maybe you should consider applying to teach English?"

"Oh, I am happy with what I am doing, what about you? Besides, I am old… at retirement age now."

"Dad, I like this place. It feels good." She pointed out the other running river just as spectacular at the southern base on the opposite side, "What's the name of the other river, Uncle Anthony?"

"That is St. Anna's River."

No wonder her mom loved this place and chose to go to school here she thought.

Andrew said, "One wouldn't get lost in a crowd here."

"Yes, Dad, I like everything about this area."

The atmosphere standing on this land gave her a celestial feeling, close to heaven. This was the gift from her mom. She felt tears dampen her eyes. She wanted to avoid emotions at all cost. The boys would take her for a weakling and she wanted to be one of them, strong and brilliant.

Diego and Daniele came to her side and she stood between the two of them. Diego put an arm around her waist and Daniele did the same.

Then he suggested "after we are finished with Agrigento, tomorrow, we take a drive to Cefalù. The ice cream fair is on and I want to buy you a gelato, it's like nothing you would have ever tasted!"

"You want me to gain weight, then you will have a fatty for a sister."

"We will love you regardless, Gracy, and I doubt you will get fat!"

"What makes you so sure? If I keep eating *cannoli Siciliani sfogliatelli*... I love those pastries. I love all the food here and the gelato idea sounds wonderful."

Then she asked them, "Tell me all you can about Mom. What was she like?"

They both opened up and were happy to share some of their recollections with her. What she felt here in their company was indescribable. The boys seemed to have been part of her life forever.

They made her promise to visit them in New York.

"Now that I have found you guys, you won't get rid of me that easily. I haven't been anywhere; this is my first trip."

Andrew was delighted to see his daughter get along so well with her brothers, they were bonding well. "Poor Gracy," he said to the Tavernas. "She has grown up frustrated at times, by being stuck with me only."

"Well," said Lora, "she didn't have a mother or any siblings. Plus, you had to live in hiding."

"Let's change the subject, it's wonderful here. I'm so glad we came and this is the best thing for Gracy," suggested Andrew.

"You are right, let's talk only about pleasantness," said Fabiana.

"I agree, let's put that part of life behind us."

Lora, as usual, was very accommodating and a wonderful hostess. She kept reminding the fellows and Fabiana to take

Gracy to Monte Pellegrino in Palermo. She told her, "Gracy, you have to go and say a prayer to Santa Rosalia. Your mother was very devoted to her. And that is the saint you have been named after, you know that."

Gracy hadn't been brought up attending Sunday mass like a devoted Catholic, but she did have the beaded rosary, and with her dad, they had prayed every night before bedtime when she was younger.

"Oh, yes, Aunt Lora, I would like to do that. Can we all go?"

They attended mass that Sunday and Gracy was in awe. After mass, Father Alfonso stood outside to greet his parishioners. He was in his seventies now, hunching over slightly with his posture, but mentally sharp. They introduced Gracy to him, "God Bless." He made the sign of the cross on her forehead. "Where are you from, young lady?"

"Australia," she answered.

"You have traveled a long way. I'm glad you found the way to this place."

Father Alfonso knew only too well of Francesca's suffering. The secret was sacred, buried deep in his soul. He was happy to see the young lady. He blessed her, silently thanking God for her safety for so many years.

Gracy looked around and felt at home, she had a notion of having been there before.

Lora was now satisfied. She had gotten Gracy to visit her mother's favorite church. Afterwards she took Andrew to one side and asked, "There is only one more place where Gracy should go, that is the cemetery, do you think she can take that?"

"I am not sure about that, let's discuss it with Fabiana and Anthony, see what they suggest."

Andrew thought he had painted a heavenly picture in heaven when Gracy was growing up, now she was eighteen and needed to face reality. Did he really want to emphasize this part at this time? He wasn't sure.

To everyone's surprise one morning after breakfast with all present Gracy asked, "I would like to visit my mother's grave. Will you go with me, Fabiana?" Then she turned to the boys Diego and Daniele, "You must come also, since you are my protectors. I must admit, you two give me strength."

The holiday was over. The goodbyes were sad. She was just as emotional as they were. The closeness with her relatives had procured love and affection.

It was time to fly to London, where Andrew was to show her around his hometown. He took her to all the sights and they were having a marvelous time. However, Gracy sensed her dad was having trouble touring London. There were signs of fatigue on his face. "Dad, we can rest one day, you know. We could do a late breakfast, read, swim at the pool, hang around the hotel. We don't have to be on the go continually. I know you're doing it for me."

"Yes, we can if you wish, honey. One thing we can't miss. I must take you to the flower market. The flowers are breathtaking. You will be re-energized by the different shapes, the fragrances, and the array of colors are spectacular to look at." He remembered when he was there last with Francesca. They had planned to return the following Saturday. Fate took care of that. As much as he hurt, he could not deny the beauty of this place to his daughter.

The four weeks had gone by so fast and Gracy was quiet on the long flight home. Andrew was glad to return to the peacefulness of the farm. He wondered about his daughter. To him this place had been his refuge. It had sheltered him and his baby from the dangerous cruel world out there. Now that their long journey was complete. He had done his duty. Gracy needed to see and experience her mother's country and culture.

They were back home and Andrew was sitting comfortably in his chair by the fireplace. The crackling wood fire was sending out warmth, soothing his arthritic knees. The pain had been bothering him lately.

Gracy pulled up a chair, "Dad, what would you say if we lived in Sicily when I'm finished school here?"

Andrew looked at her seriously, feeling sorry for her. "Are you serious?"

"Dad, I'm just suggesting it. Of course I would never go without you."

"I don't know. I'm happy here. I know it's not fair to you."

"Dad, we belong together."

"Certainly, but, I don't want to shortchange you in missing out on the opportunities in your life."

"The trip has sparked a new life in me. I love this place also. I know this is heaven for a writer, but I yearn for more"

"Of course dear, you're young. I don't blame you. You need to be out there in the world and live with the young people like you."

"Dad, you know you're my life. I would never leave you."

"Gracy, you must. You can't be stuck with an old man. I am sixty-nine."

"Dad, you are far from an old man. Maybe you should come out of your shell. How about starting to live it up yourself? Maybe we should go out more and socialize more."

"I'm pretty contented in my way. When I found your mom, I thought I had found my treasure. She was taken away from me. I have no interest whatsoever to get involved with anyone."

"Dad, believe me, I don't want to share you with another woman. I am contemplating for both of us, on spending more time with our family."

"You mean the Tavernas?"

"I miss all of them, Dad."

"I must admit they are such fine people. It would make me feel better to know they are near."

"Dad, what about your side of the family. Your brother in the U.S., did you ever think of visiting him?"

"No desire, he has never had time for me. He is somewhat of a loser. We have been on the outs for years. He wanted money you know. He also resented me for having inherited that rat hole of a flat I occupied in London."

"Oh, Dad, what a shame, and he is your only family."

"I have no use for him, or his family."

Gracy was an honor student and dedicated to her studies. Her hard work was rewarding in many ways. Her tongue, was switching fluently from one language to the other. She had mastered, French, Italian, Spanish and Hebrew. She kept in touch regularly with Diego and Daniele. They promised to visit her in Australia. She couldn't wait to see them again. She anxiously waited for their arrival.

She felt compelled to tell them in an email: *Guys, my dad and I live humbly. We only have two bedrooms. You might want to stay at one of the nice hotels in Melbourne. There are none around here. People here choose to go to farms for the weekend.*

They replied: *Gracy, I think we share the same blood of humility as you, Sis. It would be fun to share accommodation with you on the farm. I want you to know, togetherness is of more value to us.*

She read the email to her father, "You know, Gracy, your mother was like that too. I was worried sick about taking her to my flat. When I confessed my fear to her, you know what her answer was? 'Andrew, you fool, it would make no difference to me if you lived in a cave.' "

The boys were so glad to have Gracy in their life, even if she was the result of a love triangle. They wanted to love their sister. She needed them and they needed her. Diego said to Daniele, "When I see Gracy, I see Mom in her younger days. The resemblance is amazing."

"Yes, it's Mom reincarnated. We're lucky to have her. She's so sweet, she even talks like Mom."

"She is a godsend. What a miracle from Mom's devotion, to think that Mom died and she survived."

"We must see her more often. We should suggest that she live in Sicily in the summer. Do you think she would consider that? Or maybe New York?"

"If she wanted to."

"What about the Professor? You know she's very close to her dad."

"I don't blame her. He has taken good care of her. After all the trauma he has been put through."

The Frarano brothers booked themselves for Australia. They were going to see how she'd feel about their plan and find out what plans she had for her future once she graduated from university.

Andrew had gotten into the habit of going down to the forest alone and then he would sit at his desk and click away on his computer keyboard. He had written a few books since he had been at the farm. This morning was no different. He picked up a wooden stick from the ground to help him support his weak knees. There he was with his kookaburra bird whistling away. He suddenly missed the footing and before he knew it he was rolling down through the bushes leading to a river. He couldn't stop himself and he kept sliding down and down on the embankment. A bunch of eucalyptus trees were at the edge of the creek and they prevented him from falling into the rushing water. He couldn't move. His legs would not help him up. He remained there helpless. *Who is going to find me here? This is going to be the end for me,* he thought.

Only the animals frequented the area down the embankment. The dangerous wild boars with their long tusks, were roaming about. He had seen them before from a distance.

Gracy had gone to the university and wasn't due back until dusk. She was attending a conference, but she got bored. The speaker wasn't captivating. The audience looked distracted. She slipped away and returned home early.

"Dad, Dad, where are you?"

She looked for her dad around the cottage and there wasn't any sign of him. She ran over to the farmhouse and they hadn't seen him all day. Gracy ran back to the house and checked the kitchen. The breakfast dishes hadn't been washed and the computer hadn't been turned on.

Immediately she knew something was wrong. A violent fear came over her. She ran to fetch Liz and John, "Please you must help me, something terrible has happened to my dad. I know it. He hasn't returned to the house since this morning."

Gracy knew his habitual routine and the three of them started out toward the sprawling forest down the hill. She was calling out from the top of her lungs. But there was no answer. She had tracked a few footsteps, and then, no more. "Where has he gone?" She tried to remain calm. It wasn't easy. She kept calling,

"Dad, Dad, It's me Gracy, where are you?" The voice didn't reach Andrew. He had fallen asleep.

John was scouring the area attentively. It was starting to get dark and Gracy's fear was growing. She didn't know what to think. She knew in her heart he must be out there somewhere. John noticed some broken branches and a slope going down to the creek. He didn't say anything to the girls. He thought, *God help him if he's ended up in the creek.*

He studied the trail and he figured someone had rolled down. They kept yelling calling his name. Andrew woke up and heard voices calling. He tried to move, his legs were heavy. "I'm down here!" he hollered back with all his strength. "Gracy, Gracy, honey, I am here!"

She heard him, and could not control her tears. She ran toward the sound of his voice.

"Dad, Dad, we are coming, are you hurt? Tell me, where are you?"

They carefully descended the slopes to get to him. The terrain was dangerous and slimy. One wrong move and they could have easily rolled into the rushing waters of the creek. Once they spotted Andrew and made it safely to him, Gracy bent over to her dad caressing and kissing him, "Dad, I am so happy to see you, are you hurt? We will get you out of here don't you worry." She turned to John, "Uncle John, we need some help here."

John frowned, "Yes, we do." He wondered how they were going to get him out of there. "You girls need to go call for help, I'll stay here with him."

They made their way back to the house, yet none of the kids were around to help. They did not trust themselves not knowing the extent of his injury.

"Gracy, call triple zero!" ordered Liz.

In no time the ambulance, fire truck, and rescue team from the village showed up. Andrew had to be carried up on a stretcher.

Andrew's body had been battered around; he was aching badly. The paramedics took him to the emergency department at the local hospital for observation. He was lucky.

"Badly bruised and no broken bones," said the doctor on call.

The doctor released him on the promise that he would take it easy for a while and allow the swelling of his arms and legs to go down. He was grateful in counting his blessings. John, Liz and Gracy were waiting for him only too happy to take him home.

"Dad, you are never going in the forest alone ever again. You gave me such a scare."

"Sorry, my lovey, I knew you would find me." Andrew pulled her close to him in the back seat of the car.

It took a few months for Andrew to recuperate. Gracy was his nursemaid and didn't want to leave his side.

The guys from New York arrived and Gracy was so happy to see them. She needed their support.

As the older brother, Diego always spoke first, according to their custom.

"Gracy, we came here to see you and your dad of course. But more than anything, we're here on a mission." Diego, hugged her, and looked at Daniele for confirmation.

"Yes, Diego is right. We want you to move to Sicily or New York."

Diego continued: "You could have the best of both worlds, live in New York in the summer and Sicily in the winter."

"You know, Gracy. We want you near. We need you and you need us. We are family don't forget. Here it's peaceful, but too far to visit you regularly," said Daniele.

"We all miss you: Fabiana, Joseph, Aunt and Uncle especially... they are getting older. We all want you near," stated Diego.

She put her arms around the two of them; she turned and kissed them both affectionately, bursting with joy. She said, "I've got news for you. I have already considered that. I got homesick. I've missed you guys since I've been back. I'll be there as soon as Dad is ready to travel."

Diego grabbed her and lifted her up and twirled her around the room.

"Sis, this is the best news I have heard. I must tell you."

Andrew had been going through sessions of physiotherapy, to help himself and was making good progress. He got around using his crutches and sometimes if he was in pain, the wheelchair. Gracy was encouraging him and at the same time she was making arrangements for them to leave. She kept telling him, "Dad, you will have family around in Sicily. They will help you boost your immune system. You will pick citrus to eat, right from the trees. All that vitamin C and D, with the sunshine. The iodine you will be breathing from the sea. Although we have some of these great things here, but, Dad, I cannot think of a better place for both of us. It's mainly my blood relations."

Andrew, as much as he wanted to please his daughter, had his doubts. There was a pain deep in his soul when he thought of Sicily. How was he going to stop her? He couldn't. He knew she had grown restless since that visit. He didn't blame her. She had found love and support there. She had roots. Her ancestors had created them. Her mom had specifically left her that acreage. He would be doing her great injustice by keeping her back. If he didn't go, it would make her sad. After struggling with his reflections, he stood straight up pretending his legs were improving.

"Gracy, lovey. Look at me. I got up without falling over, on my own. I think we can take the long trip."

"Oh! Daddy! Daddy! Are you sure?" She hugged him with all her energy.

"I'm as sure as I am standing here, dear."

"Dad, it's a twenty and a half-hour flight. Can you take it? We can wait until you heal better."

"Nonsense, we could wait forever. The decision has been made on my part. The sooner, the better."

They were going for a longer period this time. The intentions were to gradually get the feel of their new world and eventually their plan would come into place. It did not take long to make the arrangements. Once she informed her brothers they offered to pay the trip. They only had to worry about packing.

Fabiana and Auntie Lora had written, "Gracy, don't load yourself with heavy baggage, you know we can take you shopping here for your needs."

Farmer John and Liz drove them to the airport. They were sad to see them go. Andrew and Gracy boarded Lufthansa, first class headed for Rome and on to Sicily.

Their Sicilian family was there to greet them. Gracy was overwhelmed with happiness. Diego and Daniele had flown in from New York. This was to be the happiest day in their life. Andrew watched his daughter's radiant face. He knew now he had made the right decision.

A few days later, Gracy with her brothers, took a drive to Agrigento. She stepped on her land walking proudly. She studied the exposure of the sunrise and the sunset, standing on the highest spot of the land on a rock.

"Here," she said. "I can see the river afar, the blue sky above me, and northwest is Agrigento. This rock gives me strength."

The guys listened, "What on earth are you getting at?"

"Daniele, you will design my new home. Here around this rock. An Italian villa, with the Sicilian flair."

"Is it an order, Sis?"

"Does it look like I am joking? I'm dead serious."

"At your service, madam." Daniele replied smiling.

"We need to make Mom proud," he continued.

"I will say," answered Diego.

Daniele inquired, "Why Agrigento not Palermo?"

"I gather our mom was the happiest here and so I will teach at the university. She chose this place for me before I was born. Palermo holds too many unfavorable memories for my dad."

"Whatever makes you happy, Sis. We hope you know that we would move heaven and earth for you."

"And, do you two know how much I love you?" She stepped between them and Francesca's three children dreamed of the house they would build and the lives they would live.

Andrew stood aside admiring them saying to himself, *How blessed have I been. How can I wish for more? Francesca's legacy is so complete.*

Yes. He now had a family that would be there for him.

About the Author

Gina Iafrate, is passionate about her work. Her dedication and love of literature has allowed her to also create a collection of anthologies, *Releases From My Soul*. Her next release, while working on a new enchanting novel in progress, *The Girl from the Cornfield*.

CPSIA information can be obtained
at www.ICGtesting.com
Printed in the USA
LVOW12s2131060817
543895LV00001B/2/P